BEAUTY AND THE RAKE

Endless Love
Book 1

JR Salisbury

ARE YOU SIGNED UP FOR DRAGONBLADE'S BLOG?

You'll get the latest news and information on exclusive giveaways, exclusive excerpts, coming releases, sales, free books, cover reveals and more.

Check out our complete list of authors, too!

No spam, no junk. That's a promise!

Sign Up Here

www.dragonbladepublishing.com

Dearest Reader;

Thank you for your support of a small press. At Dragonblade Publishing, we strive to bring you the highest quality Historical Romance from some of the best authors in the business. Without your support, there is no 'us', so we sincerely hope you adore these stories and find some new favorite authors along the way.

Happy Reading!

CEO, Dragonblade Publishing

Additional Dragonblade books by Author JR Salisbury

Endless Love Series
Beauty and the Rake (Book 1)
A Duke's Love (Book 2)
The Forgotten Spare (Book 3)
Love At Last (Book 4)

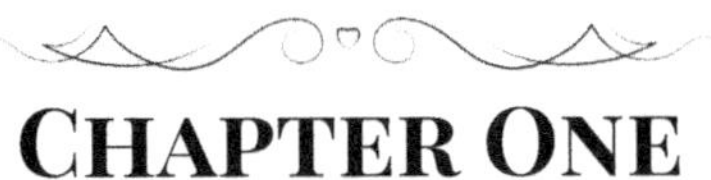

CHAPTER ONE

NEVER HAD ROXANNE thought she would miss the four distinct seasons of England. But as she glanced outside the carriage she had hired, she noted the fog from the Thames had thickened, making visibility nearly impossible, and it made her smile. Not that there was much to look at. The house she was in front of was nothing in the way of spectacular, and given the fog, it made the brick structure almost spooky.

Neither had she ever thought she would find herself in this sort of predicament. Her marriage had been one of convenience, bringing two powerful families together. Once the papers were signed and vows said, she found herself alone. As she stared at the barely visible structure, she was determined to claw herself back up the ladder she fell so far down.

She heard the driver and his man come down off the seat. The driver opened the door and put down the stair as his man began to haul her trunks to the front door. Stepping down as graciously as she could manage, Roxanne smiled at the driver. Six trunks she'd brought back from her three years stay in the south of France. There was no staff left to help. All had been dismissed by her late husband's son in accordance with his father's will.

Rather than allow her to live out the remainder of her life in the dowager house on one of his estates, Lord Casper Smith, eighth Earl of Temple instead left her a house on the outskirts of

London in a less than fashionable area. The house had once been occupied by one of the earl's mistresses until her death. Roxanne had no idea what she would be walking into. Never had she been inside. Given the key at the reading of the will, she left the attorney's office and immediately fled to her aunt's outside of Provence. If it had been Casper's idea to embarrass her and see her laughed and gossiped over by the ton, he succeeded. No longer did she live in Mayfair. Her fall from grace was his last delight.

She would have to swallow her pride and ask for help.

"Sir, my staff is not scheduled to start until tomorrow morning. Do you think you and your man could take the trunks inside to the entrance?"

He turned to study her face as he pondered his reply. He must have taken pity on her because he nodded his head of thin, graying hair. "No problem, milady. Happy to help."

Roxanne managed a smile, nodded, and walked to the front door, putting the key in the lock, opening the door for the men to enter. But before she could step aside for the men, a shiny black carriage, pulled by four black horses, stopped at the curb. She immediately recognized the carriage by the ducal seal on the door as belonging to her brother Arthur.

He sprang out of his carriage before a footman could open the door or lower the stairs and quickly came toward her. He turned to the driver for a moment. "I am the lady's brother. She won't be staying here." He nodded to his footman. "See all her trunks are delivered to my house."

"Yes, Your Grace."

Arthur continued up the stairs to Roxanne and immediately took the keys from her hand. "You're not staying here. You'll stay at Jameson House."

"But..."

"No excuses, Roxanne. I will not have my sister living in this neighborhood just because her late husband bequeathed the property to her." He leaned over and planted a kiss on her cheek.

"Very well." She watched as he locked the door. He turned, offered his arm, and led her down the stairs to his waiting carriage. Roxanne ascended the carriage with the help of a waiting footman and settled on the red leather seat. Arthur followed, choosing to sit across from her. He removed his hat and set it on the seat next to him.

"How did you know I'd be there?"

"I knew what date your ship was due."

"So you decided to rescue me?"

"Casper was a cruel man. I never did like him. He treated you horribly."

"Not only me, but he treated Thomas horribly too." Thomas was the only child she and Casper ever had. Once it became apparent that Thomas was mentally challenged and would never mature past a toddler, Casper stayed away from Roxanne's bed. According to Casper, the boy's problems were all Roxanne's fault.

"I know," Arthur said. "We have a lot to talk about."

"I suppose we do."

"How did you enjoy your time in France?"

"I liked it well enough. The south of France is quite a bit different from Paris. I saw a lot of places I might not otherwise have ever had the opportunity to visit."

The last year had gone by slowly. She had been ready to return to England. She missed her friends, Georgiana in particular. Georgiana had encouraged her to return home. After almost three years, it was time. The last thing she anticipated was finding herself left with this house which had been occupied by one of Casper's mistresses.

The fog seemed to be lifting the closer they got to Mayfair. She could make out the outline of some of the buildings and parks along the way. Roxanne glanced at her brother who was watching her. They had always been close growing up and remained so to this day. Unfortunately, Arthur had been away on a business trip when Casper suddenly died. Roxanne had sent word to him while he had been in Scotland, but he never got her missive. They were convinced Casper's son, Perry, had had something to do with the letter disappearing. Same with a telegram she sent. That was all in the past and hopefully Perry had moved on.

The carriage turned down a street across from Grosvenor Square. The ancestral family home, built by her great-great-grandfather, sat on prime Mayfair land. It was where generations of her family lived while in London. Roxanne had lived there until her father sold her to Casper. That's how she looked at her marriage. It had been a marriage of convenience. Convenient at least for her husband.

She smiled at her brother. At thirty-two, a duke and unmarried, he was one of the most sought-after men in London.

"What are you smiling about?"

"That you've still not married."

"I have no plan to marry a woman who may be over ten years younger, let alone one with no worldly experience. One of my priorities is for my wife to be able to carry on a conversation about more than just the weather or puppies and kittens."

"I see your predicament. I'm sure there is someone out there you've yet to meet that is your perfect mate."

Jameson House came into view as the carriage slowed before coming to a stop. It was a magnificent sight to behold. The brick mansion rose four stories; a dual staircase descended from either side of the front door. Roxanne never thought she'd be so happy to see the house as she was at this moment.

"I had your rooms readied," he said. Arthur linked her arm through his and they began up the stairs to the front door. The long-time family butler, Wilson, stood waiting, door open.

"You've thought of everything. Thank you."

They were in the grand hall and Arthur gestured to the staircase. "I'm sure you would like to freshen up from your journey. I'll be in my study. Come join me when you're ready."

"I will."

She turned and walked across the room to the stairs. For the first time in years, she felt a sense of calm.

ROXANNE WALKED AROUND her rooms. Nothing had changed since she left. The walls and chairs were done in a periwinkle color with white to accent it. The heavy dark-blue drapes were open. Walking over to the window, she peered down at the garden which was, as always, meticulously kept up. Hedges trimmed and the gardens full of color from the assortment of flowers.

A knock on the door had her whirl around. "Enter," she said.

The door opened and Mrs. Dunn, the long-time housekeeper, appeared with a young girl.

"Pardon the intrusion, milady, but as you came with no lady's maid, I took it upon myself to assign one to you. This is Fletcher. Amy Fletcher. She'll be attending to your needs."

Roxanne nodded and smiled at the two women. "That was very thoughtful, Mrs. Dunn. Fletcher, thank you."

"Would you care for tea?" Mrs. Dunn inquired.

"Tea would be nice." She turned to Fletcher. The girl couldn't have been twenty, and had dark blonde hair. "Fletcher, while I wait, I would like to freshen up and change. My trunks should be in the dressing room."

Fletcher nodded and walked towards the dressing room. As she did, Mrs. Dunn made her way to the door. "If you need anything at all, let me know."

"Thank you, Mrs. Dunn."

As soon as the door closed, she walked to the dressing room. Roxanne knew the poor girl was probably scared to death in her new position. If the girl was going to serve her, they should get to know each other better.

She found Fletcher bent over a trunk that carried the dresses she had made in France. "There should be a moss-colored day dress in there."

"Yes, milady. I set everything out for you. Let me know when you're ready to change."

Roxanne nodded and turned toward the door. Tea was already here.

ROXANNE STOOD IN front of the heavy oak door. Sometimes as a child, she dreaded being called to her father's study. It usually meant a stern talking to for something she might have done, like a trick she had played on Arthur. She was especially fond of going into his rooms and switching something around or locking the cat, Mr. Cat, in the day before Arthur was due home.

Her father's other reason for calling her in was her inability to act like a lady and how it sometimes drove her mother to stay in her bed. She simply couldn't understand why her daughter thought riding in trousers was perfectly acceptable or for her to spend hours in the library reading things a young lady shouldn't be interested in.

All that was in the past. A month after her marriage to Casper, Arthur had inherited the dukedom after their parents had been killed in a mysterious accident while on a voyage to India. Details had been sketchy about the incident, and to date, they had no acceptable answer. Their bodies had never been recovered, making the incident even more dark and mysterious.

She shook the cobwebs from her head and knocked, then opened the door. Arthur was seated at his desk, mulling over some papers. He glanced up at her and smiled. "Feel better?"

"Much."

"Would you like a brandy?"

"Only if you're having one," she said, sitting down on the opposite side of the desk.

She watched as he poured two snifters from the decanter

which had been sitting on the corner of his desk. "What was it you wished to see me about?"

"Who said I had anything to discuss?"

"Because you invited me here instead of the drawing room or library." She flashed him a smile as he handed her a brandy.

He sat back in his chair with his snifter and thoughtfully observed her. "You're welcome to stay here as long as you need or wish to stay. I wanted to propose something to you."

"I'm grateful."

"You're my sister, my only sibling, and I'd never turn you away. My thoughts are to see that horrid house Casper left you sold and find something in a better neighborhood. That is, if that's what you want."

"Can you do that?"

"My man is looking into it, but yes. If you want to wait to purchase something else, I'll put the money aside for you. When you find something or decide you're sick of me, we'll make it happen."

"That is too kind, Arthur."

"It's the least I can do. You've had some rough years married to that foul man. I want to help turn things around for you."

"Arthur, I appreciate all of this, but you need to think about finding a wife. You need an heir."

"I know. It'll happen, I'm sure of it," he said with a mischievous grin. "Besides, I need to entertain more in order to find a woman worthy of being my wife. You could act as my hostess. Interested?"

"I'll have to give it some serious thought. I would need to be able to go over guest lists, decide on the meal. The usual."

"Whatever you want."

"Very well, but only because you're my brother."

He ran his hand through his dark-brown hair. "Excellent. You can start tonight. I believe you know my guest, Graham Hawksbury, Earl of Otley."

She arched a brow. "Who could forget having a worm thrust

down the front of one's dress? Is he still as naughty as he was as a child?"

"He's quite settled compared to then, though I'm sure he might make an exception for you."

"Married? Children?"

Arthur snorted. "Not married. He was engaged but she called it off for someone else. Poor Graham was not expecting that. It threw him off balance for a time."

"I'm sorry to hear that."

Rising from his chair, Arthur came around his desk. "I'm afraid I have an appointment, but I'll be back in a couple of hours. Feel free to go over things about tonight with the housekeeper and Cook."

"I'll be fine. I think once I've visited the kitchen, I'll write some letters, let some friends know where I'll be."

Roxanne watched her brother as he left the room. Though this hadn't been what she hoped for, it was far better than staying in that house. Arthur always tried to make sure she was taken care of. Even when she was married to Casper, he would stay in touch by letters and checked in on her as often as he could. He had disapproved of his father's choice of a husband for her but was ignored. Their father did what he wanted, without regard to the fact he was ruining his daughter's life. Money and status were more important. It always had been, and he expected those around him to obey him. He ran his family like he would a business. He cared little for anyone's feelings; he expected nothing less than total loyalty from everyone around him. His family, his staff and business partners. Friends were treated little better than anyone else.

The past was the past, and she had a wonderful opportunity to go forward in her life. As a widow she had far more opportunities than others. For now, she would settle back into society thanks to her brother. She could do things on her own terms and at her own time.

She walked into the drawing room and continued to the far

wall where a writing desk was placed overlooking the terrace and gardens. Noting the writing paper and pens to one side, Roxanne sat down and chose one of each. She would write Georgiana first and let her know where she was and her immediate plans. Her dear friend was also a widow but had found love again. Her first husband had been similar in character to Casper, which was one more thing that drew the two women closer.

Roxanne kept writing her friend, hoping she and her new husband were happy and content. That was a silly thought. She knew Georgiana would never remarry if she wasn't madly in love with a man. For Roxanne, she wasn't sure what love was. She hadn't lived it yet because according to her father at the time he announced she would marry Casper, he told her love was made from fairy tales. Marriages like what she was about to embark on were typical to those who came before her. Marriage was to bring powerful families together. No love, no affection, only respect. Things would be different this time around. Whenever that time would be.

She was eternally grateful to her brother. She needed to help Arthur find his perfect duchess. Perhaps while staying at the family home she would be able to do that. Once she settled in and began to be invited to social functions, she would be able to meet young women and hopefully find one worthy of becoming Arthur's wife and duchess. She had kept in contact with others who in turn might point out potential women for Arthur.

Beyond the ducal estates, Arthur's business interests were many. She knew he'd sold two businesses belonging to their late father because they hadn't been performing as well as they could have. He'd taken that money and reinvested it. Though she was not completely familiar with how he did so, she could see how much happier he was not having to manage a business that bled money. Roxanne wondered if Graham had anything to do with it. Or was his appearance for dinner simply as it appeared? Two friends sharing a meal and catching up on each other's lives. Time would tell, beginning with tonight.

Sealing the letter to Georgiana, she exited the drawing room in search of a footman. The sooner her friend got the letter, the quicker they could see each other.

# CHAPTER TWO

A s Roxanne headed to the drawing room door later that evening, she stopped in front of a large, gilded mirror to check herself. She wanted to look perfect. First impressions were lasting ones, and since she hadn't seen Graham since they were children, this would obviously be a first meeting and one she wanted him to remember.

She smoothed her dark-blue silk gown. The dress was one she had picked up in Paris before leaving for London. Paris was ahead in fashion trends, and she made sure she supplemented her wardrobe with the more sophisticated gowns of the Continent. One last look, and she turned to head for the closed door.

Arthur and Graham were standing in front of the mantel talking, enjoying a glass of whiskey. If Arthur hadn't been standing alongside his friend, she would never have recognized him. Long gone was the gangly young boy and in his place was a grown man who had matured into someone muscular and tall. Both were dressed in evening attire, but it was Graham who stood above Arthur. His jacket was well filled out, and even without speaking to him, Roxanne could easily see he was articulate and confident.

Golden eyes met hers as she closed the gap between them. She was intrigued by the man she saw standing next to Arthur.

"Here she is," Arthur said, placing his glass on the mantel and coming her way.

"This can't be Roxanne," Graham's gravelly baritone replied.

"I can assure you it's me, and I must confess, the only thing I do remember is the prank you played on me."

He looked confused and turned to Arthur for explanation. Her brother, in turn, in low tones mentioned what prank she was talking about. He must have suddenly remembered because a huge smile crossed his handsome face before he let out a laugh.

"Well, I should apologize for my behavior and assure you nothing like that will happen again."

She shook her head as Arthur handed her a glass of white wine. "No need. It was a long time ago and like you said, we were children."

"Indeed," Graham said. "Arthur tells me you've just returned from the south of France. Did you enjoy your time there?"

"Yes, yes, I did. It's beautiful, and I highly recommend it if you haven't been. You can easily travel to Italy from the south of France."

He nodded. "It's one of my favorite places to go on holiday." A smug smile crossed his face.

The arrogant prig! She wanted to wipe the self-satisfied look off his face. Only problem was—his face was too handsome to risk such brutality. Nonetheless, she was not impressed by his attitude. If Arthur had caught the exchange, he'd understand. Or would he? He and Graham seemed to be thick as thieves, so for now she wouldn't let him think he could get a rise out of her. That would drive him crazy, being bested by a woman.

At that time, the butler announced dinner.

"Shall we?" Arthur said.

She led the men to the dining room and sat where she normally would. To Arthur's right. Graham took the only other seat with a place setting directly across from her and to Arthur's left. For the first time, she wished she had a flower arrangement placed in front of them. Then he wouldn't be able to look through her with those haunting eyes nor would they be able to carry on a conversation. Hopefully, Arthur and he would engage, and she would be left to her own devices. Roxanne knew from past experiences that if one listened to men when they weren't expecting a woman to be paying attention, she could learn a lot. Business, sports, politics, and an unlimited list of topics.

"Arthur tells me you'll be staying here for the immediate future," he said as the soup course was removed. The tender turtle soup had been a welcome change.

"Yes. He's most insistent I do not stay at the house my late husband left to me."

Graham nodded slightly. "Yes, he mentioned that. He's right. It's not a place for ladies of your standing."

"Her late husband was a cruel man. That's evident in how he treated Roxanne and what he failed to leave her," Arthur added.

"If I may be so bold, did he leave you with any funds to live off of?" Graham inquired. He picked up his fork and speared a piece of lamb.

"You're joking, aren't you?" Roxanne laughed lightly. "The only things I received were that house and one hundred pounds a year. A very paltry sum considering the size of my dowry he got when we married."

"Remember what I said, it's in the past and things will only get better," Arthur said.

"I'm more than ready to move on."

The evening ended up being far more enjoyable than Roxanne expected. Graham, she found, was fascinating and he genuinely listened to her. He made her feel at ease. Talking with him was easier than she originally thought it would be. He wasn't condescending like a lot of men were when talking to the fairer sex.

When the meal ended, rather than the two men staying behind for their port and cigars, they joined Roxanne in the drawing room. Arthur offered her a port and when she declined, he brought her a splash of brandy. She sipped it and listened to the latest on what was going on in London. The three years she had been away left her always inquiring for any bit of news from back home.

She was brought back from her thoughts by Graham addressing her.

"Would you care to accompany me to Hyde Park on Thursday? There is to be a concert given by an American orchestra. They're supposed to be quite phenomenal."

She was tongue tied and looked to Arthur for guidance. "I would accompany you, but I've two important meetings and I cannot cancel them."

"Very well. I accept your invitation. It sounds intriguing to say the least."

She wasn't sure of anything, and since she hadn't heard from any of her friends, it was a good way to get outside and enjoy the park and music. Roxanne had nothing else planned, and if she refused his invitation, both Arthur and Graham would know the truth. And besides, Thursday was three days off and anything could happen. Graham might have some sort of business meeting suddenly come up or it could pour down rain and everything would be canceled. Of the two, that was the most likely scenario.

"If you will excuse me, I'm tired after such a long day," Roxanne declared. "I'll leave you gentlemen to your discussions."

Arthur neared her. He placed a kiss on her forehead. "Pleasant dreams."

"Thank you." She turned to Graham. "It was nice to see you again."

"And you as well. I look forward to our outing Thursday afternoon."

She nodded and headed to the door, never looking back, or saying another word.

Roxanne dismissed the young girl waiting on her when she arrived in her rooms, despite the maid protesting. A fire was burning, the bed turned back, and the heavy draperies drawn to keep out the light and hopefully some of the London noise. Once she changed into her night rail, Roxanne sat at the dressing table and let her hair down. After removing her jewelry, she picked up the brush before her and began to brush her long hair, recalling the evening's events. She finally climbed into bed. Her eyes closed, and that was the last she remembered until morning when she heard her lady's maid rustling around the room. Roxanne cracked an eye. It was most definitely morning, but rather than blue skies, she could tell they were gray. Deciding she couldn't stay abed any longer, she slowly sat up and swung her legs over the side of the bed. Time to begin another day. Today she would catch up on correspondence, and after that she would meet with the housekeeper and Cook.

Choosing a light-gray day dress, piped with black on the collar, sleeves, and hem, she headed to the small room off the dressing area. A large copper tub was filled with hot water, the steam rising to the ceiling. On a small table at the side of the tub were a bar of orange-honeysuckle soap she had discovered in France, a washing cloth, and a towel. She dipped her toes into the water and, deciding it was just as she liked it, Roxanne immersed herself into the tub, sat back, and closed her eyes for a moment while she enjoyed the experience.

The maid helped her dress. Neither of them said much, but Roxanne wasn't much for early morning conversation. Checking herself in a mirror, she left the calm and tranquility of her rooms and headed downstairs for breakfast.

Arthur sat at one end of the table, a half-eaten plate of food before him and a pile of newspapers to his left. He stood upon seeing her. "Good morning. I trust you slept well."

She regarded her brother for a moment before answering him. Arthur was sharply dressed, everything perfectly put together, what with the gray suit he wore with the white, starched shirt and gray cravat. His hair was short, and his face freshly shaved. Any woman would love to be seen on his arm. Pity, he claimed there was no one.

"Yes, very well."

"Excellent. What are your plans for this dreary day?"

"Correspondence, meet with the cook and housekeeper. After that, I'm not sure."

"I'm sure you'll figure it out," he said with a grin. "You seemed to get along with Graham well enough."

She smiled. "He's your friend. Why wouldn't I? That doesn't mean he's still not a rake, and an arrogant one at that."

A footman placed a plate in front of her filled with some of her breakfast favorites. Eggs, sausage, toast.

"The man has a mind like a steel trap when it comes to business. He's years ahead of the rest of us. A true visionary."

Roxanne buttered her toast thoughtfully. "I'm not looking for a husband, Arthur, so don't play matchmaker."

"I'm not. Graham is a good man to know. He knows a lot of people and is well respected."

"I deduced as much. Otherwise, I would have never agreed to go to this concert in Hyde Park with him."

He snorted as he picked up a newspaper from the pile. "No, you wouldn't have agreed to it. Go, have fun. You deserve it."

She said nothing, instead choosing to finish her breakfast. Looking outside, she sighed and reached for the marmalade to spread on her bread. She had traded a life of sun for this? But, as she told herself time and time again, in the south of France she had been hiding from life and came back to face the reality that was her new life without Casper.

"That's going to take some time. When you are constantly reminded that you're only a cash cow and no one would want you, you begin to believe your attacker. Casper and I may have lived separate lives, but he always made sure I knew where I belonged in his world."

"That's something I plan to begin looking into today. I'm going to his attorney to see if there's something that might have been overlooked at the initial reading."

"I can assure you there isn't. Everything was presented as per the will."

"Perhaps. You're a woman, and that closes a lot of doors for you. Having someone like Graham in your corner can only help."

"I hope you're right."

Putting his newspaper to one side, he stood. "I'll see you later. Oh, I'll be having dinner at my club this evening, so don't have Cook go to any great lengths. Enjoy yourself."

"You as well," she said as she concentrated on her plate, the contents of which she had barely touched as Arthur exited through the door, leaving her alone with her thoughts.

Forcing herself to finish breakfast, Roxanne moved herself to the library where there was a writing desk, not to mention row after row of books. The smell of leather was intoxicating. As a child she loved to come in here and find herself immersed in books. Her grandfather had even made a section for younger readers, making sure what they chose was at their level of comprehension.

A polished black baby grand occupied one corner of the room. Immediately, she wondered if Arthur was still playing. If his schedule allowed him a few hours a week. She could play, but her abilities never came close to matching Arthur's.

Sitting at the writing desk, she took out paper from the drawer. Her first letter was to her aunt letting her know she had returned safely and where she would be staying for the immediate future. If it hadn't been for her, Roxanne wasn't sure what would have become of her during that dark time in her life. But, from the beginning of her marriage until the time of Casper's death, her very existence had been something she never wished on anyone. Though they both led separate lives, her late husband managed to find ways to make her miserable by what he would allow or wouldn't allow her to do. It had always been an amusing game to him, seeing her jump at his every command. He knew her weaknesses and vulnerabilities and fed off of them.

She shook off the morbid feelings she had whenever she thought about her deceased husband. Her letter to her dear aunt had to be upbeat and cheerful, but without overdoing it. Violet would read right through her words if she did, and she didn't want the woman scolding her or worrying about her.

The weather had seemed to change since she first awoke. The clouds had parted, leaving behind sun. Her eyes returned to the letter she was working on. It amused her how quickly English weather could change. Rereading what she had written to Violet, Roxanne finished the letter and moved on to the next. Short missives went out to a few friends she knew stayed in town. Most went to their country estates to enjoy the beautiful warm weather. Then there were others who lagged behind because their husbands were not in a hurry or whose husbands left them to their own resources. Regardless, the majority ended up in the country—even herself. She knew her brother's schedule quite well. He would be ready sooner rather than later to go to the family home in Kent. She knew he detested the hot weather, the lingering smells the city and the Thames left behind. He would expect her to join him so that she could help host his friends for various shooting matches and dinners he would want to hold. It was a part of their agreement, and she truly didn't mind. He had saved her from making a huge mistake by moving into the house left to her. Hopefully something could be done with the property before long. She was sure Arthur had someone looking into options, and in a short amount of time, the wheels of progress would be in motion. If the house were sold, she would have funds to support herself or to purchase her own home in town. She would rather have that option than be a landlord or have someone else oversee the property and its tenants.

She wanted to be completely free of any reminder or connection to that sliver of her life. Free like it had never happened.

After her third letter, Roxanne decided that was enough for the day. She needed to find a book in this room to satisfy her inquisitive thirst for knowledge. Newly purchased books had always been kept either on a table to one side of the room's center or on a shelf specifically designated for that purpose.

Quickly finding a mystery novel on the table, she decided it wouldn't hurt for her to sit back down and read for a short period of time. She had nothing but time on her hands, and a quick escape from reality was exactly what she needed. Reading had always been an escape for her and this was no different.

A knock on the door brought her back to the present. The butler nodded and picked up her letters still sitting on the desk. It was too early for her to have a response of any sort.

"Is there anything else, milady?"

"A pot of tea would be nice."

He nodded and retreated from the room, leaving Roxanne alone again. Not that she minded her solitude. It was only that she wished she had something—something with a purpose to fill her time. She could see about a charity or something similar to occupy her time, but she had to slow down. This was only her first full day. There was no time to rush. She had all the time in the world, and once she began hearing from her friends, her life would be filled with a social life and purposeful things to do.

One of her projects was going to be to assist her brother in finding a wife. He had been a bachelor long enough. It was time for him to settle. He needed an heir. Arthur seemed to have little interest in the matter, but she would change all of that. There had to be a bevy of prospective brides, even if they weren't all in London. He needed someone his equal. The last thing Arthur needed was a frail, timid bride. He needed someone who could fulfill the requirements of being his duchess.

Roxanne felt so out of touch having been away so long, but she made herself a promise that she would dive in headfirst whether she wanted to or not.

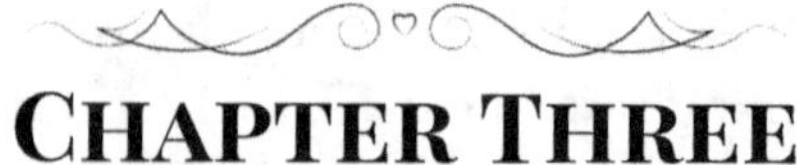

CHAPTER THREE

ROXANNE PAUSED AT the drawing room door. Inside, the Earl of Otley, Graham waited for her. Today he'd come to escort her to Hyde Park for a concert by a renowned American orchestra. She'd been looking forward to this for days. The only problem was that the sky was gray with clouds that threatened to burst open at any time. Not to be deterred, she walked into the room. The earl stood at the window looking out.

"Do you think the weather will cooperate?" she asked as she neared.

"This is London. Hard to say," Graham said as he turned to face her.

"True. Can I get you some tea, or shall we just get going?"

She had chosen to wear a sapphire-colored cotton dress trimmed in black piping. Graham obviously was drawn to her because he hadn't stopped looking her up and down since she walked across the room. She desperately wanted to say something but held back, thinking it a bad idea. They were reacquainting themselves with each other, and what she had in mind to say might make him think twice about the invitation he extended to her.

"I think we should head towards the park. There are quite a few tea shops we can stop at should you like."

It took her a few seconds to come up with an answer. Why

was she so tongue-tied talking with this man? He was far from her type, though she wasn't even sure what type of man she liked. Besides, a man in her life was the last thing she needed. She had Arthur, and that was more than enough.

"Very well. Shall we?"

He nodded and gestured for her to walk to the door. Roxanne couldn't help but notice he was attired to the most minute detail in a dark brown suit. A starched white shirt with a matching cravat completed his dress and, in all honesty, Roxanne could hardly keep from staring at him. He was one of the most strikingly handsome men she had ever laid eyes on. He was meticulous, not a hair out of place and not a wrinkle in his attire.

Graham stood by as Roxanne gathered her shawl and hat. He picked up his hat as they went through the door.

"We'll take my carriage just in case the sky decides to open up."

"Very well," Roxanne said as she let him help her into the carriage. She caught a whiff of his shaving soap as she ascended the steps to his carriage. It was spearmint and leather combined into one. The scent was one she would not soon forget. She scolded herself for having thoughts like that and hoped her face didn't give her away.

She settled on the tan leather, tufted seat and waited for him to join her. She was looking out the carriage window when she heard the carriage door close and the carriage shift as he settled on the seat across from her. He tapped his cane on the roof of the carriage. They were on their way.

Graham finally broke the silence between them. "Today people will know you've returned to London and invitations should begin to arrive."

"True, but when they see I'm with someone other than Arthur, they're going to immediately conclude there is something more at play between us."

He chuckled. "Ah, I see how it is. Roxanne, you really need to stop worrying what other people think. You're a widow enjoying an afternoon out with a friend of the family. Nothing more, nothing less."

"And you, sir, need to learn to be less arrogant and condescending. I understand why you're not married. No woman would have you with those qualities," she said, turning her head from him to the hustle and bustle of London outside the coach.

"You certainly have grown wiser than your years, dear Roxanne."

"Don't call me that."

"What?"

"Dear. I'm not your dear anything."

"I'll keep that in mind," he said smugly.

She inhaled deeply and turned her attention back to the creature before her. She studied him. He was broad of shoulder, tall, and dangerously handsome. His dark hair nearly brushed his shoulders, and a well-trimmed beard shadowed his jaw. Above the sharp cheekbones were a pair of startling golden-brown eyes. This was the man she'd been in love with since she was a child. A man who melted her heart until her father sold her off to Casper. Roxanne silently cursed herself as she felt those old feelings surfacing from where they had lain dormant for years.

No! This is not possible!

Roxanne's thoughts were interrupted by that familiar voice. "What are you so deep in thought about?"

"Nothing."

"Liar," he said with a smirk. Something she wanted to slap from his face.

She turned her attention instead to outside the carriage window. The traffic was thick, meaning they were nearing the park. The horses had slowed to almost a crawl. More people were out walking. The day wasn't that dreary not to walk. Everyone headed in the same direction.

"Roxanne?"

"What, Graham? Can't we ride along in peace? Conversation is not necessary, I can assure you."

"I was going to ask if you'd like to walk the rest of the way. We may be a while if we wait in this."

How should she respond? If they continued in the carriage, she would have to endure his drivel. If they got out, it would be too noisy to try and hold any sort of conversation.

"We might as well walk as we're almost to the park gates."

He tapped the ceiling of the carriage once again. One of the young men opened the door to see what Graham needed. "Tell the driver to stop. We'll walk the rest of the way."

"Yes, milord."

Moments later, the carriage came to a halt and the pair descended. He paused to say something to the driver before returning to her and offering his arm. Roxanne hesitated for a second, but moments later linked her arm through his after being jostled by passing pedestrians. Everyone, it seemed, was not letting the possibility of rain ruin their plans today.

The farther into the park they went, the more the crowd thinned out.

"Should we head to where the concert is going to be given and make sure we can catch a glimpse of the orchestra?" Roxanne asked as they continued to walk.

"We can, though we might be better off on the edges in case it begins to pour."

"Come on, Graham, live a little. What's a bit of rain?" she taunted.

He glanced upward towards the heavens. "If those clouds do in fact open up, everyone is going to be soaked."

They continued walking towards the grass where the concert would be held. Roxanne could feel eyes glaring at her, or them. She wasn't sure which. Something caught her eye in her peripheral vision. She turned her head ever so slightly to see that Lady Mulbury was holding court with a small group of women. It was obvious who they were talking about. Being the center of the dragon lady's gossip didn't bother her. At least the ton would quickly know she'd returned from the Continent. She was sure they were also speculating about her and Graham being together. She detested gossips, but sometimes they could be useful.

Graham bent down and lowly spoke to her. "I see the dragon isn't afraid of a little rain."

"So it seems, and we seem to be their gossip. Pity they don't have anything better to do."

"Everyone will know you've returned, so that sort of gossip is good, isn't it?"

"It depends on what is being told," she said.

Graham nodded. "I see your point."

They continued on their path. Roxanne prayed simply acknowledging the group would be good enough for now. She had no desire to be lured into the group. Unfortunately, today she wasn't going to be so lucky.

"Lady Smith," Lady Mulbury said with some distaste dripping from her mouth. "I heard you'd returned, though I didn't expect to see you here. I understood you to live in a less prestigious section of the city."

Roxanne glared at her, refusing to be spun into her web. "If you consider Grosvenor Square a less prestigious section of Mayfair, then yes."

She didn't dare look up at Graham. That would be suicide because she'd burst out laughing and Lady Mulbury would have her for a snack.

"You're staying at your family home?"

"Yes."

"You must come for a visit sometime and tell me all about your stay in the south of France."

She nodded. "I would like that, Lady Mulbury."

Graham, at that time, bent down and whispered, "No cause for alarm, but we need to turn around and head to my carriage. The skies are about to open up, and it's not going to be good."

She glanced up. The skies were a yellowish-gray with a much darker color rolling behind it. Quickly she addressed Lady Mulbury. "It was nice to see you again. Lord Hawksbury is anxious to find ourselves a good seat."

"Good day," the dragon said.

Graham's strides were long, and it was hard for her to keep up as he headed to where his carriage sat. Upon seeing them approach, the door to the carriage was opened just as drops of rain began to fall. "Faster; we're almost there."

Just as he handed her up into the carriage, the black sky opened up. Graham quickly shut the door as he settled onto the seat across from Roxanne. He removed his hat and grinned.

Looking outside, she saw people scurrying to their carriages or anywhere dry. She could see Lady Mulbury and the ladies with her rushing towards the waiting carriage. They were going to be soaked by the deluge as fast as they were going.

"Well, drat! I was looking forward to hearing some music," she said.

"Another time."

"Absolutely," she said. "Why don't we return to the house and have a cup of hot tea?"

"Sounds amenable to a wet, dank afternoon."

Roxanne focused her attention away from Graham to the scenery outside. She had forgotten what a gorgeous man he had become. Not that he wasn't always handsome. Now he had the maturity he lacked all those years ago. And like a long time ago, she still found herself drawn to him. Like there was some force at work. She would have to be careful. She didn't need a broken heart, and she didn't need to be involved with any man. She needed to enjoy life as a widow because a whole new world had opened up to her the moment Casper died.

Being friends with Graham was all she needed now. He'd always been kind and caring to her, and she could trust him with some of her secrets. He kept them to himself, not even revealing them to Arthur. There were some things better off not being told to her brother. After all, a lady needed an air of mysteriousness.

"Where are you, Rox? You're deep in thought and haven't heard a word I've said."

"I'm sorry. I was just woolgathering. Since I've returned, I find myself doing that quite a bit."

"A lot has changed since you were gone, and your life isn't as it was when you left for France."

"I want to do something productive. Not that overseeing the house for Arthur isn't, but there has to be more. I just can't figure out what it should be."

"Don't be in a hurry. Just take your time to settle in. You have a unique opportunity to do so. Allow yourself time. I'm sure if you do, a plan will emerge to you."

She smiled. "Thank you, Graham. That is very sage advice."

"I'm glad you feel that way," he said with a lop-sided grin.

She felt her heart melt just a little. What was this? She'd never remotely thought of Graham as anything but her brother's closest friend. That wasn't entirely true, but she would never let the world know of that little fact. She may have enjoyed his company today, but it went no further. No further at all. He was still the rake she remembered him to be. At least Arthur had settled some since he inherited his title. Graham seemed to still have that coltish, I-can-do-no-wrong attitude. Not as bad as he used to be, but it was still there.

THE DRAWING ROOM was warm and inviting on such a wretched, gloomy afternoon. As they waited on tea to arrive, Roxanne padded towards the hearth and sat down in her favorite chair, a cream and blue damask high-back. She motioned to Graham to join her. He sat down in the other high-back and stretched his legs in front of the hearth.

She pulled a letter the butler had given her upon their arrival. A long-expected letter from Georgiana.

"Feel free to read it if you wish," Graham said. His eyes were closed as though he were napping. Obviously, his hearing was in perfect working order.

"Thank you. I just want to see where Georgiana might be. I would love to go for a visit. We haven't seen each other for several years now."

Graham grunted.

She carefully unfolded the letter. Georgiana and her husband, Jeremy, were spending the summer at his family estate on the Isle of Wight. Georgiana invited her to join them. The pair had a lot of catching up to do.

That was as far as she read. She didn't want to be rude. She had a guest. Even if it was Graham.

The correspondence was returned to the pocket in her dress just as tea was being brought into the drawing room. The footman brought the trolley and stopped it in front of them. Just as stealthily, the young man in red and gold livery left the room, closing the door behind him. Roxanne eyed the cart closely. There was cake, sandwiches, and more cake. She recognized the latter as being seedcake, which she remembered was Graham's favorite. Obviously Cook remembered his fondness for her cakes.

She poured tea for both of them and handed the cup and saucer to Graham who was now sitting straight in his chair. He accepted the tea and set it down on the table in between them. She passed him a small plate with a piece of the seedcake, which he immediately began to eat.

"Your cook is to be commended. Her seedcake is the best I've ever tasted."

"I remembered you liked it, and I'm sure she did as well. She used to give us a piece of whatever she might have baked that day. Always looking out for us. You and Arthur were growing young men, you know."

"I'm sure," he said, his mouth half full of cake. Instantly he reminded her of the boy from a long time ago.

Her thoughts were interrupted by the door opening and Arthur walking in.

"Horrid day for a concert," Arthur said as he stood next to the hearth to warm himself.

"It never happened," Roxanne said. "We were rained out before it was time."

"She's right. It seemed anyone who was anybody was there. Even that old dragon, Lady Mulbury," Graham added.

"I would love to know if she made it to her carriage or if she got rained on," Arthur said with a cheeky grin.

"There were a lot of people scrambling to get out of the rain as we departed," Roxanne said.

"Sounds like you two were the wisest, leaving as quickly as you did."

"Yes, we were. Now, would you gentlemen excuse me while I go upstairs and change into something dry?" She eyed Graham. "Don't dare leave before I return."

"Yes, milady," he said.

She hurried across the room and up the stairs to her rooms. She wanted to read Georgiana's letter in detail in quiet. She wasn't damp in the least, but it offered a good excuse for her. She'd not be found out either. She would change regardless. First, the letter beckoned her. Roxanne sat at her dressing table and began reading.

Georgiana gave her a rundown on what was happening on the tiny island. She invited her to come visit if it was possible. Roxanne was sure that unless Arthur had something for her to help him host, she could go visit Georgiana. Further into the letter, her friend shocked her with the news that they were expecting a child. Travel this summer would be on a daily basis as she was miserable from being sick every morning, though she was hoping it would pass as quickly as it began.

Roxanne refolded the letter and placed it in a drawer until she could answer it.

She changed into a moss-colored cotton day dress. Immediately she felt better, having to admit she may have been damper than she let on. Returning downstairs, she found the drawing room empty. Not to be deterred, she turned and made her way to

Arthur's study. Knocking lightly on the door, she was summoned to enter.

Arthur sat behind his desk reading a paper. He looked up. "Graham said to apologize to you, but he had an appointment he completely forgot about. He'll be in touch."

"He said all that? Funny, he never mentioned having an appointment. He led me to believe he was free all afternoon." She shook her head and sat down in the leather chair. "Of course, we're talking about Graham, so this shouldn't surprise me."

"Must you always be so hard on him?"

"I haven't even gotten started being hard on him. A gentleman would have waited or at least written a short note explaining the situation. Or he could have mentioned his so-called appointment before I went upstairs. He'll never change. He's still the arrogant prig I remember."

"It must have been important because his valet came, handed Graham a letter, mentioned something to Graham. He left as soon as he finished reading the letter. So try and ease up on him."

"I shall try," she said.

What was it about the male sex that made them so insensitive to others? The aristocracy was the worst.

CHAPTER FOUR

GRAHAM PULLED THE letter out of his coat and reread it. The words on the page were the same as when he read it at Arthur's. The contents of the letter knocked him off his foundation. This wasn't something he could share with anyone, not until he had time to let it sink in and he was clear-headed to make decisions.

He had kept a mistress for the past two years. He ended it and when he did, Frannie hadn't taken it well. Despite him having furnished her with a place to live and funds, she still refused to believe he would walk away. That had been almost a year ago. After the initial shock, he never heard from her, leaving Graham to believe she had moved on and found someone else to support her.

Never in a thousand years would he have thought she'd give birth, let alone be with child without getting word to him. Perhaps the child wasn't his or she wasn't sure who the father was. He doubted the latter. Frannie was never kept by more than one man. Even if tempted.

She would have never left the child at his door in a basket. His valet had told him the infant couldn't be but perhaps a day old if that. So Graham sent the man to Frannie's house to check out how she was and what she was about.

The carriage slowed as the four-story, red brick home came

into view. His grandfather had built the house after the original burned to the ground after a freak lightning strike. At the time it was built, it was one of the largest homes in Mayfair. Now it would be considered a smaller residence.

A footman opened the carriage door and Graham climbed out and headed up the front steps as fast as he could. The butler, Fredericks, opened the door just as his feet hit the last step.

"Where is the child?" he asked as he divested his hat and coat and handed them to Fredericks.

"In the kitchen. The ladies are getting her warmed up and fed."

"So it's a girl?"

"Yes, milord," he said. "A very striking child for just being born. Most look like shriveled up prunes."

"They're certain the child has just been born?" Graham asked.

"Yes, quite certain."

"Fetch the doctor just to be sure. I'm going to the kitchens."

"Milord, I can have one of the ladies bring the babe to you. No need to go to the kitchens."

Graham shook his head. "Nonsense. I don't mind. Just see word is gotten to the doctor."

"As you wish, milord."

He rushed down the back stairs and through the kitchens where he found Cook and his housekeeper looking into a basket at what he presumed was the child. As he approached, they moved away, giving him a chance to see for himself. What he saw was a tiny, dark-haired infant sleeping. A babe that favored his late sister Mary. His sister had died of influenza as a child, but Graham always remembered her violet eyes and coal black hair.

"How is she?"

"Better now," Cook said. "We changed her, and she drank some milk. What would you like us to do, milord?"

"The doctor has been sent for, so let's wait and see what he says. The nursery needs to be made ready immediately. Until it is, please bring a cradle down from the nursery. Have it cleaned and put into the yellow guest room. She can stay there until the nursery is ready."

Both women agreed, nodding their heads, looking between themselves. He knew what was going through their minds. There was no denying this child wasn't his own. And Cook, having been with the family since she was a young girl when her mother ran the kitchens, knew better than anyone. She and Mary had been friends, even though his mother frowned on the idea at first. His mother quickly understood the friendship was good for Mary since she was schooled by tutors at home and had no other girlfriends.

He took one last look at the babe before backing away. "I'll be in my study. Please send someone for me when the doctor arrives."

"Yes, milord."

He turned and made long strides out of the kitchens and up the stairs. Minutes later, he was in his study, pouring himself a whiskey. He deserved one considering what he had just discovered. Frannie had been with child and never told him. He would have to call on her. His man would be back from Frannie's residence and would hopefully have some news.

Graham knew from laying eyes on the babe she was his. There was no denying it. What was he supposed to do? He wasn't going to send her off. She was his flesh and blood. Regardless of the fact he was a bachelor, he would see she was raised properly. He could send her to one of his estates with a nanny, but that would never do. They would never share a bond if he went that way.

There was no reason for decisions to be made until the doctor came. He also intended to pay Frannie a visit and see what she was about. His solicitors would draw up the papers so he would be recognized as the girl's father. Why Frannie didn't want the babe was beyond his comprehension. The only thing that came to mind was that the child reminded her too much of him. That and Frannie had never voiced a desire to become a mother.

He took a long swallow of his whiskey and shut his eyes for a moment. In the blink of an eye, his life had been forever changed. Graham wondered what Roxanne would think about all of this. Why she mattered in the scheme of things, he wasn't sure. The feelings he had for her were new to him and he didn't want to ruin what little progress he'd made with her over this. He would need to think things through and concoct some sort of story to tell.

The doctor arrived, and while he was examining the girl, Graham paced the floor outside the door of the bedchamber. It didn't take long, but he felt every second he waited. The doctor emerged, holding his hat in one hand and his medical bag in the other.

"By my estimate the child can't be but a few hours old. She appears in perfect health. You'll need a wet nurse, of course. I'll arrange one to stop by and introduce herself to you."

"Not necessary. As long as my cook and housekeeper are comfortable with the woman, that is good enough for me."

"Very well. Send for me should the need arise, but as I said, the babe is in perfect health."

Graham knew the older man wanted to know more but wasn't about to ask him. Smart man. It was no one's business—at least for the immediate future.

"Thank you for your discretion," Graham said. He followed the doctor to the stairs and walked behind him down to the front reception hall.

Donning his black hat, the man nodded and left. Turning around, Graham caught the outline of the young man he'd sent to Frannie's. Perhaps he had some news.

"Did you see her?" Graham asked.

"No, milord. Her man said she had left two weeks ago, taking all her personal belongings. She told him she was going to her sister's to give birth. He had no further information about where her sister lived. She had hired a carriage to take her to wherever she was going instead of using the one you furnished her."

"Very well. See if you can find out anything further. I would think someone would know something of her whereabouts."

The man nodded. "I'll get straight on it, milord."

"Thank you."

Graham had no knowledge of where any of Frannie's family could be. He knew her parents had died years ago, when she was just a child, but that was all. No mention of siblings, cousins, or where she came from. The only thing she did let slip once was that her father had been a sailor. His attorney would have to investigate this further. If necessary, he'd have the man hire someone to look into Frannie's background and find her, because from where he stood, she did not wish to be found.

His mind was spinning now. He had a lot to have taken care of. He would retire to his study and write what correspondence needed to be sent. It was important to get in to see the attorney.

First, he needed to see his housekeeper or Cook. The babe was going to need clothing and whatever else someone so tiny required. He took to the steps two at a time and entered the yellow bedchamber where he found his housekeeper speaking with a young woman.

"Sorry to interrupt, but I just wanted to let you know to purchase whatever is needed for the child."

"Thank you, milord. This is Jane. She is going to be helping Cook and me out with the child until a nanny is hired."

"She has experience with babies?"

"Yes, milord," Jane said. "I'm the oldest of eight children. I always helped out with the younger ones, especially the babies so Ma could get things done."

"I see. That will work until someone is found."

"Was there anything else, milord?"

Graham shook his head. "No. I simply wanted to make sure you purchased whatever is needed."

The babe was sleeping, but Graham could still see that shock of black hair in the cradle. He smiled and turned to leave for his study.

He sat down at his desk, took a sheet of fresh paper, and began writing, requesting to urgently see his lawyer. Once he finished, he rang for the butler, requesting the missive be delivered immediately. This was the most important thing to be done. Being named the child's guardian as soon as possible was important as it would allow him to raise the girl in the manner she should be.

He chuckled at the thought of some of the dowagers and other older ladies of the ton getting ahold of the news that he had an infant to raise. One of dubious origins. It would be the center of gossip. There was nothing stopping that. He never paid them any mind. The whispering and looks at his next social engagement would prove quite interesting. But they would move on quickly the moment something else captured their attention. The ladies were like that. The babe would be old news, and they would move on to the next gossip.

The one they called the dragon lady would be the one who led the charge and would lead the ladies of the ton as to how to accept him now.

Which led him to his next dilemma—Roxanne and Arthur. He needed to let them in on what transpired. Neither needed to hear it through the gossips. They needed to hear it directly from him. His next letter was to Arthur. Without spilling exactly what was going on, he simply told his friend there was an urgent matter he needed to talk to him about and that Roxanne would need to be informed as well. In person. A letter would simply never do.

He poured himself a whiskey and sat down in front of the hearth, where a fire had been set, to contemplate his life.

Since the day he was born, his life was one of privilege. As the heir to his father's title and all that entailed, Hawksbury found life wasn't as easy as one might think for the heir of a great man. His father, as was his father before him and his grandfather, all the way back to the first earl. The men were cold, emotionless, and carried a temper few could match. His father rarely showed interest in his heir, preferring to leave his upbringing and education to the earldom to others. He spent little time with his son, and when he did, his father would often fly off into a rage if Graham missed a target or when hunting with his father and failed to kill prey.

His mother, on the other hand, was a loving, kind woman. One who deeply loved her two children. That changed when Mary died. His mother never recovered from her loss. Where she had once defended her son from his father's tirades, she now spent most all her time locked away in her rooms, grieving.

His mother had been his heart, and he lost a huge piece of it the day she died.

Now he had been given a child, albeit a bastard, something that would follow her for her entire life unless he could invent her story. First, she needed a name, one befitting a little angel. Mary Charlotte, after his sister and mother. He couldn't think of a more fitting tribute. The babe would also carry his surname in spite of the fact she would become his ward. Perhaps that could change if he ever found a woman worthy of being the girl's mother.

CHAPTER FIVE

"**H**AWKSBURY HAS INVITED us to dinner this evening," Arthur said. He walked across the room where Roxanne was seated near the windows, a book in her hands.

"Have you replied?"

"No, I wanted to check with you first."

Roxanne arched a brow before responding. "I have nothing planned. Do you?"

He shook his head. A wayward strand of dark brown hair fell into one of his eyes and she watched as he pushed it back into place. "He would like us there at seven."

"I'll be ready."

"What are you reading?" Arthur inquired.

"Keats."

"I like Keats. Excellent choice."

"I wrote to my friend, Georgiana. She and her family are on holiday on Wight. She has invited us to visit."

"I don't think I can get away that long."

"Come now, brother, we need to get out of the stench of a city for a while. Wight would be perfect. Or we could go to Gloucester for a month or so."

"I'm not sure that would be such a good idea. You'd want to host a house party."

"No, I wouldn't. Arthur, just about everyone has left the

city."

"If you want to visit your friend, make the arrangements and go. You don't need my permission."

"I know."

Arthur pushed himself to his feet. "If you'll excuse me, I have an appointment with my tailor within the hour."

Roxanne nodded and tried not to grin. Her brother had always disliked trips to a tailor or anyone else for clothing. Funny how things change. "I'll see you in time to leave for Graham's. He has me curious."

"Me too. Makes me wonder what he's up to."

"Perhaps it's something as simple as just wanting friends to share a meal."

"And we shall find out."

He leaned over and kissed her on the cheek. "Enjoy your afternoon."

"Thank you, I shall."

She watched as her brother quit the room. He seemed to be in a jovial mood. Perhaps there was something more to his afternoon than a visit to his tailor. Curiosity piqued her attention as she wondered if there was a lady he might be calling on. Someone he wasn't ready to share with her. He hadn't mentioned anyone but that meant nothing. It was well-known that Arthur was one of a handful of men who was still unmarried after all these years. He was also highly sought after by the mothers, all of whom thought their daughter would be a perfect match for him. Perhaps one of her own friends might suit him. Something to ponder, though matchmaking her brother was not at the top of the list. That was why he needed to get out of London and go somewhere like the seashore. Even his country estates wouldn't do where finding love was concerned. Too secluded for her taste.

Putting her book aside, she stood and walked to the door leading to the terrace. The sun was shining bright, the sky a magnificent shade with white fluffy clouds floating across the blue backdrop. She stepped out onto the terrace and gazed out at the bed of roses. Tending to roses was something she found very satisfying when she was with Casper. It gave her solitude and a way to keep her sanity. Perhaps the head gardener needed to be approached about her wish to tend the blooms. The same could be said for the garden in Gloucester. Roxanne remembered it being her mother's pride and joy. She had enlarged the beds and added hardy new varieties her gardener had helped her graft. Her mother had been well known for her roses and her knowledge of anything to do with them. That was where Roxanne picked up her fondness for roses. Now, until her brother married, she would carry on the tradition and hope Arthur's wife would do as well and not be one of those women who wouldn't be seen doing something as menial as tending roses and insist the gardener keep the beds up. She, in the meantime, would have better things to occupy her time, and Roxanne prayed he didn't take such a woman as his wife. Another reason for her to monitor her brother's choices. She needed to get him out of London. And soon.

She returned to the house to gather her things. It was best to make the most of days like today when the weather was dry. There was a bookshop on the far side of the park. Roxanne wanted to check out their selection of history books and see what they might have on one of her brother's favorite subjects: Roman times in England. He had a vast array of books on the subject, but she knew there were some which eluded him. They were either hard to find or had to be ordered. Arthur's birthday wasn't until the end of summer, so ordering one of them now would be the smart solution to her usual dilemma of what to get her brother on his birthday.

With her list of titles in one hand, Roxanne neatly folded the paper and placed it in her reticule and headed towards the park. It was never as crowded as some of the other parks in the area, but still, if one wanted to be seen by other residents without going to say, Hyde Park, this was the place to go. People were scarce, as most residents fled the city during the summer months. Or at least for the hottest part. London was not at her best this time of year.

The bookshop, Hanson & Son, Booksellers was not busy. A few gentlemen browsing, and that was about it. The shop had been here for as long as Roxanne could remember. Arthur would bring her once their father had said a bookshop was no place for a woman. Women were supposed to let their husbands choose and approve what they read. Since she wasn't married, he would pick out what he considered suitable or let Arthur do it in his place. Arthur usually always approved of what she wanted to read.

Roxanne wandered over to a table near the window which featured newly released books. Sam, the grandson of the owner, approached her, inquiring if there was something he could help her with. He had always been quite knowledgeable, which was to be expected since he'd practically lived at the shop in the afternoons after school, assisting his father and grandfather with whatever needed to be done around the shop.

"Is there something I can help you find, milady?" he asked with a shy grin.

She pulled out her list and handed it to him. "I'm looking for a gift for my brother. These are some titles he's mentioned."

He eyed it closely. "Yes, he's come in a few times looking for a couple of these titles. They have to be ordered, I'm afraid."

"That's fine. Choose two you think he'd really like. I'll order them for his birthday."

"If you'll follow me, I'll get all the information I need."

"Thank you, Sam."

Roxanne followed the young man to the counter and waited as he wrote down everything he needed for the order. As she was standing there, she felt someone approach the space beside her. She didn't acknowledge whoever it was because she didn't want to start a conversation with a perfect stranger. Her goal here had been to find Arthur something for his birthday. Sam handed her a paper he'd been writing on and asked her to make sure everything was correct.

"That's some heavy reading for a young lady such as yourself," the voice from her right said.

She drew in a deep breath and contemplated how to defuse this before it got started. But her mouth had other plans. "Is that so? Just because I am of the fairer sex, doesn't mean I haven't had an excellent education."

"I never meant to imply…"

"No, I'm sure you didn't. If you'll excuse me, I need to finish my purchase," she said, turning her attention back to Sam. "Sam, please send the bill to me, and not my brother. I don't want him paying for his own present."

"I can have it ready when you come to pick up the order if you like."

She nodded. "That would be perfect. Just send a note around when they've arrived."

"I shall, milady. Is there anything I might interest you in?"

"Not today. I appreciate all your help, Sam. Thank you." She turned and began to walk away, ignoring the man who'd spoken to her moments ago.

"I'm afraid we've gotten off on the wrong foot. Allow me to introduce myself. I'm Franklin Brown. I recently arrived in London."

"I wish you all the best, sir."

He hesitated before leading into, "May I be as bold as to invite you next door for a cup of tea?"

"It's really not necessary. I don't even know you."

"I've told you my name."

She arched a brow. "And that you've recently arrived in London."

"Yes. I received word my older brother, Marquess of Lowshire, died unexpectedly. Since he had no heir, I was called back."

"So now you're the reluctant marquess?"

"Not in the least. It was what I was raised to be in case something this tragic occurred."

"I'm sure you'll make him proud. Now if you'll excuse me."

"Wait, you still haven't told me your name, milady."

"I know. Perhaps I don't wish you to know."

"You have me there."

"Good day to you, sir." She continued to the door and pulled it open, when the newly minted marquess was at her side, holding the door so she could pass. She didn't dare look up at him, but somehow, she caught a glimpse of him anyway. An average man. Dark-blond hair and height. He apparently spent a good deal of time in the sun. Nothing striking about him otherwise.

She crossed the street and headed back to the park. Though she had planned to spend more time looking into the shop windows, this insistent man made her change her plans out of pure caution. Part of her wanted to turn and look behind her, to make sure he wasn't following her, but she didn't dare. He certainly had nerve to be so insistent.

The entrance to the park neared.

"Lady Roxanne? Is everything all right?" a familiar baritone said from her left.

"Yes. I was just headed to the house."

"In such a rush?"

"Well, I…"

He did something completely unexpected. He removed his hat, leaned over and kissed her cheek. "You're a terrible liar. Who is the man you're trying to distance yourself from?" He placed her hand on the crook of his arm and placed his hat back on his head.

"He's following me?"

"Might be. Would you like me to have a word with him?"

"No, if you could escort me, though."

"It would be my pleasure," Graham said.

After a few minutes of silence between them and once they were inside the park, Graham turned his head and looked around as discreetly as possible. "Where did you run into this fellow?" he asked.

"At the bookstore. He approached me at the counter," she

said. "Is he still following?"

"No, but that doesn't mean he isn't still around."

"I swear I did nothing to encourage him. If anything, I was a bit rude."

"I hadn't thought of this before, but he could be someone your stepson hired. I'm sure he knows by now that you didn't move into that house."

Roxanne stopped. "Why could what I do now be of interest to him? Everything was settled. Or so I thought."

"Perhaps learning you aren't living in the house piqued his interest. Why, I don't know. We'll mention it to Arthur and see if he has any thoughts on the matter. In the meantime, we're going to exit the park at a different entrance, and I'll escort you through the kitchens."

"That sounds amenable. However, if this man's done his research, he'll know where the family home is."

Graham chuckled and patted her hand with his free one. He started to walk once again. "I imagine he does, but this way I can get you home without him seeing you return, and we can look out one of the front windows and see if he's out there."

"You don't need to involve yourself in this. I'm sure Arthur can take care of the situation."

"I'm sure he can, but I'm involved, and I'll not see you bothered by some stranger with nefarious intentions."

She sighed, knowing she wasn't going to change his mind. "Then let's go. I had other things planned for the afternoon that didn't involve ducking around alleyways."

He barked out a laugh and they continued at a more rapid pace.

The kitchen staff barely noticed them as they entered through the kitchen garden door. Roxanne and her brother were regular visitors using the door as a means of escape back when it was needed. Roxanne caught the eye of the housekeeper and asked the woman if any of the staff had noticed anyone hanging around the alley. She said she hadn't but would inquire with the rest of the staff and ask everyone to be vigilant.

Climbing the stairs to the main floor, Roxanne and Graham stopped in the front hall. "If you want to speak to Arthur, I'll see if he's returned home."

"Not necessary. We can discuss this at dinner tonight," he said.

"I look forward to it, and yes, we can talk about it with Arthur then."

"I'll take my leave and see you this evening. Don't leave the house, just to be safe."

"Don't you want to see if he's outside?" she asked.

"I doubt he's going to be that brazen. I'll keep a lookout for him."

"Very well. Thank you for escorting me safely home."

"The pleasure was mine."

The butler had appeared out of nowhere and had the door open. From Roxanne's viewpoint, she could see no one lurking across the street. The only people were those headed somewhere. She stood and watched Graham disappear. The butler closed the door.

"You have some letters which arrived this afternoon. I placed them on your desk in your chamber, milady."

"Thank you."

She turned and headed upstairs to her bedchamber. Entering the room, she removed her shawl and placed it along with her reticule on a chair. Nearing the desk, she noted a silver salver with several letters. Before sitting down, Roxanne picked up each one and studied the handwriting if there wasn't a return sender's information. One was an afternoon musicale with tea from Lady Winters. She smiled at how easily the ton left in London for the summer could gossip. That was the only way Lady Winters could know of her return. The wagging tongues never slept, she mused.

Picking up another, she recognized the familiar script of one of her friends, Lady Pamela. Pamela and she had become close friends as children since her family lived only two doors down.

She went on to marry the Duke of Middlesex, only to have him die a year ago in a mysterious riding accident at their Surrey estate. He had been an expert equestrian and was said to be able to ride any horse presented to him. He had been riding his stallion, one he'd had since birth, when all of a sudden, out of nowhere, the beast spooked. Something the stallion never did. The horse had always been fearless. Roxanne had been unable to make it to the funeral and it was a month before word reached her in France of Middlesex's demise.

She sat down and opened the missive and began reading. Pamela had recently arrived on Wight at Georgiana's invitation as her period of mourning had ended and she wanted to get away from anything reminding her of her husband. As they had only two twin daughters, the late duke's brother had taken the title. He'd given her the dowager house, but Pamela was quite frank in that she had trouble living there with what had happened. Everything reminded her of him. Pamela went on to say she hoped Roxanne would consider making the journey to Wight so the three of them could catch up on their lives. Perhaps she could talk her brother into going as well. Finding a house to rent would be impossible, but a hotel may have rooms available. Roxanne would broach the idea again this evening at dinner. If her brother still didn't want to go, she would tell him she was going. She needed to visit both her friends. They hadn't seen each other in at least three years. There was much to catch up on.

She picked up the invitation one more time before deciding to accept. It would be a good way to dip her toe back into London society. Her reply to Pamela would wait until morning. She wanted to be sure of her plans before writing her friend.

CHAPTER SIX

ROXANNE HAD SEEN no reason to mention the stranger nor the possibility he had been following her to her brother. They were en route to Graham's for dinner and the subject would be best broached with their host since Graham had indeed rescued her. Somehow, sometime this evening she would approach her brother about a short holiday in Wight. She knew she'd be more at ease knowing Arthur would be accompanying her, but if need be, she would go alone. It wouldn't be the first time. She had, after all, traveled all the way from the south of France to London alone. Widowhood allowed her to make the journey alone.

No sooner had they entered the grand hall of Graham's home than their host appeared to greet them. Pleasantries were exchanged before Graham led them to the drawing room. Roxanne glanced about the room. It was done in a deep shade of red with a wall covering that complemented the décor. Gold, deep red, and cream damask furniture fit the room perfectly.

Graham poured both himself and Arthur a whiskey and Roxanne a glass of red wine. "I'm so glad you came. I'm not much on hosting anything, not even dinner with friends."

"You need to do it more often," she said as she accepted the glass.

A grin crossed his face. "Perhaps I will."

He then arched a brow, giving her what she assumed was a

signal that they needed to tell Arthur about the incident earlier that afternoon. "Roxanne, why don't you tell Arthur about what happened this afternoon."

"What happened?" Arthur said, looking between his sister and Graham.

"A man approached me in the bookshop. He randomly came up to me while I was trying to finish a transaction and began talking to me."

Arthur took a swallow of whiskey. "Why do I sense there is more to this than you've told me?"

"There is. He tried to force me to have tea with him. I began to leave; I was outside, and Graham appeared. If he hadn't, I don't know what I'd have done."

"I'm sure you would have figured something out. You always do."

"He tried following us," Graham added. "I brought her home through the kitchens to try and throw whoever this man was off."

"Thank you," Arthur said.

"I think he may be someone my late husband's family hired."

"Why?" Arthur asked.

"Word got out that I'm not living in the house Casper left me. He's trying to find out everything he can about where I am and what I am up to."

"Interesting."

"Do you think you should have your man look into it?" Roxanne asked.

"I'll request a meeting with him and see what he suggests."

"I think that's a wise move," Graham said dryly. "It was un-nerving for Roxanne."

Arthur turned to his sister. "Don't worry about it. I'll have the matter looked into."

"Thank you. I'll feel much better knowing who hired him."

At that point the butler popped his head in the room after knocking and announced dinner was ready. The trio walked into the dining room together. A long mahogany table sat in the center of a room of gold and cream.

A footman pulled out a chair and Roxanne sat, noting she was to Graham's right. Since there were only the three of them, options were limited. Roxanne wondered if Graham used the room when alone or if he dined in a breakfast room or perhaps even his study.

Soup was served as soon as everyone was settled. Roxanne peered into the bowl as the footman placed it in front of her. Squash soup. Popular with the aristocracy but not one of Roxanne's favorites. Still, she politely tasted it and consumed several spoonsful. There would be many more courses, and no one wanted to fill up on the first one. She decided to approach the subject of a holiday on the Isle of Wight now.

"Arthur, I had a letter from Pamela. She's staying with Georgiana on Wight and has invited me to join them. Since we've discussed the fact that you need a holiday out of the city, I thought this would be perfect. We could stay at a hotel for a week or two, then head to the country. I think you'll find the sea air a big help."

She didn't have to wait long for a reply. He set his soup spoon on the plate which held the bowl of soup. "If you want to go visit with your friends, go. I plan on leaving for the estate by week's end. The seaside does not interest me. Not at the present time."

"But…"

"Enough. You're a widow, a dowager countess. It is much easier for you to travel without a man to accompany you. You do not need me to go with you."

Turning to Graham, she posed a question. "What do you think? Should I go alone or go on to the country with my brother?"

Graham's eyes had a twinkle to them. He knew exactly what she was hoping to accomplish. "Don't bring me into this. I have no opinion on the matter, nor should I. This is between you and Arthur."

She blew out a breath, frustrated. Men! They stuck together

no matter what. "I should have expected this."

"Expected what?" Graham asked with a smirk on his lips. Lucious lips, is what Roxanne always thought. For a second, she wondered how they would feel and taste on top of hers. That could never and would never be. He might be cordial and a gentleman, but there was still a cheeky rake that waited in the background for the perfect situation to come to life.

"The answer I got. Very well, I'll go by myself."

"I could accompany you. I need to go check on a project near Brighton. I could take you as far as you can go before taking a ride to get over to Wight."

"I appreciate the offer, but I can make it to Wight on my own."

Graham nodded but didn't say another word or try to change her mind. She saw him cast a glance at her brother. The two of them were probably in this, thick as thieves.

"Do you know how long you'll be in Wight?" Arthur inquired. "I had a missive from Uncle Charles that he and Aunt Violet would like to drop by the estate for a visit on their way to Dover."

Her agreement with Arthur had been to hostess social events when she returned from France. "Do you know exactly when they'll arrive? I'll make my plans around their arrival."

"I'll check when we return home. I know Uncle Charles gave me a time frame."

A smile crossed her face. It would be good to see their mother's sister and her husband. As they had, until recently, lived in India, a visit was always most welcome. It was where her parents were going when they were mysteriously killed. Murdered. Her aunt and uncle had returned to their home on the border of Scotland while she was still in France. Roxanne figured she hadn't seen them since her wedding to Casper.

"It will be good to see them."

"Yes, it will," Arthur agreed.

Dinner progressed without another incident. Roxanne was

impressed with Graham's cook. The dishes served were quite amazing, not only in presentation, but taste. She knew he was trying to impress her. For a moment she wondered if perhaps he had hired a more experienced cook for the evening because a lot of what was being served was a bit more sophisticated and complex than one's everyday cook might prepare.

She decided not to broach the subject because that would only encourage Graham, and she truly only wanted to enjoy the meal and not get into a deep discussion about any of it. She knew he was waiting on her to do just that. Roxanne was having no part of it. Besides, frustrating him was more fun to watch.

Once dinner was finished, Roxanne started to excuse herself and take tea alone in the drawing room, leaving the men to the port and cigars. It was a ritual she never understood other than it was a time for men to have times without the women and allowed them to speak of subjects too intense for delicate feminine ears.

"Please, Rox, there is something I need to tell both you and Arthur. It's of a personal matter, and I need your opinion and suggestions," Graham said. He rose from his chair and walked to a sideboard and picked up another glass. He poured a splash of port into it and handed it to Roxanne before returning to his chair. He picked up his own port and downed it in one long swallow.

"I had a surprise recently. It was completely out of the blue. The butler went to answer the door and when he did, he found a basket with a newborn baby girl."

"This isn't the babe…" Arthur began to ask. He stopped to let Graham reply.

He turned to Roxanne who was eyeing him carefully. He wondered what she was thinking at this very moment. Clearing his throat, he continued. "I've had a mistress for the past couple of years. I had ended things with her and never knew she was with child. I understand she was going to go to her sister's to have the child. She changed her mind."

"You weren't expecting her to drop off the child for you to raise?"

"No."

"Have you thought about a foundling home or know of a childless couple who might raise her as their own?" Arthur asked.

"No one comes to mind, and no, she won't go to an orphanage."

"Graham, you're a bachelor. People will talk as soon as they learn you're raising a child," Roxanne said.

"Let them talk. I had thought to say her parents died. She was my cousin. Something like that."

Arthur swirled his port thoughtfully. "Have you spoken to your solicitor about this?"

"No, I wanted to talk with the two of you about it."

Roxanne grinned ever so slightly. She loved seeing him dazed like this. "You've certainly gotten yourself in a predicament."

"What do you suggest I do?"

"See your solicitor first. If you're going to raise her yourself, you'll need the mother to sign her over. That protects you. My only other suggestion would be to raise her at one of your estates. At least for the first couple of years. One close enough you can go visit the child." She sipped her port and watched his face.

He nodded. "Would you like to see her? She's not much to look at right now, as newborns seldom are."

"She's here?" Roxane exclaimed.

"Yes, she's in the nursery. I've hired a wet nurse and another woman to help with her."

"Perhaps another time," Roxanne replied.

"I would have thought you would have sent her on to the country," Arthur said.

"No. Nothing happens until I've seen my man."

Roxanne finished her port and set the glass back down on the table with a large thunk. "You're positive she's your child?"

"Yes. Let me mention something I've been thinking about. What if I do find a couple willing to take her? What's to say I'll ever marry or if I do, wonder if my wife cannot have children? This child wouldn't know who I am, and I would have no heir."

"I'm afraid it isn't the first time a quandary like this has happened," Arthur said.

"Yes, I'm aware."

"See what your solicitor says first. If you wish to continue the discussion with Arthur and me, let us know."

"Thank you both," Graham said.

She and Arthur didn't stay long after that. Her brother feigned an early morning meeting. Roxanne made a point to thank Graham for a delicious dinner to which he thanked her, telling her how he looked forward to seeing her again. Simply nodding her head, she slipped past him to the waiting carriage.

The ride home was quiet and once inside the house, she made her announcement. "I'm going to leave for Wight in two days' time. If we haven't heard back when Uncle Charles will arrive, you may get word to me as soon as you do."

"Very well. Do you think a fortnight will be enough time to visit with your friends?" he asked.

"I'll make it work, and thank you, brother. I look forward to seeing our relatives."

"As do I. It's been a while since we've had company."

"It has."

"Graham is quite befuddled about this baby, isn't he?" Roxanne said with a laugh. "I don't think I've ever seen him unable to make a decision."

"This is different. This is his daughter, bastard or not. He wants to do right by the girl. Giving her to someone else to raise is going to be a hard decision, if that's what he's left with."

"True. I guess now it's dependent on what his solicitor advises," Roxanne said.

"Yes. It's late. I'm going to bed." She stood on tiptoe and kissed him on the cheek. The scent of the cigar he had and the port still lingered. The combination brought memories back of their father. "Good night."

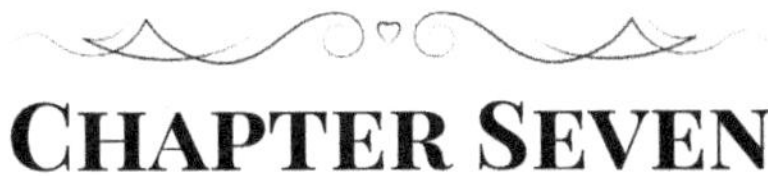

CHAPTER SEVEN

THE CLOSER SHE got to the house, the more excited Roxanne became. The Italian renaissance style home was exactly as Georgiana had described it. Large and an off-white in color, Georgiana and her husband, Jeremy Black, Duke of Dorset had purchased the home after falling in love with the structure the first time they saw it on a walk they'd taken on the beach. Her husband had made discreet inquiries and paid over market value for the property. This was where they spent their summers now while the duke had his country estate renovated. A long overdue project and one he wasn't rushing.

To look at the home, one would think nothing else while passing it by. Just another luxurious home of a member of the aristocracy. She wondered if Georgiana had been inspired to incorporate the property into one of her books. Her friend was a novelist and often weaved real places and people into her novel. This would be fun.

The carriage slowly began the journey down the long, crushed-shell driveway. If she remembered what her friend told her, the front looked out on the street from a distance while the back of the house overlooked the sea. There was a beach where Georgiana mentioned they could use her bathing machine to swim. Bathing machines had become all the rage along the beachfront villages which dotted the coast. Roxanne had always wanted to try one, but it never seemed to work out.

A few moments later, the coach came to a stop. She waited for the door to open, but Georgiana had rushed down the stairs and flung open the door. It was obvious from the first glance at Georgiana that she was happy. One day Roxanne hoped to find that same kind of love and happiness.

"I can't believe you're here," Georgiana exclaimed as she pulled Roxanne from the carriage.

"Neither can I. For a moment, I thought it might not happen."

"Come, you can tell me everything. I'm sure you'd like to freshen up first, after which we can have tea and catch up."

"Has Pamela arrived?" Roxanne asked.

"No, she'll arrive tomorrow. She made a quick stop to see her sister."

"I can't wait to see her. It's been ages since I've seen any of you."

Georgiana hugged her after she exited the carriage. "I know. Let's get you to your room. I think you'll like the room I chose for you."

"I'm sure whatever you chose is going to be beautiful."

The pair walked up the stairs arm and arm and into the great hall of the house. It was magnificent with its black and white marble floor and a dramatic double staircase toward the rear of the room. Vases of flowers graced various tables along the walls and one in the center of the hall.

"This is breathtaking, George."

"Thank you. We fell in love with the house the moment we stepped foot in this room. It sets the tone for the rest of the residence."

"It does, and I haven't even seen anything beyond this room," Roxanne said.

"Follow me." George smiled.

Roxanne followed her friend up the stairs and down a hallway to a closed door. Inside, the room was breathtaking. Done in shades of lavender and purple, Roxanne thought it was the most beautiful bed chamber she'd ever seen. A small sitting area surrounded the fireplace while a huge white four poster bed dominated the far wall. Lastly, a large window let lots of light into the room.

"The dressing area is just beyond that doorway. I hope you'll make yourself at home."

Roxanne walked around the room, taking in all the detail put into the décor. "May I ask a question?"

"Of course you may."

"Did you and Jeremy purchase the house furnished or did you do all this yourself?"

"The house was completely empty when we purchased it except for a couple of heavier pieces which remained. I was able to use those. The job is not quite finished."

"I imagine it was quite the undertaking." Roxanne gazed around the room, taking in all the details.

"One I've enjoyed immensely," George said. "I'll let you get settled. When you're ready, join me in the drawing room. We'll have tea and catch up."

"How will I ever find it?"

"The footman I've posted outside your room will escort you. The house can be like a labyrinth if you're not familiar with its layout." George headed to the door. "I'll see you shortly," she said with a smile and disappeared.

Hearing her maid rustling around in the dressing room unpacking her trunks, Roxanne headed in that direction. "Are there any dresses ready for me to wear?"

"Yes, milady. The sage colored one is ready."

"Good. I'll change into that. Be sure something is readied to wear to dinner."

"I will. I was thinking the dark-blue silk."

"That will be perfect," Roxanne said.

A short time later, Roxanne left her chamber dressed in sage-colored cotton. The footman was diligently keeping post at her door. "Drawing room? Can you tell me how I get there?"

"I'll show you the way, milady."

Roxanne knew she wasn't going to get out of the young man escorting her, so she didn't even try to talk him out of it. Instead, she followed him through the house until they ended up at two large oak doors. He opened one door and stepped back so Roxanne could pass. Attention to detail was evident in this room. George had done it in shades of red and cream. The damask covered furniture complemented everything else. The pleasant red complementing cream made the furniture stand out.

"What do you think? Too much?" George asked.

"Not at all. You've tied everything together quite nicely."

A knock on the door kept her friend from saying anything. A footman pushed a cart into the room as the butler watched from the doorway.

"Come, let me pour you tea," Georgiana said after the door closed. "I think you'll find everything to your liking."

"You're spoiling me, and I've only just arrived."

Georgiana smiled. "You're on holiday. Enjoy being fussed over."

"I've been on holiday for three years."

"I don't consider those years a holiday for you. You had just lost your husband, regardless of the situation."

"True."

"Now tell me all about what you've been up to since your arrival in London," George said, raising her teacup.

"I'm staying at Arthur's, acting as his hostess if the need arises."

"How's that working out?"

"Good. Casper had left me a derelict house in an unsavory neighborhood. Arthur stepped in and offered to see the property sold, and until I could find a place of my own, I could stay at the family home."

"Have you found anything? A townhome?"

"I haven't begun to look. For now, I'll stay with Arthur."

"What about men? Has he introduced you to any of his friends?"

"No, he hasn't. The only man I've had any contact with is his friend Hawksbury, but I've known him since we were children."

George arched a brow. "Is he a contender?"

"Heavens, no!" Roxanne snapped back. "He's still the same arrogant, brash man he's always been."

This time George bit back a laugh. "You certainly were quick to dismiss him."

"Bollocks! He's never nor will he ever have a chance with me. He needs to look elsewhere for a good time. I'm not going to be one of his playthings."

"I'm sure if you mentioned what troubles you to Arthur, Hawksbury might settle."

Roxanne shook her head. "The man will never change, George. I'm merely civil to the man when I see him."

"Jeremy and I plan to host a ball while you and Pamela are here."

"You shouldn't."

I don't want to hear anything about it."

"You know I can only stay a fortnight."

"I know. I read your letter. Pity you can't stay longer but I understand family comes first."

"Then know I plan on cramming every hour of the day and evening with somewhere to go." She was too. Her promise to her brother would never be broken and she looked forward to seeing her aunt and uncle. They were about the only family they had on their mother's side of the family. A handful of cousins, one being their daughter. Until she had to return to London, she would have the best time.

"That's what I want to hear."

The next two weeks seemed to go by in a flash. She and Georgiana kept busy every day with shopping, rides along the seaside, and sitting in the garden talking, reading, and painting. Georgiana would spend time writing in a notebook with ideas for an upcoming book. Roxanne was amazed with how her friend made it look so easy. How could she take scribbles of notes and turn them into a bestselling novel?

Word came from Pamela that she was having to postpone her holiday because her father had fallen ill and she had promised her mother she would stay on for a while. Her mother hated to be alone during a time like that, and since none of Pamela's other siblings were coming, she felt it was the least she could do for the woman who had birthed her.

"I'm sorry I won't get to see Pamela," Roxanne said as she and George sat on an iron bench in the garden. The afternoon was delightful with a blue sky and big fluffy white clouds ambling slowly across the sky. She sighed.

"As am I. I was looking forward to a reunion," George said.

"We'll have to make plans and do it next summer for sure."

George nodded. "We will because this visit hasn't been as expected. Not that I haven't loved seeing you, I have."

"It's just that life seems to be getting in the way, doesn't it?"

"I couldn't have said it better."

"I will give you the name of my modiste I use in London. That is, if you need one," George said.

"I would appreciate that," Roxanne said.

George's butler appeared at that very moment and handed her a calling card. "He says it's urgent."

"Show him in and make sure tea is served on the terrace," George said.

She passed Roxanne the card. A scowl crossed her face as she read the name. Hawksbury. What did he want and how did he find her? "I told you he was a rogue," she said as they rose from their bench and walked to the terrace.

"Let's not jump to conclusions. I've never met the man."

"I specifically asked him to leave me alone if he happened to come to the coast. The man can't even follow simple instructions."

As they neared Hawksbury on the terrace, Roxanne couldn't

help but admire him. In spite of his infuriating personality, she had to admit he cut a fine figure. But what was he doing here? He'd been one that for years broke all the rules. Whatever it was he wanted, she was not going to let him off that easily. How dare he blatantly ignore her wishes.

"He is a handsome one," George drawled.

"Yes, and he's well aware of it."

They were at the table and Graham stood and let her introduce everyone. "I apologize for the intrusion, but Arthur asked me to seek you out."

"My brother is incapable of that. What sort of shenanigans are the two of you up to?"

"I have no idea what you mean, milady. Arthur instructed me to do whatever it took to take you back to London. Even put you over my shoulders if that's what it takes."

"You wouldn't dare!"

"I'm simply following instructions."

"I'm sure you are," Roxanne said.

George, who hadn't sat down, cleared her throat delicately. "I'm going to see about some tea." She disappeared, leaving Roxane and Graham glaring at each other.

Roxanne sat down across from him and watched as he lowered himself into the iron chair. For a second, she had to admit George was right. He was a handsome man. His chiseled jaw and kissable lips were highlighted by deep golden eyes. Kissable lips? For someone perhaps, but never her.

"I know you don't wish to see me, and I never intended to disrupt your holiday. Arthur asked me to come get you and escort you back."

"Why didn't he come for me himself? Why send you?"

"I have no idea, Roxanne."

"Is something wrong with our aunt and uncle?"

"It is futile for you to keep asking me questions I don't know the answers to," Graham said, tapping the top of the table with his fingers.

"Yes, I suppose it is. You wouldn't tell me even if you knew the answer."

He made a point of changing the subject. "You've had a nice visit with your friend?"

She nodded. "I have. Our friend Pamela was supposed to join us, but her father took ill, and her mother asked her to stay."

"That's what happens when one has aging parents," he said.

"Yes." She looked directly at him, trying to get some idea of what he was really all about. "Did your meetings in Brighton go well?"

"They did. A good start to a prosperous project."

"I found it an unusual place for a business meeting, but I assume he's one of those who holidays at the seashore."

"He and his wife have a cottage there, I'm told, and he keeps an office there."

"His business won't suffer with him being out of London."

"No." He gazed around at the house behind them. "Quite the house your friend has."

"It is, isn't it. The moment I walked in, I could see how George fell in love with it."

"Perhaps you'll live in something similar should you remarry," he said.

She smiled at him. "Impossible. I have no desire to remarry."

He chuckled at her statement. "Never say never, Rox."

Georgiana returned and sat down, glancing between the two of them. "Have I interrupted something? Because if I have, I can come back."

"No, don't be silly. I was trying to find out how soon I must return."

"As soon as you are packed. I'll have tickets for us to take the late afternoon train to London," Graham said.

"No, I can assure you I cannot. That's simply unacceptable."

"You'll go upstairs and change. Your maid can follow with your luggage. You will come with me, and we'll head to the station."

Georgiana was pouring tea but looked up at Roxanne. "I'll see she and your luggage make it to the train station."

"No, I will go nowhere until I know why I'm leaving."

"I've told you I don't know, Roxanne. The only thing I've been told was to make sure I get you back to London as soon as possible. Whatever is going on must be serious for your brother to send for you."

"What if I refuse?"

"Roxanne!" Georgiana exclaimed. She handed her friend a cup of steaming tea and one to Graham. "You will do no such thing. Whatever is going on, Arthur wants to tell you in person. So you will go to him."

She felt like everyone was working against her, but Georgiana was right about one thing: whatever Arthur wanted to tell her was serious enough that she had to return so he could tell her in person.

"Very well, I'll go."

Roxanne sat in silence as she drank her tea and pondered what could be so important for her brother to interrupt her holiday. Nothing immediately came to mind, and she knew she'd drive herself mad if she kept trying to guess. Why send Graham? Why not send a telegram? She wouldn't question a telegram, but sending his friend irritated her. And to make matters worse, he seemed to delight in knowing he was causing her such discomfort. She would ignore him all the way back to London. There was no need for them to converse. He was simply Arthur's errand boy.

She reached out for a piece of seed cake. She had better eat before they left. There might not be a chance until they arrived in London. Roxanne decided rather than share a meal with Graham, she would go without until she arrived at the family home. Besides, that journey was going to prove interesting since she wasn't talking to him. She wouldn't let herself fall into his trap of pretending to care for her when he actually only wanted to turn her into one of his conquests and move on. He had a lot to learn about her or women in general.

Pushing the plate and cup back, Roxanne rose. "If you two will excuse me, I'm going to change and talk to my maid about packing."

"Don't dawdle too long. We need to leave for the station within the hour," Graham said.

She ignored him and walked toward the drawing room door. Stopping for nothing, Roxanne was in her room in no time. Her maid was already beginning to fill one of the trunks.

"I need to change into something for traveling."

"Yes, milady. Her Grace already came and told me you were returning to London. I hope it's nothing serious."

"Knowing my brother, it's probably not, but he knows how stubborn I can be, so he sends an escort."

"Yes, the earl. I don't understand why you act the way you do around him. He thinks a lot of you."

"He's arrogant. One thing I cannot abide in a man."

"Yes, milady. I left your blue traveling gown out. Let me go get it."

"Fine."

While she was waiting, Roxanne took off her shoes. She would have to be unhooked out of this dress, as the buttons were all on the back. She was becoming more appreciative of the ones that a woman could do on her own.

An hour later she descended the stairs, ready to leave, only to find Graham pacing the floor between the great hall and the drawing room. He looked up at her, a storm cloud of fury crossing his face. She pretended not to notice, and he scowled. "I'm glad to see you changed. We can leave at once. Georgiana is in the drawing room."

She nodded and headed in that direction, not saying a word. This could be quite fun not talking to him. It would frustrate him and that was part of what she was after. Georgiana walked with her and Graham to the carriage at the bottom of the stairs.

"Promise to write as soon as you know what's going on."

Roxanne took her friend's hands in hers and squeezed them. "I shall. I promise."

"Good, because I'd hate to have to involve Arthur."

She climbed up into the carriage and sat back on the leather tufted seat. As soon as Graham joined her on the other seat, the carriage door closed, and the four black horses began to walk forward. Roxanne leaned against the seat and closed her eyes, or pretended to. From under her lashes she observed him pull out a book and open it. She closed her eyes the rest of the way and found herself drifting off to sleep. At least that would make time go by faster and she wouldn't be forced to converse with that man.

Why was he always around? He knew how she felt about ever remarrying but still found reasons to be around her. He hadn't tried to kiss her, which she found puzzling. Most men like him would have at least tried. It was almost as though he thought of her as a sister, which was how they'd always been growing up. They were grown adults and if they kept this up, people would start to think there was indeed something going on between them. She wasn't ready to give up her newfound freedom to any man.

CHAPTER EIGHT

GRAHAM GAZED ACROSS the carriage at Roxanne. With her eyes closed, she appeared to be asleep, but he knew better. She was angry with him for having ruined her holiday. It couldn't be helped. Arthur asked him to help get her back to London. He was in the area and if he'd simply written her requesting her return to London, she would have ignored his request. Then he'd have to see if Lady Georgiana could assist him, and she wouldn't be able to convince Roxanne without telling her the truth of Arthur's request. He didn't want to have to do that. This was bad enough because she would ask him if he knew, and he knew how that would end.

He tried to get his mind back into the book he was reading but found it nearly impossible. The lull of the carriage was going to have him asleep if he wasn't careful. His lips twitched as he tried to avoid a smile as he continued to watch her. He was of good mind to get up and sit next to her and kiss her like she needed to be kissed. Heaven knew Casper had never been capable in that. He ignored her and avoided her at all costs.

He averted his eyes. If he kept gazing at her and thinking inappropriate thoughts about her, like taking her here, she was going to wake up and find him with his trousers tenting. He was having difficulty trying to leave those thoughts somewhere else. Right now, his main concern was handing her over to Arthur.

The one thing he did know was that if anyone deserved something good in her life, it was Roxanne. She'd been through enough. Before Casper died, he deliberately took away all her cameras and photographic equipment out of spite. It was one of the things Roxanne loved doing, but Casper told her women weren't meant to use cameras or to develop the images. It was an art form left solely to men. Arthur had shown Graham a couple of her images and he was overcome with emotion, which he was sure was what she was trying to accomplish. Perhaps, he could get her interested again. She was going to need something to occupy her time, a way to get her out of the house. This was something she enjoyed and was good at.

He sat back, his head against the back corner of the seat. Not realizing it, he sighed rather loudly. Once again, his eyes were heavy and though he had his own matters to ponder over, he couldn't help but give in to sleep. To make it even more lulling, a rain began to fall on the roof of the carriage. Not uncommon being close enough to the seashore. Hopefully, it would dissipate before they made it to London.

He wished he'd followed his instincts and purchased tickets for the train back to London. Something distracted him, and he completely forgot to do it. Now, with the rain, they wouldn't get into London until much later than planned.

Closing his eyes, listening to the gentle sound of the rain, Graham fell asleep. For how long he was unsure, but he was pleasantly surprised to hear Roxanne's voice quietly trying to wake him up. Her hand was on his knee in her attempt.

"We're entering London," she said gently.

"Already?"

"Yes, we made good time despite the rain," Roxanne said.

"They're pushing the horses. That's too much distance to cover in a day. They've got to be exhausted. The driver is a fool. I told him we'd stop for the night and start fresh in the morning."

"They did stop. They changed out the team. So see, you have no reason to be grumpy."

He said nothing. He never woke up easily and yes, Roxanne was right; he was grumpy first thing in the morning. "Humph."

"You were sleeping. I saw no reason to wake you."

"I normally don't sleep so deeply," he said.

"Obviously, you were tired." She smiled. "You look so innocent when you're sleeping. Did anyone ever tell you that?"

"I don't usually leave myself that vulnerable."

"What are you going to do when you marry?"

He arched a brow. Interesting. "I never plan on marrying."

"You can tell that to someone who doesn't know you so well, Graham. This is me you're talking to."

"True, but we haven't seen each other in years. For all you know, I'm Jack the Ripper."

She shifted on the seat. She was smiling. Something he wished she'd do more of. But as soon as they got to her home, all of that was going to fly out the window. Once again, her life was going to be changed forever.

"Some things about a person never change. They remain with you forever. It doesn't matter how long it's been since we've seen each other. You're still the same decent man you were then as a boy. Though I will say one thing. You know something. You know the reason why you came to get me. Arthur just instructed you not to tell me."

"You imagine too much," he said. He hated lying to her, but Arthur had instructed him, and he respected his friend's wishes.

"Do I? You and my brother may think you're protecting me, when in fact I know when the two of you are up to something." Her lips were pursed, and her face told him she was agitated but was trying hard not to let it show. He didn't know how much longer he could continue this. He had to figure out a distraction at least part of the way through London. He'd kiss her. By doing that, he hoped he would leave her befuddled and speechless. There was, however, the possibility she would react negatively. She considered him a childhood friend, almost to the point of being like a brother because of his association with Arthur. It was a predicament.

Without another thought to the situation, Graham switched seats. He moved quickly, sitting next to her. The scent of oranges and vanilla woke his senses. He always thought of her when he smelled this combination. That and being this close to her did other things to him. It made him want to ravage her right here in the carriage.

That's when he placed his hand on her cheek and lowered his lips to hers and kissed her like there was no tomorrow. Fortunately, either caught off guard or as eager as he was, she responded to him. His tongue pushed open the seam of her lips and tasted her. She opened to him, one hand holding on to his shoulder as though she depended on him.

"Graham, what are you doing?" she asked moments later. Her mouth wasn't but inches away from his.

"I'm kissing you. I'm kissing you thoroughly."

"Don't stop. I rather like it. You're a very good kisser."

"Hmm," he responded as his lips found hers again. "I was going to say the same about you."

They sat there in the middle of London, in a carriage, kissing each other as two long separated lovers might. He couldn't get enough of her. He wanted more, but a carriage wasn't the place for it. A thousand thoughts ran through his head. This was the woman he'd been waiting for his entire life, and he wasn't about to lose her again.

Quickly he opened his eyes and looked out the window of the carriage, trying to see where they were and how far they were to their destination. They were close, too close for more.

What time they had spent seemed like hours instead of mere minutes as he once again found his way to his seat. She would be in no frame of mind for anything but grief shortly, but he felt that this time she would allow him to comfort her. They had bonded, or feelings that had been smoldering for years and years had now been brought to the surface.

Graham felt anxious as the carriage came to a halt in front of the house. He dreaded what was about to transpire. Gazing up at the door, he found nothing black to tell people this was a house in mourning. A smart move if Arthur were trying to wait until Roxanne had been told. Most people didn't even know Roxanne had a son. Because of Thomas's afflictions it had been something the family kept quiet about. Her late husband saw no need and blamed Roxanne in fact. Graham wondered how much time she had spent with her son over the years. Did he even know who she was? It was a heartbreaking situation. There was so little known about diseases of the mind. For Thomas he never matured past being a three-year-old. A heartbreak for any parent. Luckily, Roxanne's late husband had been able to afford to make sure Thomas got better care than if he'd just been placed in there like someone off the street. That in and of itself showed that Casper had a heart and some emotion towards his son.

He followed Roxanne up the steps and into the grand hall. Nothing had been said between them after leaving the carriage. Was she regretting what passed between them or was she merely anxious about finally finding out why Arthur had her brought back to London?

She turned to him and cocked her head to one side. "For being so insistent I return, one would think my brother would be waiting at the front door with open arms. Instead, he's nowhere to be found."

A lone figure appeared at the top of the staircase. "I am here. In the drawing room."

Roxanne said nothing as she ascended the stairs. Graham followed, arching a brow in Arthur's direction as he passed and continued to follow Roxanne into the drawing room. He heard Arthur shut the door behind him and watched Roxanne closely as she walked to the fire, where she dramatically turned to face the two of them and began taking her gloves off.

"Arthur, you have a lot of explaining to do. You practically had poor Graham here kidnap me, for what I do not know."

"I know, but I also know how stubborn you can be," he said.

"Why don't you sit down?"

"Just tell me what is going on so I can go to my rooms and change," she responded as she pulled off the second glove and flung it on the chair where she had thrown the other.

"Roxanne! Sit!" Arthur exclaimed. Graham could tell she was frustrating him and all he wanted to do was get this over.

She sat in the cream damask wing chair where she had thrown her gloves. "Someone certainly got up on the wrong side of their bed."

"This is no laughing matter, sister."

"Would you please tell me what's going on?"

Her brother knelt in front of his sister, taking her hands in his. It was almost more than Graham could take. He felt like bolting.

"It's about Thomas," Arthur began.

"What about him?"

"There was a fight. Somehow Thomas was in the fray…"

"Oh my God. No! Is he okay?"

Arthur cleared his throat. Graham could see him tighten his grip on her hands. "I'm afraid not. He died from his injuries."

Saying nothing, Roxanne merely stared at Arthur in disbelief. "No, no, no. You must have misheard. Thomas was gentle. He would never get involved in a fight."

"I'm afraid I haven't misheard. He's gone, Roxanne, and I'm so sorry to have to be the one to tell you."

She nodded, tears streaming down her cheeks. It was all Graham could do to remain where he was when in fact, he wanted nothing more than to take her in his arms and comfort her.

"No one knew of Thomas's existence. It will be a very private funeral. No one outside the three of us. No one else. The house must not go into mourning. It would cause too many questions, and I will be judged if we did," Roxanne said tearfully.

"Whatever you want, I'll make it happen." Arthur let her hands go and rose to his full height.

"Thank you. Now, would one of you pour me a drink? I'm finding myself in need of some fortification after that news."

"Wine, whiskey, or brandy?" Graham asked.

"I think a glass of wine will suffice."

Graham walked over to a sideboard lined with decanters and glasses. Arthur followed, pouring a whiskey for himself. He poured a second while Graham was pouring the wine. They looked at each other, trying not to let their faces show any emotion.

"Arthur, do you think we could have the burial at the estate?"

"Of course. Whatever you want."

"I can contact the vicar on your behalf. I assume you would like to use the family chapel for the service?" Graham said.

"Yes," Roxanne said.

"I'll get word to the staff and have everything readied. When do you want to go?" Arthur asked matter-of-factly.

"As soon as it can be set up." She turned to Graham who was standing by the hearth. "You'll be in attendance, won't you?"

"Yes, of course."

"Thank you."

"Are you going to invite Casper's son?" Arthur asked.

Roxanne shook her head. "I see no point in it. It's not as though Thomas had a will. Any money sent from Casper's people will end as soon as they hear the news, which I'm sure they have."

"Agreed," her brother said.

She rose from her chair and faced the men. "If you gentlemen will excuse me. Unless there is something else I'm needed for, I'm going to lie down for a while."

"Of course. I understand," Arthur said.

"I hope you feel better," Graham added.

She gazed at Graham without any emotion. "Thank you. I'm sure you've had a great lark with all of this."

He looked puzzled. "I'm sorry, I don't follow.

"You know, playing the concerned friend, bringing me back to London while all along pretending you knew nothing of why I was truly being brought back."

"I asked him not to tell you," Arthur inserted.

"It matters not now, does it?" She placed her glass onto the table between two chairs and walked out of the room without another word.

A look passed between the two of them after the door closed. "She's hiding her feelings," Arthur said lowly.

"Yes, she is. I can't imagine having to live with that. I'm sure she feels as though she failed him as a mother," Graham said.

"Casper never gave her a choice or a say in the matter."

Graham went to refresh his drink. Arthur followed. "I had an idea. You know how Roxanne enjoys taking pictures? I was thinking of purchasing her whatever she needs to take and develop her own images. Your estate might be the perfect place to get her started," Graham said.

"I think that's a wonderful idea. I'm not sure if she's going to accept such a lavish gift from you."

"I know, but if she rejects me, I'll just leave it there, and I think she'll be too curious to let it just sit."

Arthur turned and glanced at the clock on the mantel. He took a sip of his drink. "I have a feeling Rox isn't going to feel up to a big dinner. Why don't we go to the club for dinner?"

"One of their steaks might just be what we need," Graham said.

"Indeed. Let me tell the butler. He can break the news to my cook, and he can tell her Roxanne might wish a tray."

Graham grunted and threw back the contents of his drink. Now he needed to figure out what was going on with regards to what transpired between them in the carriage earlier.

ROXANNE DIDN'T WAIT for her maid. Instead, she kicked off her shoes, walked straight over to her bed, grabbed a blanket she kept at the foot of the bed for cold winter nights, and climbed up. She lay down on her side and closed her eyes. The first thing that crossed her mind was that her son was in a better place. That he didn't have to suffer the horrors in that asylum any longer was like a dream come true. Though her late husband tried numerous times to tell her the place was one of the best, and if anyone could help Thomas it was them, she knew better. She'd researched and read anything she could about facilities like this one, and what she'd found out scared her to death. There was little hope for someone like her son. She knew he'd never get better, but Casper thought by letting her believe he'd one day be cured, he was doing her a favor keeping the atrocities from her. Indeed. Just like she wasn't to speak of Thomas in the house. It was forbidden. As far as Casper was concerned, the day Thomas left home, he no longer existed in his mind. His own son.

Blame, of course, was put directly on her. It was her fault he was born with such a malady. Horrors such as that were always the result of faults in the woman's family blood or some such nonsense. He refused to believe it just happened. Everything happened for a reason, and he vowed to never forgive her for giving him such an inferior child.

She would probably never know the joy of having children and a family of her own. Such was her cross to bear. She would get through it with grace and dignity and move forward in her life. This was her time, and her brother had given her a way to start anew, at least for the immediate future.

Then the thought of Graham kissing her in his carriage brought all sorts of conflicting messages. From everything such as how dare he to how she longed for more.

This wasn't fair. She was in control of her life now. She never had a man who appreciated her for who she was, and she doubted Graham was such a man. On the other hand, he and Arthur were childhood friends, and she couldn't see her brother allowing Graham such liberties unless Arthur didn't know. He wouldn't have allowed her to travel from the seashore to London with only Graham if he did.

Finally, her eyelids grew heavy and she succumbed to much needed sleep, complete with reminders of how life would have been, should Thomas have lived. Her plans had included taking him out of the madness and taking him home, even just overnight. She had thought getting him away from all the mayhem and chaos he might have an opportunity to see what outside those walls was really like. Would he even remember her?

For three years she'd stayed away, hoping when she returned the nightmares would be a thing of the past. But that wasn't to be. The torment started almost immediately after her return. It still raised its ugly head by making sure she couldn't even visit friends. But this mayhem wasn't going to win. No indeed. She was.

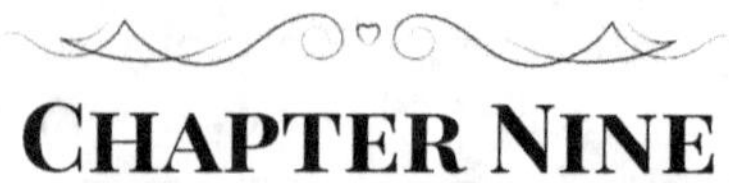

CHAPTER NINE

TWO DAYS LATER, the funeral for Thomas was held. As per Roxanne's request, no one outside of herself, Arthur, and Graham attended. The vicar had met with her the day before and was quite understanding of her wishes after they talked over tea. He had been at the local church for as long as Roxanne could remember. He was a kind man who treated all his parishioners as equals. To him, it mattered not what a person's social status was, or how much money they did or didn't have. Everyone was equal in the eyes of God.

At Roxanne and Arthur's request, the vicar and his wife walked to the house with them where luncheon was waiting. Given the fact the vicar had been given no notice about presiding over the funeral and burial of Lady Roxanne's son, it was the least they could do. That and a significant donation to the parish in their parents' memory. Her mother had done what she could, participating in various projects the women kept going. She was very proud of whatever she did, especially for those less fortunate. She had tried to instill those qualities in her daughter, and Roxanne liked to think her mother had done herself proud and she would beam at her daughter and how strong she was.

Refusing to give into grief, Roxanne decided to enjoy the afternoon outdoors in the garden. The vicar left, and she had made it quite clear she was not to be disturbed. She took a novel she'd been trying to read for the past week but had not gained much ground in. Today might not be the day to try, but she had to try. She couldn't let this consume her; what others thought was of no consequence to her.

She walked to the center of the gardens where a fountain sat, water moving in a rhythm. She sat on one of the benches overlooking the fountain. Laying her book aside, Roxanne closed her eyes momentarily to listen to the soothing sound of the water. Finally, she opened her eyes and watched the water splash. This had also been her mother's favorite place to come when she didn't want to be disturbed.

But then she heard an all-too-familiar voice to one side. Graham. How did he seem to know exactly where she was at any given time? A recent development, and it could be annoying. If she didn't watch herself, she'd be telling him just that.

"I'm not disturbing you, am I?" he asked. It was hard for her to tell in this light, but she assumed he'd changed from what he'd been wearing earlier.

"Would it matter if it did?"

"Probably not since I come bearing gifts."

"Really? To what do I owe the pleasure of a gift?"

"Nothing, no strings attached. I've seen the photographs you've taken, and you're quite talented. I thought I'd take the liberty of helping you set up your own studio."

Roxanne tried hard to keep her tongue in check, but lately with this man, she found it increasingly hard. Could it stem from what they shared in the carriage?

"Why? Why would you do something without consulting me first? I have my own money. I can afford to set my own studio up if that's what I choose to do."

He'd come closer to where she was sitting. His face was bordering on anger. She hoped she hadn't pushed him too far.

"You are the most ungrateful woman I know. You weren't raised to be, but with all you've been through, you've become a hardened version of yourself."

"How dare you speak to me like that!"

"No, how dare you." He flung a key at her. "If you're inter-ested, everything is set up in the attic. Frankly, I don't care what you do with it."

With that he turned and stomped off.

She shook her head and yelled after him, "You're a pompous ass, Graham!"

If he heard her, he didn't acknowledge her remark. He just kept walking until he was out of sight. How dare he? Staring down at the key, she wrapped her hand around it and put it in the pocket of her skirt. Knowing Graham, he would think she would be trotting right up to the attic to see what he'd left. She wasn't going to give him the satisfaction. She would wait for the right time. When he wasn't here. Since his own estate was very close, she knew he wouldn't be spending the night. He'd return to his own home to lick his wounds. Served him right, the arrogant rake.

She would admit since she was forced to marry Casper, she'd become a hardened shell of herself. He made her that way. She hadn't known who to trust, and he couldn't be trusted. He lied to her, talked down to her, until Thomas's birth, and he sent her to his farthest estate so he wouldn't have to look at either of them. She couldn't open up to anyone, and that included Graham. He would get over their row eventually. Graham was moving too fast, and he needed to be reminded of that. If he didn't, it would be sad, but then she had no interest in remarrying. Not even to him. She had come to enjoy her newfound freedom in France after Casper died.

Unable to find any solace from the fountain after their con-frontation, she rose and began to walk to the garden's edge. Walking towards the stables, she decided watching the two newborn foals run about on their unsteady new legs was better than too much thinking by herself. The babes were carefree, ignorant to the ways of the world.

As she approached, she noted her brother leaning against the fence to the small paddock where they'd been put with their mothers until they were a little more steady on their feet. He was laughing at something they were doing and didn't hear her as she drew near.

He turned his head towards her as she joined him at the fence. "What did you do to anger Graham this time? I passed him coming here, and he stalked right by me without so much as a word."

"It's not important. He'll get over it."

"Roxanne, tell that to someone else. I've known the man for most of his life, and it takes a lot to anger him like he was when he marched past me."

"He does things without consulting me. Did you know he… never mind. Of course you know he purchased cameras and other equipment and put it in the attic. He could have at least spoken to me about it first."

"Here's some free advice. Accept his gift and move on. You've made it very clear you have no interest in any sort of relationship. Stay friends with him. You never know when you might need one."

She giggled and pointed to a black youngster who was in the middle of the grass, running circles around his mother. Kicking his heels up, they landed on his mother, which prompted the mare's ears back and teeth bared as she reprimanded him.

"I won't apologize," she said, still watching the horses.

"Of course you won't."

"Please, give me some time. Since I've returned, I have done very little for myself. My visit to see Georgiana was cut short. Thomas died unexpectedly, and I haven't had time to accept anything new."

"Well, I should tell you, the Marquess of Norfolk will be coming with his daughter for a short visit. He is looking for a couple of saddle horses. Graham also has a few he wants to look at as well."

"Do you know when?"

"They are scheduled to arrive next week. The nineteenth."

"Find you how long they intend to visit, so I can plan menus and other things."

He smirked. "Of course."

"Do you know how old his daughter is?"

"I believe she's ten and eight or thereabouts. Why?"

"I don't want to plan activities for a child if she's older."

"She loves horses. One of the horses her father purchases will be for her."

"I suppose we could ride about the estate," she said.

Arthur arched a brow, turning to look closer at his sibling. "You could, but I know how riding has never been one of your favorite things to do."

"It's not, but if it helps you secure a sale, then I will do what I can to help."

"Thank you for that. I know if the lady wishes to ride one of the horses her father deems suitable, he or myself will have to ride with her," he said.

"She might choose to act inappropriately on a horse she does not know?"

He nodded. "I understand her mother died when she was quite young. Her father indulged her, and the result is a spoiled young woman."

"I understand," she said. "You needn't explain any further."

"I knew you'd know what to do, given the circumstances."

"Yes. Make sure I know the details of their stay as soon as you hear. In the meantime, I will see the housekeeper and Cook now so they may begin readying the house."

Arthur watched the foals one last time before pushing away from the fence. "Well, I was going to go for a ride myself, but the sky looks as though it's going to drop rain."

"You're right. I had not noticed the clouds moving in. I'm going to walk back to the house."

"I'll join you. I've got lots to keep me busy in my study."

"It's a never-ending job, isn't it?"

"It can be if you let it get out of hand, if you don't keep up to date on the estate's ledgers. Lucky for us, we have an estate manager who is quite competent. He brought me the ledgers for me to review, first thing this morning."

"Mr. Mawbry has always been good at what he does. He's been around for as long as I can remember. Doesn't he have a son who will take over from him when the time comes?"

"The elder Mr. Mawbry had a series of strokes while you were in France. When it became clear he could no longer function as estate manager, I brought in Felix. I gave his father a pension and a cottage to live in for the remainder of his days," he said.

"That was kind of you."

"He was born on the estate and inherited the position after his father died. That was at the end of Grandfather's life."

"Amazing," she said. "How does Felix seem to be doing since he took over?"

"Extremely well, but then he learned from the best," he said.

The house loomed above them and both walked the steps to the terrace and into the drawing room.

"I'm going to check my correspondence and try to start planning this visit. Let me know when our guests will arrive."

Arthur nodded with a cheeky grin. "I'm afraid Graham will need to be invited to dinner. There are a couple of animals he raised that are of interest."

"Meaning he'll be around more than usual?"

"Yes."

"I'll try and be on my best behavior, but you know how he can be."

"Methinks the blame lies with both of you."

Roxanne arched a brow before taking her leave. "I'll pretend I never heard that. By the way, have you heard anything about his daughter? What his solicitor might have said. He's been rather tight-lipped about it all."

"I know he's become her legal guardian, at least for the moment. They're trying to locate the mother."

"Has he decided where he's going to raise her?"

"Not at the moment since she's a babe."

"Sounds like things are proceeding, even if slowly. If you'll excuse me, I shall see you later."

There was too much to do, and she really didn't want to waste any more time. There would be a lot to do to prepare for this, and this was to be her first official dinner party. She left Arthur staring after her.

⟫⟫⟫✕⟪⟪⟪

THE MARQUESS OF Norfolk's carriage came to a stop in front of the house the following morning. The dark, ominous skies had opened with a vengeance earlier in the morning. The carriage door was opened and a young woman with hair the color of buttercups descended. She stared at her surroundings as an older gentleman, her father, the marquess followed as the footmen held out an umbrella to try and help keep the water at bay.

Roxanne stood at the door and greeted both guests and showed them into the front hall. Their outerwear was immediately taken from them. She then introduced herself.

"Your brother? I would have expected him to have been here to greet us when we arrived," the marquess's daughter, Lady Prudence drawled.

"There was something that required his immediate attention. He sends his apologies."

"While we're waiting for him, I require a hot bath."

"More than happy to accommodate whatever you need."

Her father, for the most part, had remained quiet, saying little. "I would like to freshen up after that carriage ride."

"I'll have a footman escort you to your room. If my brother hasn't returned by then, I'll show you to the library since the weather isn't going to break anytime soon."

"Thank you."

"I expect you to show me to my rooms, and I'll require some hot tea as well."

Roxanne tried not to show any emotion to the demands of this spoiled girl. It would do no good and it humored her that she would talk down to her given Roxanne's station.

"Very well. Follow me, please."

The pair walked in silence until they stepped into the guest room. Lady Prudence immediately made her way to the windows and looked out. The room looked out to a luscious green meadow with a small forest at the far end.

Lady Prudence sniffed and looked around. "This won't do."

"I apologize, but what did you say?"

"I said, the room won't do. I abhor the colors and I need accommodations that have less light."

Thinking for a second and wondering if anything could please this young woman, Roxanne contemplated the surrounding guest rooms.

"There is a nice room nearby. It is done in shades of periwinkle. It's a bit smaller, but I've always liked it for its coziness."

"Show me," she said.

Lady Prudence followed Roxanne and stepped into a room a mere two rooms down. She knew the moment the young woman stepped into the room that she liked it.

"This is perfect, and I don't mind it being smaller since I probably will be out anyway, riding potential mounts and such."

Trying to maintain her poise, Roxanne glided over the carpets to a table and rearranged a couple of books placed there. "I'm glad you like this one. I can have the room refreshed if you like, though I know the staff did so a couple of days ago in readiness for your visit."

"Some flowers might be nice, but I'll be fine for the rest of the day. If someone could find my maid and let her know where I am, I can bathe."

"Very well. I'll go in search of your maid. I'll be downstairs should you need me."

"Thank you."

Roxanne was never so grateful to leave the company of such a spoiled young lady. She needed to be taken over her father's knee and spanked, but the marquess didn't seem the sort. The man would do whatever he could to give his daughter what she wanted. Even if she was rude. At least the girl had enough to keep her busy for a couple of hours. It would give her time to breathe.

She wondered how her brother and Graham would react to Lady Prudence's behavior. The young lady would probably be on display for the evening so the men would fall under her spell. Then she would show her true colors. They both would be eating out of her hand by the time the evening was through. Young ladies such as her had a book on how to play their attention seeking game to their advantage. Roxanne also wondered if marrying a rich, well titled husband might be on her agenda as well. Her father was quite well off financially and Roxanne was certain his daughter's dowry was large beyond words. Surely Graham and Arthur were smart enough to see right through her game and see her for who she really was. Neither were that naïve, at least she didn't think they were. They might be flattered by the attention she would lavish them with, but in the end that's as far as it would go. Sighing, she went in search of the housekeeper to get the girl's maid. She was sure the young woman expected to be tended to immediately and that no excuse would do. A clap of thunder caused her to startle. She hadn't been expecting it. Roxanne hated weather like this, especially the thunder and lightning.

CHAPTER TEN

AFTER ONE LAST quick meeting with the housekeeper, Roxanne hurried as quickly as she could to the drawing room. She paused at the door and smoothed her skirt. She had decided on a deep-emerald silk gown for the evening. The gown had been made just before she left France. She knew the moment she found the fabric it would be perfect for a gown she'd found on a fashion plate in Paris. Her instinct had been perfect.

Nodding to the footman to open the doors of the drawing room, Roxanne entered regally. The men were standing around the fire and Lady Prudence sat on a dark-gold damask chair. Even at this distance, Roxanne could tell the young girl was flirting with Graham and Arthur. Served Graham right after the way he'd been acting toward her. It was amusing seeing him squirm.

"I apologize for being late. I had a few things to check on in the kitchen."

"Don't you have someone to do that for you?" Lady Prudence inquired.

"Yes, I do."

Arthur glanced at her. "Would you care for some wine while we wait?

"Please."

"Are you going to show the marquess and Lady Prudence some horses in the morning?" she asked Graham. She couldn't help but notice he was slightly uncomfortable, making her want to give him a huge grin. Instead, for now she hid behind a mask. The evening was early, and she wanted to enjoy every morsel of it.

"Yes, and since Lady Prudence is an accomplished horsewoman, I'm going to put her on the bay."

"That ought to be interesting. He takes a firm hand from what I learned riding him," she said, accepting the glass of wine from her brother.

"Perhaps your riding skills are meant for something gentler," Lady Prudence said with a smirk. Roxanne ignored her and turned to Prudence's father. "My brother tells me you recently lost your personal mount and that he was quite old."

"You would be correct. Pegasus was twenty-four when he died. Colic. I've tried some of the other horses we have, but none measure up. Pegasus was fearless. Someone could shoot a cannon next to him and he'd stand there as calm as he could be."

"You'll know him when you see him," Graham said. "Something will click when you first lay eyes on him or when you first pet him. You'll both know."

Lady Prudence laughed. "How can he possibly know unless he rides this imaginary horse?"

"Of course, your father would ride him. That would be the final bonding," Graham said.

"Does this phenomenon happen to everyone?" Lady Prudence asked with an unladylike snort.

"I believe there's always some sort of bond between rider and horse. The only exception I can see is if the horse picks up on a bad trait that person holds. Some horses would be apt to let their feelings be heard by biting or being stubborn."

Thank goodness the butler took now to announce dinner. Roxanne was certain this conversation might not end well. It seemed their guest had to prove everyone wrong. Her original plan for seating was to have Arthur at the head of the table, with Lady Prudence to his right and her father on his left. Graham was seated next to Lady Prudence and Roxanne on the marquess's left. Everyone took their seats and Roxanne thought everything was working out until she figured out Lady Prudence was trying to monopolize Arthur and Graham's attention, leaving her and the marquess together.

The older gentleman was quiet, and an easy dinner companion. Roxanne found herself enjoying talking current events. At one moment she glanced across the table at his daughter who had been dominating the conversation she was having with Graham and Arthur. She was staring at her with a look of fury on her face. Evidently Roxanne had broken some silent, unspoken rule regarding her father, the marquess. Women weren't to speak with him. Lady Prudence was not going to have her father remarry. If she were that selfish regarding her father, what would she be like if she found a man genuinely interested in her? Would she remain so self-absorbed or would she finally grow out of this nasty phase of her life?

Roxanne chose to ignore her. Lady Prudence was laughing louder than some might deem appropriate for a dinner party. She couldn't tell who said something funny, Graham or Arthur. Not that it mattered. This was Lady Prudence's way of dominating the conversation. She felt a smile cross her face as she tried to imagine what this girl would be like in the future. If her actions weren't curbed right now, Lady Prudence might end up a dragon lady. It wouldn't matter whether she married or not, she would be a domineering figure in the ton, and not in a good way.

Arthur, the ever-charming host, was attempting to be as gracious as he could be. Her father, of course, was his guest, and Arthur attempted to respond to something the marquess said, when Lady Prudence interrupted. Not to be swayed, she continued a conversation with Graham who was in the middle of eating the main course of lamb to try and ignore her. Poor Graham indeed.

While the men stayed behind in the dining room for cigars and port, Roxanne led Lady Prudence to the drawing room. A pot of tea awaited them. She began to pour as the younger woman looked on.

"You don't like me, do you?" Lady Prudence said as she arranged herself on a settee.

"What would make you say something like that? I barely know you."

Accepting a cup Roxanne handed her, she finally spoke up. It was as though she were carefully choosing her words, though Roxanne didn't know why she would start now.

"You need to stay away from my father. He has no interest in marriage to any woman after my mother."

Roxanne bit back a laugh as she stirred her tea. "Your father is a guest of my brother. It would be rude of me to ignore him. Second, if it's any of your business, I am a widow, so your father and I do have that in common. We understand what the other has been through."

"That's what I'm for. I understand my father and his feelings. At least when he shows them."

"Losing one's spouse is much different than, say, losing one's parent. To ease your mind, men rarely let their feelings show, so don't take it as personal."

Why she was offering advice to this horrid girl was beyond her. She probably had few friends, and now, with the passing of her mother, felt she needed to be there for her father.

"Thank you for that information. Papa's always been a little distant, but I've never not been able to talk to him."

"You've got a good relationship. I wouldn't worry about him. Give yourselves time to heal."

"I will."

Roxanne wanted desperately to tell the young woman to quit flirting so outrageously with the men, but she imagined it would do little good. She could only hope her father could see his daughter needed a woman, a female relative to assist him with his daughter's social skills. Lady Prudence desperately needed someone of the feminine sex to guide her through these important upcoming years.

The pair continued getting to know each other for the short period of time they had before the men rejoined them. Roxanne found out she had a passion for photography, which hit home for her. She told Lady Prudence of the equipment she had, though she said nothing about not having taken the time to use Graham's gift. Lady Prudence brought a camera along on her trip and was hoping she'd find some things to photograph in the country. Roxanne offered to take her about the estate where she could make plenty of stops along the way to use her new camera. This excited her as she had been afraid she might be limited to where she could go on the estate unless she walked, and Roxanne knew that was never happening.

After their guests retired for the evening, Arthur poured the three of them a brandy.

"I think that went well. Except perhaps the tension between Roxanne and Lady Prudence," Arthur said, passing them both a snifter.

"I'm hoping we've worked it out for the most part. She's lost her mother at a very important time in her life. She and her father are both healing."

Graham leaned back in his chair and unfolded his long muscular legs in front of himself. "Any idea which way he's leaning when it comes to the horses?"

"Weren't you there in the room with us, Graham?" Arthur said with a smirk. "Too busy thinking about the ladies?"

Graham bit back a laugh. "Not that one. She's trouble."

Roxanne said nothing. She had said what she wanted and wouldn't betray anyone's trust by talking about private conversations.

"To answer your question," Arthur drawled, "I believe you are going to be the lucky one. He's leaning toward the gray gelding for his daughter and is quite interested in the bay stallion."

"Excellent! That's what I like to hear. No hard feelings?"

"The sale is not final. He may have a change of heart come tomorrow."

"Not likely," Graham said. He glanced over at her and with one hand, pushed his black unruly hair back.

"I think I'll leave you two. Lots going on. Guests leaving, guests due to arrive," Arthur said.

"Sleep well, brother," Roxanne said as she watched her brother walk through the drawing room door.

She turned in Graham's direction. "Thank goodness he's gone. Now we can talk more freely."

"I thought you didn't want anything to do with me."

"Quit with the dramatics, Graham. Tell me what's going on with the babe."

He chuckled. "She is under my protection. Since she's so young, I'm thinking of taking her to my estate outside Leeds."

"You'll hire the necessary people to look after her?"

"Of course I will. I understand through my solicitor that word has reached the babe's mother's sisters, and they think they ought to be appointed her guardians."

"They see money," Roxanne said. She swirled the amber liquid left in her glass but didn't drink. "Have you named her?"

He smiled proudly. "I didn't think it would be appropriate to use family names, but I've decided to name her Mary."

"I love it, Graham. Excellent choice. If I may ask, why did you decide to send her away, and to one of your lesser estates?"

"I'm glad you like my choice. I go to Leeds only a few times a year. Virtually no one knows I have family property in the area. So I think it's perfect."

"Sounds like you've put a lot of thought into this."

"I have." He glanced at the clock on the mantel. "It's late. I best be leaving."

They both stood, and as they did, Graham approached Roxanne. "I had a delightful time. I will see you tomorrow?"

"Yes. I suspect if these deals are finalized, they are going to want to leave for home."

Graham arched a brow. "Yes, I imagine her father will want to be getting her back home. And I'll bet you she's back to her old ways tomorrow."

"If you want to lose, you're on. I'm quite confident she's seen the error of her ways." She wasn't so sure; she agreed with Graham's observation of the situation.

"Thank you for a lovely evening, Rox."

"My pleasure."

At that precise moment he took both her hands in his and pulled her closer. She didn't resist as they gazed into each other's eyes. One of his hands cupped her cheek as his lips met hers. When he saw he was going to get no resistance from her, he deepened the kiss. She sighed as his mouth ravished hers. He tasted like the brandy and port he'd consumed with a hint of cheroots they'd partaken in.

He loosened his grip, and the kiss ended. "I could ravish you all night."

"Yes. I want more."

"Soon. I don't think tonight would be the proper thing to do," he said and added, "but soon."

He kissed her again. This time gently on the lips before heading out the front door.

As the door shut, Roxanne's fingers wandered to her lips to perhaps feel where his had been. *Damn you, Graham!*

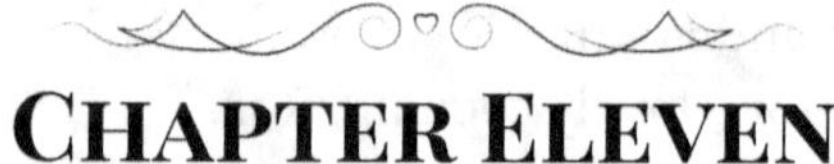

CHAPTER ELEVEN

T HEIR GUESTS LEFT late the following afternoon, taking with them the two horses Graham had brought for them to consider, and Roxanne spent that day going over the preparations for their next guests.

As she entered the breakfast room the following morning, she found Arthur behind a newspaper eating his breakfast as usual. She shook her head and wandered to the sideboard where all sorts of choices for breakfast were held. She made her selection and sat down in her usual spot to her brother's right.

"Good morning," she said.

That was answered with a grunt.

Agitated by this rude ritual Arthur had, she pulled the newspaper out of his hand. "Don't be rude, Arthur. I said good morning."

"And I answered you."

"With a grunt and your face hidden."

He sighed. "Very well, have it your way. Good morning, sister."

"That's better," she said. "Now what has you in such a mood?"

"I received word that Aunt Violet and Uncle Charles will arrive a few days later than planned."

Roxanne blinked and stared at her brother. "Did he give a

reason?"

"Something about a carriage spring, and Aunt Violet refusing to travel any further unless it's fixed."

A laugh escaped her. "Can't blame her. It would be near impossible to ride in it… I can see it now. Poor Uncle Charles."

"Indeed. At least you get a few days' reprieve."

"Yes, that will be helpful. Let me know when you hear when they'll be here."

A knock on the door and the butler appeared. He carried a silver salver with a missive of some sort. He walked right up to her. "A bouquet of pink roses arrived. I placed them on a table in the drawing room unless you prefer them elsewhere."

Taking the note, she opened and read it. Twice. It was from Graham asking her if she would like to have lunch with him at his estate and that he'd send his carriage for her. The last sentence mentioned something about wanting to share something special with her.

"I take it that's from Graham?"

"Yes. He would like me to have lunch with him today. Something about wanting me to see something."

"You're going to go, aren't you?" Arthur asked. He picked up his coffee cup and took a swallow, watching her face closely for any expression she might give up.

"Yes. I think I'll go write out my response and send it directly. It would be a nice afternoon. I haven't seen the house in ages."

Arthur chuckled. "For someone who could barely stand to be in the same room with Graham, you've certainly changed your opinion."

"It's nothing like that. I must admit he can be pleasant company, but that's all."

"Uh huh, tell that to someone who doesn't know you so well. I've caught glimpses of the two of you staring at the other."

"Now you are truly imagining things," she said with a grin.

"We'll see," Arthur said. He finished his coffee and put his newspaper back on the table. "If you'll excuse me, I have some correspondence to tend to before I meet the estate manager. It seems there's a portion of wall that's crumbled and I need to see what he suggests."

"Then I'll see you later," she said. She rose from her chair and grabbed a piece of her toast. "I best write out a response to Graham's request."

"That you're going?"

"Yes. He has left me too curious."

"I bet he has. Enjoy."

She watched the back side of her brother as he left the room, grateful at the relationship they shared. Other friends couldn't say that. If their brothers weren't married, they were more inclined to socialize and be part of the family when it suited them. Certainly, Arthur had his moments, but after their parents' tragic deaths he took his title very seriously.

THE DAY WAS so nice, Roxanne decided to go outside to wait on Graham. Even though a lady shouldn't, she thought it antiquated since the two of them were such old friends. She had no desire to be stuck inside on such a sunny day. Standing in the large drive, she caught a glimpse of a gig coming closer. She realized immediately the driver was Graham and smiled. Like her, he was a bit unconventional when it came to some things. He never thought twice about how he thought life should be lived. He maintained his duties and businesses as a man of his social standing should, but when he was home, he did things his way.

The gig pulled up next to her and Graham jumped down and walked over to her. His black hair was windblown with wisps having fallen to his face. He pushed it back off his forehead.

"Beautiful day for a drive, isn't it?" he said.

Roxanne nodded. "It is. I had to come outside to wait for you rather than stay in that stuffy old house."

"I agree. We get too many cloudy, rainy days as it is."

He helped her up on to the gig, then rounded the front, checking the horse's harness before climbing up next to her. He clucked to the bay to move forward.

"Where are we going?" she asked.

"Remember I told you I had something to show you?"

"Yes."

"We're going there now. After, I thought we could ride out to my lake for lunch."

"That sounds perfect, though you're certainly being secretive about what you insist on showing me," she said.

"No, that's just your imagination." He grinned.

His smile reminded Roxanne of when they were young. It meant mischief. But for one of the first times, she couldn't read him. They rode along in quiet until his family home appeared. Then she heard him begin to hum a tune.

"I don't know what you're up to, Graham."

He grinned again. "Can't I be in a good mood? It's a beautiful day, and I'm with one of my most favorite people in the world who happens to be a great kisser. What's not to be happy about?"

She arched a brow. "And as I've told you, that was a mistake. A one-time incident which I promise will never happen again."

"Never say never," he said as he guided the gig into the round drive. There was a large bed of various perennials which encircled a statue of some past earl. As he brought the gelding to a stop, a young stable boy appeared seemingly out of nowhere. Graham jumped down and gave the boy instructions before helping Roxanne out of the gig. By the time they neared the front door, the butler opened the door and let them pass into the main hall. Roxanne had always loved the pink and gray marble floor. Staff had kept it clean and well maintained over the years. It was the original floor.

Graham took her hand and led her over to the staircase. "Come follow me."

Snatching back her hand, she stopped. "What are you doing?"

"Taking you upstairs to see something."

"Why? Why not bring it to the drawing room?"

He let out an exasperated sigh. "You certainly ask a lot of questions."

"Curiosity is part of my make up."

"Roxanne, just follow me. I promise I won't do anything inappropriate."

She smoothed the front of her dress and silently counted to ten. "Very well."

Extending his arm, he waited for her to start up the stairs. She passed him without so much as a glance at him and began to climb the stairs. At the top were the main rooms: one of the drawing rooms, a ballroom, and a multitude she couldn't remember. Roxanne climbed the next set of stairs which she remembered led to the bed chambers.

Once on that floor, Graham took her up the stairs that led to the nursery and storage rooms. Beyond the end of a short hallway was a shut door. On the other side were the staff's quarters. Turning to Graham, Roxanne realized why he brought her here. His ward, his infant daughter lay inside the nursery.

Entering the nursery, she noted the walls were freshly painted in a pale yellow. In a corner just right of the fire was a cradle. Immediately Roxanne walked across the room and gazed down into the cradle. The babe was swaddled in blankets, and the only thing she could see for sure was a shock of black hair. Just like Graham.

"You can pick her up if you like," he said.

She shook her head. "Your nanny and nurses would be quite unhappy with me if I were to wake her."

"Bloody hell if they'll voice any sort of opinion as to who can hold the babe and who can't."

"Very well," Roxanne said as she leaned down and picked up the tiny bundle. The babe was deep asleep and the only sound she heard was that of herself breathing. There was no mistaking this child was Graham's.

"What do you think?"

"She's beautiful. She looks a lot like you."

"Yes, she does. She seems to be a good-natured child."

"You've decided to raise her here?" Roxanne asked.

"Yes. It's close to town and I can be here relatively quickly if I'm needed."

She gently rocked the child. "You've thought this through quite a bit and you're happy with your decision."

"Yes, I am."

"She's at some point going to need a mother figure in her life."

"I know. And of course her mother's family. They might try to take her."

"I thought your attorneys were working on this," she said as she gently placed the infant in the cradle.

"They are. I'm not worried about them. I'm merely concerned of the babe being raised without a mother."

"Perhaps you'll find the perfect woman to marry who will love the cherub as much as you do."

He walked to the window and back in deep thought. "Are you ready to continue our afternoon?"

"I certainly am, and thank you for sharing this moment with me."

"There is no one I'd rather have shared this with than you."

A short time later they were on their way to the lake on Graham's estate. The lake had been off-limits to them as young children, but the rules changed as they grew older. It had originally been a small pond, but Graham's great-grandfather had it enlarged and deepened. In the middle was a small "island" with a statue of Graham's great-grandmother. It seemed his family liked having statues made of family members.

Finding the perfect spot to sit and eat lunch, Roxanne found a blanket in the back of the gig and laid it on the ground a few feet from the shoreline. Graham followed with a basket his cook had prepared. He set it to one side and began to sit down. As Roxanne unpacked their lunch, he picked up a bottle of wine he'd had the cook include. There was a plate with ham and roasted chicken, red cheddar cheese, fruit, freshly baked bread, and butter.

"This looks quite inviting," she said as Graham passed her a glass of red wine.

"It does, doesn't it? I thought this would be a nice spot. The lake has always been one of my favorite places on the estate. I used to come here frequently when I needed some time alone. A perfect place for contemplation."

She prepared a plate and passed it to him. "I imagine it would be a perfect place to come and read."

"I've done that a few times, but I find coming here if I need to figure something out lets me do it with fewer distractions." He took a sip of wine, followed by a slice of bread.

"We all need to have at least one place like this."

"Indeed," he said. "Do you have such a place?"

Roxanne pushed the chicken and ham on her plate around as she attempted to decide how to respond. "Not since I was married off to Casper. When I was growing up I either went to the attics or sat in an old apple tree if it wasn't raining."

"If you need a place, you're always welcome to come here."

"Thank you, but I don't want to intrude."

He reached out and took her free hand. "You wouldn't be intruding. You're more than welcome here."

"You're too kind."

"It's not an act of kindness. I have concluded that I've fallen madly in love with you."

"Graham, it's not nice to tease."

"I'm not. Despite both of us declaring there was not the first bit of feelings between us, there is."

"I don't know what to say."

"Say nothing. Let's just see what develops."

She arched a brow. "Is that why you brought me here? To meet your daughter and get swept off my feet by you?"

"Of course not. My feelings for you are real, always have

been. Bloody hell, Roxanne, I want to marry you and spend the rest of my life together with you."

"Like you said, let's see what happens. I'm not saying no, and I'm not saying yes. Give us some time to get to know each other as a couple."

"I can live with that, but if you break my heart, I don't think I'll ever recover."

She laughed and tilted her head, so she wasn't looking directly at him. "Must you be so melodramatic?"

The next thing she knew, he was so close to her she could smell his shaving soap. Musk with a hint of citrus. Gently he pushed her down on her back and began kissing her passionately.

Suddenly, Graham broke their kiss, and he leaned on one elbow, gazing down upon her. She couldn't play his games. "What the bloody hell, Graham?"

"As much as I would like nothing more than to make love to you, I want our first time to be private and personal."

She grinned up at him for his thoughtfulness. "So do I, and anyone could come riding upon us and see what we're up to."

He responded with a hearty laugh. "I promise it won't be long."

"You know, my aunt and uncle will be here in a day or two. We could share that we're courting once they arrive."

He nodded. "I suppose I should speak with your brother, so he won't be surprised."

"I don't think he'll be surprised, but sharing with him first will mean the world to him," Roxanne said. "I wish he could find someone."

"What about any of your girlfriends? Any you could match him up with?"

"Perhaps, but we should concentrate on us first, though I will keep prospects for Arthur in the back of my mind," she said.

"That's what I want to hear come from your lips." He smiled. He righted himself and looked toward the basket. "I could have sworn I saw some of Cook's delicious chocolate cake."

"I think you might be right. Would you like a piece?"

He nodded and situated himself to pour two more glasses of wine while Roxanne retrieved the cake out of the basket. She tried to concentrate on the task at hand and not what they had just discussed, because if she were truthful with herself, she would have to admit to Graham that she had been in love with him for years.

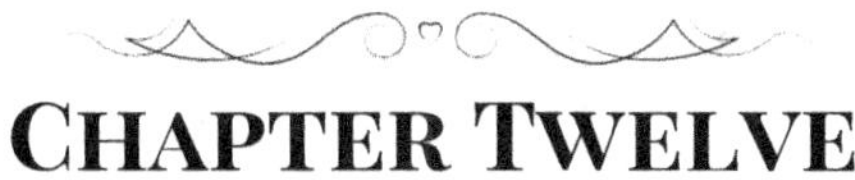

CHAPTER TWELVE

S EEING HER AUNT for the first time in many years, Roxanne felt like a piece of her had come home. She couldn't explain it other than she never realized how much she missed her mother until now. Leaving home at such a young age into a forced marriage to Casper had alienated her from everyone familiar to her.

In the past two days Roxanne had managed to avoid Graham. Not that it was hard to do. He had mentioned there were some matters on his estate needing taken care of, and she wanted to make sure everything was perfect when her aunt and uncle arrived. She knew his reasoning was over-exaggerated but was thankful he wasn't pushing her.

She and her aunt were sitting on the terrace enjoying lunch, her first full day with them. The butler had just brought her a letter from her friend, Pamela. It sat to Roxanne's left unopened.

"You wrote me telling me about your lady friends; how you all shared one common connection. Your husbands had all died. Have any remarried?"

Roxanne turned her head, fighting to get out of some fog that had surrounded her. "We were all friends before we married. This just brought us closer together. Georgiana remarried and is gushingly happy."

"Have you thought of marrying again?"

"No, not really. I was under Casper's thumb for so many years that I would like to enjoy some freedom on my own. If it's meant for me to marry again, I'm sure I'll find the right man."

"I have no doubt you will," her aunt said with a sly grin. Roxanne watched the older woman pop a piece of cheddar in her mouth, still looking a bit too triumphant for getting her view in.

"You and Arthur! I swear I get no peace from him, and now you. Perhaps the two of you should start a business for matching people up because he's been working overtime trying to get Hawksbury and me together," she said.

At that, Aunt Violet burst into a fit of laughter the likes of which Roxanne had never seen before. Her aunt was always so dignified. Now she was showing her a playful side Roxanne didn't know existed.

Wiping the tears from her cheek, she grinned at her niece. "I've seen the way Hawksbury looks at you."

"You haven't seen him since when? When he and Arthur were at university?"

"Even back then. The man is desperately in love with you. He looks at you like a big, brown-eyed puppy." She began to laugh again but stopped when she saw Roxanne wasn't humored. "I think you feel the same way. You're just scared to entrust your love to someone new after you had such a bad experience the first time."

"If Papa hadn't forced me to marry Casper."

"That's in the past. Get over it, Roxanne. You'll never find happiness if you don't let go."

Roxanne quietly contemplated her aunt's words. She knew the older woman to be right, but she just didn't seem to follow her own advice to herself. "You're right, of course. I need to work harder on it."

She was about to add something about Graham but was interrupted by Aunt Violet's finger pointing to the sky. To the west the sky was black as night. A storm was fast approaching.

"Come inside," Roxanne said, rising from her chair and grabbing her letter and putting it in the pocket of her dress.

Staff was already bustling around them gathering the food and plates. The butler mentioned to Roxanne they would reset everything in the breakfast room. Since she was still a bit hungry, she agreed and ordered a fresh pot of tea.

Violet reentered the breakfast room after having gone to her room and returned looking refreshed. "Do go put on something warmer, my dear. There's a chill in the air now with this storm."

"You're right. I'll just run and grab a shawl." She was met in the hall by the girl who had been looking after her since she arrived in Kent. She had a thick, dark-gray shawl in her hands and helped Roxanne get it over her shoulders.

"Thank you," she whispered to the girl before turning to walk back to her aunt.

Aunt Violet glanced up as she walked into the room. "That looks warm."

"It is. I found it in Scotland a couple of years ago. Before Casper died."

The housekeeper entered with a footman carrying a fresh pot of tea. The older woman dismissed the boy after he placed the teapot down.

"His Grace just informed me there would be one more for dinner tonight. I thought you would like to know."

"Don't tell me, Hawksbury?" Roxanne inquired.

"Yes."

"The storm seems to be bringing in the masses. I'm sure Cook can handle it."

"Yes, she can."

"Thank you for telling me."

Violet cackled the moment the housekeeper walked out of the room. "Hawksbury?"

"What about him? He and Arthur have business together, plus you know they're best friends—have been for life."

"Yes, I remember," Violet said. "Now if you will excuse me, I think I'll lie down before dinner. I hadn't realized how a long carriage ride can wear one out."

"Come. I'll walk with you to your rooms."

"Thank you."

The pair walked up the stairs and down hallways to get to the guestrooms. Roxanne stood in front of a white door. Inside, the walls were a delicious apricot color. One wall was covered with a wallpaper that matched the paint color wonderfully.

"I hope these will do. Uncle Charles's room is right through that door," Roxanne said.

"This is perfect."

"If you need anything just ask the maid or pull the rope and someone will come."

"Thank you. You've thought of everything."

"I'll see you at dinner."

Retracing her steps to another hall, Roxanne entered her bedchambers. She threw her shawl on a chair and walked to the bed where she took Pamela's letter out and began to read.

Pamela was back in London, getting ready to meet her mother in Dover. Her younger sister Jem was about to give birth and wanted Pamela to escort her to Dover. Jem wanted to spend some time with Pamela before she had to give her time to her family. Pamela had always had a flair for healing, even if her parents did disapprove in the beginning. The man she married had been a physician and he never discouraged Pamela from pursuing medicine. It was after his life was so tragically taken in a freak accident that she began to practice what she was successful doing. Basics. She was at an age when women were few and far between as physicians. She did what she could and assisted when necessary. Thus, why she was going to be present at her sister's birth. Her mother wanted her to oversee the event. So, being the dutiful daughter, she would go.

Her friend inquired as to her photographs and was she more at ease with the bulkiness of the cameras. Truth was, she hadn't taken any photographs. Everything had arrived in London, but she'd had no time, and she'd fussed at Graham for such an extravagant gift. She would love to get some photographs of Graham and the babe. It would be something he'd always have. She hadn't asked him, but as soon as they had a moment, she would.

Putting the letter down, Roxanne repositioned herself on the bed, putting her head on the pillows. She sighed in relief as she settled in. She wished she could tell Pamela about Graham's daughter, but she had promised she would keep it all to herself. At least for now. And there were doubts and whispers for a while when news first got out. But all would turn out fine because Graham didn't care a bit about what the ton or anyone else thought of his decisions. He wasn't the first man to have this dilemma and wouldn't be the last. Most men, however, didn't have anything to do with the child's upbringing. They might help financially, but that's as far as they would venture.

She needed to respond to Pamela's letter, but her eyelids were getting heavy, and she doubted she could stay awake much longer. Pamela's visit would be a welcome one. She could find more reasons for going into the village than anyone she knew. It would be nice to enjoy the company of someone closer to her own age. Roxanne placed the letter next to her and closed her eyes. The next hour she dreamed of going off into a field after a battle to confirm the casualties. Now what did this have anything to do with, other than she and the animal would be a place for all the estate's animals. She began to see what, if anything, might be possible. She needed to clear her mind. This was more than she was used to.

"Is Hawksbury running late?" Roxanne asked as she effortlessly entered the room. She was wearing a cobalt-blue silk gown she had purchased in Paris before her return to England. She had loved how well the gown came together, hanging on the edges of her shoulders.

She walked to where everyone was gathered near the fire.

"I'm afraid he sends his regrets. His aged stallion is quite ill, and he doubts the animal will make it through the night," Arthur said, handing her a glass of wine.

"Not Zeus! Hawksbury's had him for years."

"Yes, that's the one. Anyway, he won't be joining us," he said, turning to his uncle. "Hawksbury's had the horse since he was born. A gift from his father."

The older man nodded. "Losing the stallion will be like losing a part of his father. I understand."

Roxanne excused herself shortly after leaving the men to their cigars and brandy. She feigned a headache to her aunt, and Aunt Violet insisted she go to bed and get a good night's sleep. Whether the older woman believed the headache excuse or not, Roxanne quickly climbed the stairs and found her bedroom.

Kicking off her shoes, she walked straight into her dressing room where her maid was waiting. "My dark blue riding attire."

"You're not going out on horseback at this late hour, are you?"

"The moon is full and nary a cloud in the sky. I'm not going far, and I'll be fine."

Riding as fast as she thought safe, Roxanne soon arrived at Graham's stables. A single lamp shone, and apart from that, she couldn't see anyone. As she swung her leg over her mount's back, a stable boy appeared out of nowhere. His face looked as though he'd been crying.

As she headed for the open door, the boy spoke up. "You don't want to go in there, milady."

"I'm here to see…"

"He's at the house."

"Oh, my," she whispered half to herself. "Thank you."

She walked toward the house. Deciding to enter by the kitchen, Roxanne pulled the door open. There were a few gathered at a table in the room. All heads rose upon seeing her enter.

"I'm sorry to disturb, but I'm looking for Hawksbury," she said.

"You'll probably find him in his study, poor man," a man she recognized to be one of Graham's footmen said.

"Thank you. The stallion couldn't be saved?"

All heads shook. "No."

"I was afraid of that. Don't let me disturb you any further," she said, heading to the stairs that led up to the main floor.

There was no response when she knocked on the door to Graham's study. After pounding a third time, she heard a voice telling her he didn't wish to be disturbed. Well, like it or not, he was going to be disturbed. She hadn't ridden out at this time of night just for him to push her away.

She opened the door slowly and walked in. The only light was coming from the hearth. Sitting in one of the well-worn brown leather wing-back chairs sat Graham, a glass of brandy in his hand as he stared into the flames. As she walked closer, he still did not acknowledge her presence.

"I came as soon as I heard," she whispered.

He nodded ever so slightly. "You didn't have to. He went down and no one could get him up. You know he'd have never recovered once that happened, so I made the decision to put him out of his misery."

"I know that had to be the hardest decision to make."

"It was the only decision at that point."

"Look at it this way, he's out of pain and misery," she said, sitting in the chair next to his.

"He is, but it still wasn't an easy decision to make. I've had him all his life. He's known no one else."

"I know," she said, watching his face closely. She stood. "If you'd rather I leave, I can."

He glanced up at her and shook his head slowly. "No, I'm glad you're here." He set his snifter down and unfolded himself from the chair. "Would you care for a brandy?"

"Yes, yes I would."

Taking his glass, he poured them both a glass of the amber liquid. When he neared, he handed her a snifter. "Sit," he said.

Roxanne held the crystal with both hands and sat down again on the chair in front of the fire. She took a swallow of the smooth French brandy. Graham always kept some of the best liquor from the Continent.

"How is the babe?" she asked.

"To be honest, I don't know. I got so caught up in Zeus's ordeal that I never made it to the nursery. I'm sure she is fine."

"That's understandable."

"Humph."

"Would you like me to go to the kitchen and see what I can find for your dinner?"

He shook his dark locks. "No, not right now. I'm enjoying your company. Thank you for coming."

They sat in his study by the fire and talked for a long time about Graham's memories of his beloved stallion. In one instance he recalled when Roxanne hounded him about riding Zeus. No one rode Zeus. No one until that summer afternoon when Graham spoke to Arthur about letting her try. He let her get relaxed atop him. It was then that the animal snorted, pulling aside and running. Arthur watched in dismay as he eyed his sister trying to regain control of the situation. One thing was for sure, she had no control, and the stallion certainly wouldn't cease his bad behavior.

Roxanne slid out of the saddle and directly her bum hit the ground. She moaned as she got to her feet and dusted her dress off. She never let on if she were in any pain.

Walking past Arthur and Graham, who were still laughing, she mumbled something about that stupid horse. Neither heard her comment. Exasperated by both, she walked past them and headed towards the house.

"I suppose we were a little insensitive, but if you could have seen yourself flying off Zeus..." He snorted, then took a drink of brandy.

"I'm sure it was quite amusing to you and Arthur, but my bum hurt for several days afterwards."

"Served you right."

Slowly, with both hands on her face, he drew her towards him. He leaned down and caught her lips with his. Her hand curled around his nape, running her fingers through his hair while the other drifted up to his chest. She shivered as he nibbled at an earlobe.

"Someone might enter."

"No one dares enter without first announcing themselves," he replied.

"I'm not used to this."

"What? Being with a man outside the bedroom?"

He stood and headed across the room.

"Where are you going?"

"To lock the door. I'm going to make love to you."

He dropped to his knees in front of her and lifted her skirts. Quickly removing her undergarments and parting her legs, he gazed down at her. Her breath hitched in anticipation of what came next. He ran his fingers over her hipbones before running his tongue along her folds.

She moaned low as his tongue pressed against her nub before sucking and making her quiver with anticipation. He lifted her legs and raised them over his shoulders and continued to tease her with his tongue. Finally, all the buildup exploded, taking her over the edge. She reached for his cock and found the tip wet. She smeared the wetness onto her thigh, then guided him to her opening. Another small orgasm raced through her as he penetrated her. He pushed farther.

"Don't stop," she whispered.

He continued deeper into her and pushed until he was seated to the hilt. He began to slowly thrust in and out as they established a rhythm together.

"You feel so good," he gasped.

"Graham!" She cried out his name as she met him stroke for stroke.

Finally, he exploded inside her. Her name and filthy words flew from his mouth as he finally slowed and pushed one last time. They remained like that for a few moments. He didn't know if it was mere seconds, a minute, an hour, or a day. He was in utopia and never wanted it to end. He wanted to carry her upstairs and take her again, this time completely naked, where he could taste her breasts and feel the rest of her flesh against his.

"I want more," he murmured. "I want to touch every part of your body. I want you to touch me."

"I do too."

"You do?" He hadn't expected that from her.

"Yes. Is the tower far from here?"

"Far enough, but it sounds like rain is hitting the windows.

"Drat," she replied. "I suppose we're left with no choice but to stay in your chambers, milord."

He laughed and kissed her. "Get dressed."

They put themselves to right and then left the library and stepped into the hallway. It was eerily quiet, but then Graham's servants knew how to disappear into the woodwork. Taking her hand, he led her up the stairs to his chamber.

As soon as the door closed behind them, he locked it and bent down. His mouth covered hers, and he kissed her deeply, his tongue slipping past her lips to toy with hers. He tasted like liquor and perhaps cigars. She felt his fingers working her clothing until she was down to her chemise. Slowly, he pulled it over her head. His hands reached for her breasts, stroking them tenderly before he pinched her nipple. He led her to the bed and quickly undressed before kissing her neck.

"Graham," she moaned.

She ran her hands down his back. He was nude, his skin hot to the touch. He lay atop her, his weight settling between her thighs.

She felt the tip of his cock nudge her as he found her entrance and thrust inside. He shifted back and rocked, gently, each small thrust pushing him deeper. He hooked his hands under her knees and lifted them over his shoulders. He kissed her mouth, then feathered kisses to her breasts, torturing her.

He was in control and would make love to her in the manner he desired. She arched up, silently asking him to touch her more. She ran her hands through his hair and hung on, kissing him back and moving submissively under him.

He groaned as his hips worked a little faster, his cock deep inside her. She felt each thrust and moaned, wanting more. She arched her back and met him with equal fervor. She wanted this man more than life itself.

He broke their kisses and slid his fingers down her side, between their bodies. He pressed his thumb down on her throbbing nub.

"Come with me," he rasped. His shoulders were bunched with muscle, strands of hair clinging to his face as his eyes stared wildly into hers.

"I can't."

His thumb circled her nipple as his cock continued to fill her.

She arched her head and cried out, his mouth catching the sound. She'd never experienced anything like this before. He propped himself up on his elbows and kissed her gently as he made love to her, then threw back his head as his body jerked into hers. He called out her name as his seed flooded her.

"My God, Roxanne, what are you doing to me?"

Slowly, he withdrew and lay on his side, pulling her close to him. Roxanne had never felt such bliss before. She absentmindedly ran her fingers through his chest hair, feeling his chest rise and fall as he settled.

"I could ask you the same thing."

"What?"

She sat up. "I've never experienced the closeness I felt when we're one."

He smiled. "Good to know. There is so much more I want to teach you. That is, if you're interested."

"Yes, I'm interested."

"I was hoping you would be."

⟫⟫⟫❈⟪⟪⟪

IF ROXANNE HELD any chance of not being seen returning from her late-night ride, she was mistaken. Of all people, it was Arthur she faced on the path between the stables and house. He was dressed for riding and she hadn't the energy from lack of sleep to get into any sort of discussion with her brother.

"I assume from the hour you keep, things did not go well."

She shook her head. "No, Graham ended up putting the animal out of his misery."

"Probably best, given his age."

"I sat with him, let him remember."

"Breakfast awaits, unless you ate already."

"No, I haven't."

"I have a meeting. I'll see you later."

"Men and their meetings," she sighed with a grin.

She heard Arthur's footfalls grow faint and swore she heard him chuckle as he walked.

Roxanne walked through the door of the bustling kitchen. As she made her way across the room, she caught the eye of one of the young girls and asked her to have a fresh pot of tea brought to the breakfast room. Though she was exhausted from lack of sleep the night before, she was determined to have something to eat. It would also give her a chance to glance through the newspapers. Then and only then would she gather herself up and retire to her rooms for a hot bath and change of clothes.

The breakfast room was quiet as it normally was. It was one of her favorite rooms in the house because she could look out over a meadow where she loved to ride when she didn't want to wander too far into the estate. She made her way to the sideboard and picked up a porcelain plate and chose toast and marmalade.

Once she was settled in, she picked up one of the papers and began scanning the page for anything which might be of interest to her. She smiled to herself and shook her head. This was how she spent her breakfasts when married. Alone. She had grown used to it, the solitude she faced. One day she hoped things would change but for now, she accepted what hand she had been dealt.

Her mind wandered to Graham and the intimacy the two of them shared after all these years. There was a deep attraction, and neither could deny it. It certainly was not a one-time thing. There was something more and they were both going to have to stop making excuses for their obvious feelings.

She picked up a piece of toast and spread marmalade on it. As she took a bite, the butler entered the room. He carried with him a large bouquet of assorted flowers. He handed her a sealed envelope. "These just arrived for you. I'll have them placed in water."

"They are gorgeous. Have them placed in the drawing room so everyone can enjoy them."

The man nodded and turned and left her to read the note in privacy. She already knew the flowers were from Graham because she had seen these exact flowers at his estate and had remarked to him how lovely they were. After rereading the note, she slipped the letter into the pocket of her skirt. She would send him a note thanking him for the flowers. It would be rude to do otherwise.

Her thoughts turned to Graham's daughter. If things were to progress, what would happen? Would she be expected to help raise the child as her own? Questions flooded her head. What had his people been able to find out? Would the babe go off to live with her mother's family, or would she stay to be raised as an earl's daughter? This needed to be addressed and soon.

Roxanne had always wanted more children, but after her son and his defects that led him to an asylum, she had closed the door to any further children. Her husband refused to share a bed with her after Thomas's birth. In Casper's eyes, she had been responsible in bearing a devil's child.

"It's awfully early to be so deep in thought," a voice behind her said.

Turning in her chair, Roxanne noted her aunt Violet standing in the doorway. Her aunt was still a striking woman despite her advancing years. Though her hair was light as snow and her face carried more lines than previously, Violet continued to carry herself as the regal woman she always had been.

"Good morning. Please join me," Roxanne said.

Violet walked toward the sideboard and instructed the footman what she wanted before turning and sitting at the table.

"Beautiful day, isn't it?"

A pang of guilt swept over Roxanne. How could she have been so negligent of her dear aunt? "It is. Is there anything you'd like to do today?" She watched as her aunt began to thoughtfully smear marmalade on a piece of toast.

"You don't have to entertain me, Rox. I can keep myself amused if needed."

"I wouldn't be much of a hostess if I did such a thing. I simply wasn't sure how tired you'd be after your journey. I know you tire easily after long distances such as this. I simply didn't want you to feel forced to do anything if you indeed needed more time to recover."

"I'll be fine just taking a walk or something simple like that."

"I have a couple of things to go over with the housekeeper and answer a couple of letters. Then I'll be free."

"I need to tend to some letters myself as well. When should we meet and where?"

Roxanne smiled. "Two hours in the drawing room?"

"Perfect."

Two hours went faster than Roxanne anticipated, but she was finding she could accomplish quite a lot—a lot more than she first believed when she accepted Arthur's offer. Remembering something she picked up in Paris for her aunt, she returned to her rooms to get the new embroidery threads. She remembered when she was choosing colors for herself that her aunt loved to embroider and was quite good at it. Besides, Violet rarely bought anything for herself. Not that she and her uncle couldn't afford luxuries like that. That wasn't a problem. Her aunt always put others above herself.

"This is for you," Roxanne said as she handed a small parcel wrapped in tissue.

"You didn't need to go to any trouble," Violet replied, accepting the package and studying it intently.

"I can assure you it was no trouble at all. I was in Paris for a couple of days. I wanted to shop, of course, and saw these and couldn't resist."

Violet began ripping the tissue from a small bundle, squealing in delight as she laid eyes on the threads for the very first time. She picked up a dark green from the top of the pile and fingered it. "These are exquisite. Thank you."

"I'll give you the name and address of the shop. You may want to visit them while you're in Paris."

"I would be most appreciative."

"I'll give you the other shops for dresses and such. They are willing to ship your purchases to you."

Placing the threads to one side, Violet nodded at Roxanne's statement. "That is good to know. I'm hoping we'll be there long enough so I can be fitted with one or two new dresses."

"You deserve it."

"I can't believe I haven't ever been to Paris, though. My father believed women didn't need to travel to faraway places and that they should be satisfied with staying close to home."

"Well, Uncle Charles is changing all that. Take advantage of every stop you make and embrace everything a city has to offer."

"I plan on that," Violet said with a huge smile.

"Good."

"You deserve a chance at marital happiness, Roxanne. Someone who will be your equal. Someone who will encourage you. Someone who's a great listener."

Roxanne grinned. "It might be difficult to find a man like that."

"He's out there. I know you don't want to remain a widow for the rest of your life."

"No, I don't, but I'll accept whatever hand I'm dealt."

Violet arched a brow. "I've never known you to be someone who doesn't fight for what they want. Someone who simply settles."

"You ought to have endured what I had to when I was married to Casper."

"I can only imagine, but you've got to move on. It's been years now. This is your time, Rox."

"I know, and I'm trying hard to do that."

"While you're searching for a bride for your brother, why don't you eye the eligible men?"

"I've been trying just that. That's easier than trying to find a bride. I suppose once we return to London I'll be able to work more at what young ladies are available."

"True. Have you thought of hosting a country ball or house party?"

"It had crossed my mind, though a house party is something for the future."

"Then a ball it is! I wish I could be here for it, but I know you'll do splendidly."

Roxanne watched her aunt as she continued to examine each skein of thread in the basket next to her. "I wish you could be here as well."

⇛⇚

HER UNCLE AND aunt's time seemed to fly by. Charles had not given them much chance to stay because he and Violet were excited about the next leg of their adventure, the Continent. It was only after she persuaded their uncle to spend some time upon their return to England that her aunt agreed because she felt, given the time, there would be many changes by the time they returned.

After seeing them off, Roxanne headed to the rose garden to pick some blooms. She hadn't been able to spend time alone with Graham and she was anxious to find out how his young charge was doing.

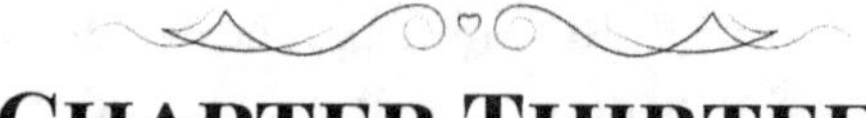

CHAPTER THIRTEEN

HAVING SENT GRAHAM a note regarding the babe, Roxanne began to question herself. Though she hated to admit it, her feelings had only deepened for the man. They both acknowledged that there was something between them that was far more than plain friendship. They had made love, sharing the deepest intimacy a man and woman can share. He seemed to have become more settled of late, but she was sure that was due to the fact he'd found himself a father in charge of raising a mere babe. She was sure it was daunting to him. Especially because she was a girl, and her needs were different than those of a boy. She was going to need a mother or mother figure but until Graham found himself a bride, he was going to have to rely on others. Nannies would be filling in until then.

Growing tired of waiting for his reply, Roxanne had the gig readied. This way, she didn't have to ride, and she could take a few baked goods for him with her.

As she turned down the drive leading to Graham's house, she noted movement to one side of the trees lining either side of the long drive. Upon moving closer, she realized it was Graham in the company of a young woman. She was on a dark bay horse who was on a long lead which Graham seemed to be in control of. Roxanne wondered if she was the daughter of a friend of his and was here for a lesson upon a horse her father had purchased from Graham. The girl appeared to be an adequate rider but that didn't mean a thing when she was in a controlled environment.

She continued to sit in the gig watching what was transpiring in front of her. She listened as Graham gave the woman a thorough critique of her efforts. A smirk briefly crossed the rider's face before becoming solemn once again. It occurred to Rox at that moment the young girl was attempting to flirt with Graham. And not doing a very good job at it because he quickly became agitated by her lack of seriousness. He said something to her, bringing the bay to a stop. Nearing the horse, the two began to have some sort of conversation. He was putting an end to the lesson and asked her to dismount the horse. She acted as though she hadn't heard him. He repeated her task and stood and waited for her to do as he asked. Bending over, she appeared to be looking at the ground, saying something. Graham shook his head and made it clear if she didn't dismount, she could sit in the side-saddle while the horse was led back to the stables. Finally, she slid off the bay and stood as close as she could get herself to Graham. He backed away, and she quickly threw her arms around his shoulders and kissed him firmly on the lips. Graham untangled himself from her, said something to her before turning and gathering the bay's reins, leading him back to his stables. She stood there for a moment, scheming before joining Graham as he walked back to the stables.

Roxanne smiled at this turn of events and waited until the pair were out of sight before continuing to Graham's house. The butler and footman greeted her as she slid down off the cart.

"He's finishing up with his pupil, so he should be here shortly," she said as she tried hard not to show her amusement at what she'd just witnessed.

The butler followed her into the entry hall. "Would you care for some tea out on the terrace, and will you be joining the earl for lunch?"

"Tea would be wonderful. As far as lunch, you best consult the earl. He doesn't know I'm here as I simply decided on a whim to come."

"I'm sure he'll be happy to see you. Now if you'll follow me, milady."

Roxanne began to follow the older gentleman. She knew Graham's butler had been employed by the family for years. He'd always been here. In fact, she thought she remembered the butler's own father had worked in the position before retiring and handing over his responsibilities to his son. She wondered if he had a son of his own to pass the torch to.

Upon arrival at the terrace, the older man made his excuses to see about tea and lunch and left after seeing she was seen to. Sitting at a table, she took in her surroundings, marveling at the well-maintained gardens that lay before her. The only real sound she heard was that of birds happily chirping.

The unexpected sound of a door shutting just behind her caused her to jerk her head around to see Graham coming toward her. She couldn't really tell his mood, but if the scowl on his handsome face was any indication, he was annoyed.

"I'm sorry, I don't recall us scheduling anything." He sat down across from her.

She shook her head. "No, I had some questions and thought I'd stop by and check up on your charge."

He nodded, running a hand through his thick black hair to tame an errant lock that kept falling over his eyes.

"I saw you giving lessons to a young lady as I came up the drive." She knew she'd hit a nerve because he rolled his golden eyes.

"Yes. Her father purchased the bay you saw her riding and wanted to make sure they were a good match."

"And how was she?"

"A royal pain in my arse. She is spoilt, stubborn, and rude. Thinks she knows best. I'll have to have a word with her father because I'm not sure she and the gelding are suited."

"And she bears some affection for you?"

"You saw that? That was the last straw."

"I'm sure you'll have everything under control for the next

time," she said dryly.

"Hmmm. Now tell me about why you've come."

"The babe. Have you decided how you are going to resolve the issue?"

He shifted in his chair as he thought about how to respond. "My man is still attempting to find the babe's mother with no luck to date. So we're petitioning the court to have me assigned as her ward until sufficient time has passed."

"I'm sure you'll have no problem."

"I certainly hope you're right. My being a bachelor does not work in my favor."

"So find someone to marry," she said boldly.

"And who am I to marry?"

Roxanne simply sat there and stared at him in disbelief.

"What?"

Of course, lunch made its debut, and they sat in silence until the servants left the terrace.

Once they were alone, she passed him a plate filled with roasted chicken. As he speared a few pieces off the plate, she noted he was trying not to look directly at her. He knew he'd hit a nerve. "So what is bothering you?"

Dropping her fork onto her plate, she stared at him in disbelief. "I thought we'd discussed this, and I thought there was something developing between us."

"Yes, I believe there is something profound happening between us and I want nothing more than to pursue it."

"So explain to me what you mean by pursue it. Are we simply seeing each other, are we betrothed, what?"

He turned the tables on her. "What do you want?"

"Ultimately, I would like nothing more than to marry you, Graham. In the meantime—at least through the summer, we should court."

"I can live with that," he said, popping a piece of chicken into his mouth. He was enjoying this way too much.

"I'm at the end of what I can tolerate, Graham. This going

back and forth and dancing around the subject is beginning to wear on me hard."

"I didn't mean to upset you."

"I know you didn't, but let's decide what we're doing. To-day."

"Then I propose we make our relationship public."

"What of Arthur? I don't want to blindside him, though I suspect he knows more than he lets on," Roxanne said.

"Yes, he knows quite a bit more, and I can assure you he wants nothing more than for us to marry."

"Men! You're all alike, and you band together like a bunch of naughty schoolboys. Always sticking together, and you always have each other's backs."

"Of course. Women are too petty. The claws come out and you play viciously," Graham said.

"Touché! I must agree with you. That's why my circle of women is only a select few."

"I can live with that. When we finish here, we should go to the nursery and check in on Mary."

"I would like that very much. How is she?"

"Thriving!"

"That's wonderful, Graham."

"Her nanny tells me she's finally fallen into a routine."

Roxanne found herself getting excited about becoming a part of this baby girl's life. Whether Graham knew it or not, he was the best thing to enter her short life. He could sit back and let nannies oversee this babe's upbringing or do what he was doing. Instead, he was becoming a hands-on father and loving every moment.

"That's good because I have friends whose children aren't, and it makes life a little more challenging." She picked up a piece of apple and chose some stout cheddar cheese. She studied the cheese for a moment before taking a bite. Graham's estate was well known for making some of the best cheese in the area. The estate had been making two varieties of cheddar, each aged for different lengths of time to give it the distinct sharp flavor.

"I hope she continues to be sweet."

"Don't count on it. I'm sure she'll have her moments. All children do," Roxanne said with a sly smile.

Graham threw his head back and laughed in that deep baritone of his. "The key is not to over-indulge them."

She arched her brow. "Or give in to their every whim."

He laughed again. "What is that look for? Do you really think I'd spoil her?"

"You already are. Not that it's a bad thing, but as she gets older, the more likely she'll be to just wrap you around her little finger. You won't know what happened."

"I suppose you're right, and it would be unfair to her siblings. Everyone should be treated equally."

"Siblings? You certainly are sure of yourself, aren't you? Putting the cart before the horse?"

He reached across the small table and took her hand and squeezed. "We'll have some beautiful babies. Don't tell me you haven't thought of it because I certainly have."

"Of course I have."

"You sound hesitant," he said.

"Only because of the problems my son was born with."

"That doesn't mean it will happen again."

She nodded. "I know and I'm sure I'm being overly dramatic, but having experienced it once, I can't help my feelings."

"It's all right. We'll deal with it one day at a time."

"Thank you."

He took a piece of cheese and bit into it. "Let's finish up so we can go to the nursery."

"I'll need to get back home afterwards."

"What could possibly be so important? Do you dislike my company that much?"

"You know I love spending time with you, but I'm sure you have things to do other than entertain me."

A wicked grin crossed his face, and he waggled his eyebrows.

"You know I like more than anything being able to be with you."

"Get your mind out of the gutter, Graham."

"Who, me?"

"Yes, you. Now why don't we go upstairs to the nursery?"

"Very well. Perhaps we can find an unused room in the attic afterwards. Hmmm?"

"We'll see." She removed her hand from his and finished the apple and cheese.

Her mind was running a mile a minute and no matter what she tried, she hadn't been able to make her thoughts slow down. It irritated her because she knew where Graham was concerned, she needed to be focused. He'd have them married tomorrow if he could get everything in place. There was a lot more for them to discuss before they married, and she wanted that taken care of by summer's end.

They walked into the house and Graham led the way to the third-floor nursery. He opened the door and let her pass before joining her. The rooms were quiet, and Roxanne immediately knew the child was asleep. The nanny Graham hired led them to a corner of the large room where the babe lay asleep. Roxanne studied her as she slept. She still thought there was no denying whose child she was. She even had Graham's long dark lashes.

"Would you like to hold her?" he asked lowly.

Roxanne shook her head and backed away from the child. "No, not today. I don't wish to disturb her, and I'm sure Mrs. McPhee would be most appreciative if I didn't wake her before she's ready."

He nodded with a scowl on his face that could only be likened to that of a new father who had no clue on what it really meant to raise a child. Especially one so young.

She thanked the nanny before walking out of the nursery. Graham followed. Neither said a word until they descended the staircase. Roxanne smoothed the moss-green dress and pulled her shawl tight around her shoulders.

"What do you think?" he asked.

"You got quite lucky finding your nanny."

"Yes, I suppose I did. I would still like you to spend some time together. With both the babe and Mrs. McPhee."

"And I will, but for now, I need to head back."

"So soon?" he asked with a slight pout to him.

"Yes. I have several things that need my attention. If you'd like to come to dinner, I'm sure we can use the time to not only tell Arthur, but for us to talk about the changes this is going to bring."

"Yes, I'd like to get a special license so we can marry sooner than later. But I'm afraid I have a prior commitment for this evening."

"No problem. Why don't we each make a list of anything important we want to bring to this marriage?"

"Such as?" he asked.

"Beginning with some much-needed renovations to the house. It looks like nothing has been done since probably your grandfather's time. Something like that."

"But let's not get carried away," Graham said.

"Exactly."

"We can hire someone who is more knowledgeable about these things. Someone who's familiar with it all and someone who'll take the extra incentive to assure this will happen."

They were nearing the front door. Her gig had been brought around from the stables and the gray mare stood there waiting on her. She settled and picked up the reins. Rather than cluck to the horse, she leaned down and looked at this man she'd agree to marry and kissed him on the cheek before righting herself and urging the horse along.

GRAHAM STOOD AND watched as Roxanne's gig disappeared from sight. Both expected and unexpected pieces had come to light today. Her agreeing to marry had been the greatest compliment he could receive. She had a strong personality, and few things scared her—not even his peers or business associates. The ladies of the ton would also be curious, and envious that he'd found a bride. Though he was sure there would be some snipes, which were to be expected, Roxanne would be able to hold her own without so much as having to bring out her metaphorical claws. She would be the perfect countess. Not only that, she would be the perfect mother. Not only for future babes, but for Mary as well.

He turned around with the intention of going to his study. He needed to make a list of what needed to be done by the time Roxanne moved in as his wife. Running a list through his mind, the one thing besides a special license was a ring. Not only a wedding ring, but another to celebrate their union. He would first go through his mother's and grandmother's jewelry to see if there wasn't something Roxanne might like. If not, he'd go visit the jeweler in London and if need be, take some stones for use.

In all honesty, he was surprised she had accepted. She was finally free of the atrocities Casper put upon her, but she'd had three years in the south of France to mourn or not mourn. She was ready to move on, and he was grateful it was he she chose.

Entering his study, Graham walked over to a sideboard and picked up a bottle of whiskey and a crystal glass. Placing the items on the corner of his desk, he sat down and lazily propped his feet up on the desk. Closing his eyes momentarily, he tried to recall Roxanne's face as she was bent over whispering to Mary. He never had any doubt that she would be a devoted mother. As a wife he saw them as a team. They now got along well, working together to achieve the same results. Not a lot of couples could say that. In most marriages, the wife was subservient to her spouse and agreed with whatever her husband wanted. After all, he knew best. A woman's place was to see to the house and children. Nothing more, nothing less. Thank God he was nothing like that.

Deciding he'd had enough time woolgathering, Graham righted himself and leaned over and poured himself a splash of whiskey. He took a healthy taste of the amber liquid before placing the glass at his right. He then pulled out a piece of paper from the top drawer and picked up his pen. Before he knew it, his short list had filled a page. He was trying to anticipate for any and all scenarios, and it appeared a trip to London was looming.

He would see if Roxanne had reason to go, and if so, they could travel together and stay at his residence. He would bring the photographic equipment he'd bought for Roxanne back with him. She certainly couldn't learn to use it if it sat somewhere else. She had a keen eye for detail, and he was certain her images would show such.

Flowers were also a passion of hers. He would speak with the head gardener to see if he would mind Roxanne tending to some of the many flowers. Gardeners were a lot of time quite possessive of the gardens and didn't care for an interloper making havoc with something that they'd nurtured for years. He had to find a delicate way to introduce the idea to the man.

Making Roxanne feel at home was especially important to him. He didn't want her feeling like a guest in what would be her new home. He needed to make some exceptions at first. He imagined her wanting to re-do some of the rooms. Heaven knew this was sorely needed.

The sound of the door to his study opening caused him to look up where he found Arthur standing. His friend had a solemn look masking his face. Then a broad grin replaced it. He wondered if he'd talked with Roxanne. If he were a betting man, he'd say the man had spoken with her.

"You could have warned me," he said, picking up a glass and pouring a whiskey from the decanter on Graham's desk. He sat down, saying nothing further.

"About what?" he teased.

"Don't play ignorant with me. You know I'm talking about my sister."

"What about her?"

Arthur paused. "Ah yes, I spoke with her as she returned home, and she mentioned something about the pair of you getting married? I thought you needed my blessings."

"Actually, I was going to come speak to you, but I was unaware I needed to ask your permission. She is a widow, and the usual rules don't apply. Looks like she beat me to it."

"I'm joking, Graham. I've been expecting this, though I will admit it happened quicker than I thought it would. Have you made plans?"

"That's what I'm working on. I need to make a journey to London. We'll need a special license rather than have the banns read."

"How big of an affair is this going to be?" Arthur asked.

"Very small. That and when are two things up in the air. I wanted to make sure I had the license first."

"As long as she's happy. That's all that matters to me, and I know she's made the right decision," Arthur said as he brought the glass to his lips and finished off the whiskey. He placed the glass on the desk in front of him.

"Thank you."

Arthur accepted another glass of whiskey from his friend. He swirled the contents thoughtfully. "Are you going to do a wedding trip? Or are you going to wait?"

"We'll probably do it next year, perhaps in the spring."

"That'll give you ample time to plan one out."

Graham nodded. "I concur. I wish at least my mother could be here to join in our happiness."

"Same here, though I doubt Roxanne would agree. Our mother never thought for herself without our father's input. She's always seen that as a sign of weakness. Roxanne needs to realize our parents grew up in an entirely different era than we did. Things were a lot stricter than they are today," Arthur said.

"That they were."

"I'm so grateful you and my sister found each other," Arthur said. "I'm glad to see you've moved on, and to be honest, I haven't been sure Roxanne would ever marry again, let alone have a relationship with a man."

"Thank you. That means a lot," he replied. "You know she's going to try and find a bride for you."

"She started the day she arrived. Lucky for me, you've been somewhat of a distraction."

"Don't be fooled by her innocent act. If you remember, she had quite a distaste for me at first."

"An act," Arthur said with a smirk. "The more she complains means in most cases she likes the person or situation."

Graham filled each of their glasses and sat back to savor the whiskey. "Can you find an excuse to join us in London?"

"I'm sure I can find the time. Why?"

"There's a ship I'm interested in acquiring. I would like a second opinion on the matter. The company which owns it is shifting away from maritime shipping in favor of rail."

Arthur arched a brow. "They can't do both? I only ask because rail is still not the quickest way to do business."

"Not the most direct. There is still a need to bring sugar, spices, and other goods from the Caribbean and Far East, and a lot is simply not suited for rail. I'm at a loss for why they don't see that."

"Certainly works to your advantage." Arthur was referring to the sugar plantation Graham owned. His father had purchased it years ago, sold sugar to a lot of customers, but had always had to purchase space on cargo vessels.

"I can ship more for myself to sell and distribute and keep a few loyal customers."

"You wouldn't have room for a partner or investor, would you?"

Graham chuckled and placed the glass on his desk. "You catch on fast. That's exactly what I have in mind."

"You know I've been looking for a way to invest outside of the obvious. Times are changing, and quickly. I don't wish to be locked out."

"Neither do I. That's why I wanted to share this opportunity with you."

"I appreciate you thinking of me. I really do."

"It won't be the last," Graham said as he leaned forward in his chair. "I mean, if we're going to be family, we might as well help each other out."

"Well said." He glanced at the clock on the mantel. "I should be getting back."

"Stay. I'm sure Cook can find a couple of good thick steaks that'll rival White's."

"You talked me into it."

Graham rose and found the bellpull. Moments later, the butler appeared. The man was always there when he needed him, which was more than he could say about some of the younger generation. It was easy to spot who truly wanted a life-long position to those who were merely passing through until something better came along. He informed him of the changes for dinner, and once the butler left, he returned to his desk to pick up his glass.

"Let's sit somewhere more comfortable," Graham said.

Once they'd settled, the pair sat in silence for a few minutes. Arthur stretched his long legs out in front of him and sighed.

"It's nice to just sit. I've been so busy with my estate manager, I sometimes forget to slow down."

Graham grunted his response.

Finishing his glass of whiskey off, Arthur set the glass on the table beside him. "I forgot to ask earlier, but who is it who's selling this ship and possibly ships?"

"Gregory Crenshaw."

Arthur jerked his head in Graham's direction. "Did I hear you right? Did you say Gregory Crenshaw?"

"I did."

"You do realize who he is?"

"Yes, I do. He's the man your parents were supposed to meet

in India about a business deal, but never did," Graham said.

"Why would you even consider purchasing a ship or anything else for that matter from him?"

Graham said nothing for a moment, as though choosing his words carefully. "Because he's not the man he represents himself to be. He's in great need of money to finance this new railroad scheme, and no one will lend him the money."

"So he's turned to liquidating assets in hopes of making the money he needs."

"Exactly."

"We'll have to be careful. The man's not to be trusted. Everything pointed to him being involved in my parents' disappearance, but it couldn't be proved."

Graham arched a brow. "It'll be interesting to see his reaction or lack of when I introduce you."

"Yes, it will. I take it from the way you talk, you've been looking into him?"

"Absolutely. I recognized his name immediately. I've hired someone to look into him, everything we need to know."

"What will you do? Contact the authorities?" Arthur asked.

"Once there's enough information to give them. For now, I'll rely on this gentleman I've hired."

"Do me a favor and let's not mention anything about Gregory Crenshaw to Roxanne. All she needs to know is we're looking at a ship to purchase," Arthur said.

"I concur. Planning for the wedding and settling into her new home will keep her busy for quite a while."

It was no exaggeration that Roxanne would have plenty to keep her busy for the next few months. She was meticulous about nearly everything. Since her marriage to Casper had been forced on her, she would want to plan the perfect small wedding. Graham wouldn't deny her that. Nor would he deny her wish to redecorate the residences.

A knock at the study door caught both men's attention. It was the butler. How long had they been sitting here since he took the dinner menu change to the cook?

"Dinner is ready, milord."

"Thank you. You set us in the breakfast room?" It was so much easier for just one or two people to eat in the smaller room than be lost in the large, cavernous dining room.

"Yes, milord."

"Excellent. We'll be there momentarily."

CHAPTER FOURTEEN

ROXANNE WAS GLAD to be back in London. The country estates were equally wonderful, but London had so much to offer, including shops a village wouldn't have. She hadn't seen either her brother or Graham since they hit town yesterday. Not during the day. She knew they had business affairs to attend to and Graham would be seeing the bishop about getting a special license. She had an appointment with her dressmaker today, and hopefully something could be whipped up for her wedding or the woman might have something in stock. That alone would set the tone for when they'd marry. She was hoping for Thursday, but if it was impossible to pull off, they would marry the following Tuesday or Wednesday. So much to do and her list just kept getting longer. There wouldn't be a large number of people invited; in fact, outside of Arthur, there was no one. That was fine with her because that was what she truly wanted. Something small and intimate.

There was much to be done once they were wed. She and Graham needed to have a discussion about what he expected. Baby Mary came to mind. Another thing to be discussed. Would she raise the child alongside Graham as their own? Would they at some point tell her the truth about her birth mother? Graham had discussed perhaps telling people she was the daughter of a cousin who, because of his cousin's sudden and unexpected death had left the infant under his protection. Yes, they needed to have the matter settled quickly.

Though she wasn't going to redecorate until after she settled into Graham's residences, Roxanne decided to begin to make notes of what she wanted to change, colors, carpets, wallpapers, and furnishings. She would try and write down things she found in shops, perhaps bring samples home. Graham had already mentioned speaking to the gardener about letting her have a bed so she could grow what she wanted. He was also giving her an older greenhouse to use. Once she cleaned it, she could use the greenhouse to grow startups and seedlings. It wouldn't happen overnight, but the idea of having space of her own made her happy. And another new project she was going to have to learn to be efficient in was all that photography equipment he'd purchased for her when he first found out what drew her to go beyond painting. Though she was adequate at painting certain things, she never felt she'd captured the essence of her subjects. In her mind, there had to be a connection.

She arrived at the dressmaker for her appointment with lots of ideas and expectations. While she waited on Mrs. Levi, Roxanne admired some of the new fabrics placed on a table. She wanted the gown to be something she could use again. Something elegant but practical. A deep-plum silk fabric caught her eye. She could see herself in it, perhaps with lavender for piping. First, though, she needed to study some of the many fashion plates to find something similar to what she'd sketched a few days prior to leaving for London.

Studying a fashion plate with a recent design from Paris, she sighed. It was a style she loved but knew in the back of her mind that it was not one that looked very flattering on her body type. There were too many ruffles. She needed a dress that wasn't so exaggerated.

"Your note said you needed something for a special occasion," Mrs. Levi said as she approached Roxanne. The dressmaker was, as usual, dressed impeccably, not a hair out of place. She had lived in London for ten years and stayed after her husband suddenly died. The woman was quite popular and sometimes it took weeks to garner a time slot.

She studied the woman for a moment. "I need something I can use as not only my wedding dress, but also for other occasions."

"You're going to be a bride? How wonderful! Who is the lucky man? And when is the wedding?" Mrs. Levi said in a rapid-fire response.

"The groom is the Earl of Otley, and no date has been set until he obtains a special license, which he is off doing as we speak."

"You snagged one of the most sought-after rakes in London?"

"I don't know if snagged is the proper term to use. I've known the earl since we were children. I have never known the rakish side of him. Not really, but I will say he's settled as he's gotten older."

Mrs. Levi cocked her head. "Let me check in the back. There is a dress that was canceled by the lady, and I think it would be perfect."

"What about making one?"

"I'm short staffed and I doubt I could have it ready in time."

"Very well. Bring it on," Roxanne replied. She watched as the proprietress hurried out of the room. This wasn't what she planned but understood the woman's dilemma. Roxanne knew Graham wouldn't accept putting off their wedding because of a dress. That would be selfish on her part. She would see if what the dressmaker had might suffice.

She gazed up to where Mrs. Levi had disappeared and saw her with a dress in one hand, the other hand beckoning her. Roxanne walked across the shop. The dress in Mrs. Levi's arm was a deep mauve color with black piping. Mrs. Levi placed the gown on a table as she tried to sell it to Roxanne.

She had to admit, it was a beautiful dress and worth her further attention. "I like it, though I'm not sold on the color."

"Come with me," she said as she began walking in the direction of her workroom.

Undressing and redressing was a ritual women had to endure. She peered at the woman staring back at her in the mirror. The dress would need a few alterations. Mrs. Levi clapped her hands as she admired the transformation. "I have to admit I love the design."

"It looks as though it was made for you. Stunning."

"You really think so?" she asked as she turned around in front of the mirror.

"Yes."

The woman seemed to recognize her hesitation. "What's wrong?"

Roxanne stood in front of the glass. "You know what? I believe you're right. This dress was meant for me. Though I had something else in mind, this one is simply perfection."

"Wonderful. Is there anything else?"

"Yes, I need everything. I want all my undergarments new. I'm starting a new chapter of my life, and I deserve new."

"Agreed," she said. "Let's take care of what will need to be altered and then we can look through the undergarments I keep readymade."

After finding everything she needed or wanted, Roxanne settled up with Mrs. Levi, with the dress being delivered the following afternoon for a last fitting. Roxanne felt like a great weight had been taken off her shoulders and there was one less item on her list.

Before she went home, she made the rounds of some other shops. One was a bookshop she remembered Arthur and Graham frequented since their time at university. She needed a wedding present for Graham and since he loved books, especially old ones, she decided to see if the shop might have something.

Entering the shop, she found it quiet.

"May I help you, milady?" The man was the son of the proprietor and knew books even better than his father. He was of average height, with glasses and balding hair. He fit his shop perfectly.

"I'm looking for a gift. A wedding gift for my betrothed."

"Do you know what he likes to read?"

She smiled. "Yes, but you may know his tastes better than I. He and my brother have been coming here for years. The Earl of Otley?"

"Oh yes. The earl is quite the rare book collector. Shakespeare is the top of his list," he replied. "I do have a first edition of *The Tempest.*"

"That would be a wise choice because I know he has one shelf in his library dedicated to Shakespeare."

"This is one he's been searching for, and this particular one is in excellent condition. Let me go in the back and get it. I've been keeping it there in case he came by."

She watched as the man disappeared and returned with a cloth-covered leather-bound book. He unwrapped it and pushed it across the counter for her inspection.

"You're right, it is in superb condition. It's been well taken care of." She looked up at him. "I'll take it."

"Excellent choice. It's the best I have to offer at the moment."

"Can you send the bill to my brother? I don't need the earl paying for his own gift."

"No, you can't. Just let me wrap it for you unless you have some more books in mind."

"Just the one for today." She glanced out the window and noticed how the sky was changing to a menacing dark gray. She needed to get back to Jameson House before the rain set in. Turning back around, she found the proprietor coming out of the back room, his hands full with a package.

"Here you are," he said.

"Thank you." She took the package from him. "I know he's going to love it."

Heading outside to her waiting carriage, Roxanne felt the first few drops of rain hitting her face as she ascended the steps. Today had been successful, and it was time to return home. She wasn't one of those women who spend an entire day shopping. The meager funds Casper provided her as pin money had been so dismal. If there was something she really wanted to purchase, she would have to save for it, and by the time she had the funds the item was usually sold out. Now she could be as frugal or extravagant as she wanted. It just made her feel good knowing she had a choice.

RETREATING TO JAMESON House just as the rain began to come down in droves, she ran across the reception hall and up the stairs to her bedchamber. She placed Graham's gift on her desk, noticing letters which had been delivered today on the right of the desk. Turning her attention back to the book, she unwrapped it, making sure the rain hadn't gotten to it. It was as dry as it had been in the bookshop, so she picked it up off the desk and put it in a drawer in a small nearby chest.

It was then she returned to the desk and took off her damp shoes. She picked up a letter she'd opened and began to read it. It was from a childhood friend, Lily, who had married an American and was living with her husband in Baltimore. He was an attorney and had quite a few public figures as clients. They were doing well and had welcomed a son, Matthew, into the family six months earlier. She apologized for not letting Rox know, but everything was upended surrounding the birth and time had gotten away from her.

She continued to read the words. There was talk of a trip to the Continent and London. Partially a working journey for her husband, with the stops in London and Amsterdam being where he had meetings. It would be nice seeing her friend again and hearing all about her life in Baltimore.

As she finished reading, Roxanne put the crisp white paper

aside. Hearing a rustling behind her, she turned to find her lady's maid, her arms filled with boxes from the dressmaker. Roxanne had to smile. "Why didn't you get a footman to help you with these?"

"I did, but I wasn't going to allow him to come in here, even if it was through the back door."

"That's very thoughtful," she replied. "Why don't you put them on the bed. They're new undergarments I purchased from the dressmaker."

"Did you find a dress?"

"I did, but it was one a customer had abandoned. It's not what I had in mind, but it's elegant and I'll be able to use it again and again. She will be here in a day or two for the final fitting. Just to see if there are any changes needing her attention,"

"You're going to be a beautiful bride, milady," she said as she arranged the boxes before opening each one with care.

"Thank you. I never thought I would ever marry again. My previous marriage was arranged, and it was nothing like what I expect my marriage to the earl to be."

"You've got a keeper with him, if I may be so bold to say."

"You may." Roxanne had never had much interaction with the maid she had before, but the woman wished to stay with Casper's family, and she wasn't going to deny her.

Remembering her correspondence, Roxanne turned back towards her desk but thought twice about it. She really wanted to take another look at everything she'd purchased. "It's getting close to time for tea. Would you see that it's served in the drawing room? I'll be down momentarily."

"Yes, milady."

"You may put all of these away while I'm having tea."

She waited until she was alone to sit on the edge of the bed and run her fingers over the silky material. Not that she hadn't had fine undergarments before, but this time it was different. It wasn't just a necessity, it was something special, to be shared with someone important. The lingerie she'd chosen for her wedding night was probably the most beautiful of anything else she'd chosen. An off-white gown with the nightrail matching with detailed embroidery around the collar. She smiled, knowing good and well they wouldn't be on her very long on their wedding night.

Graham had been after her since their last encounter, but it seemed as though there wasn't an easy way for them to be together. She reminded him he needed to control his rakish ways and wait until their wedding night. It would be worth the wait.

Rising from the bed, she walked back to the desk and arranged the correspondence before placing it into the center drawer. She'd read all of it when she returned to dress for dinner. She reminded herself she needed to make a trip over to Graham's to go through it and decide what, if anything, the home might need. It would be better to ask Graham if he would be present and answer any questions. Asking the housekeeper before she was married might be considered bad manners and or forward on her part. Besides, Graham's staff seemed quite efficient, and she had decided to let things continue before she made any changes. If any were needed.

Tea was brought into the drawing room just as she arrived. She walked to the doors leading out onto a terrace while the staff were preparing the tea tray. The rain was still coming down and Roxanne was grateful she'd made the decision to return home rather than spend the afternoon running errands in the cool, damp rain.

The tea, cups, plates, and delights had been placed on the same familiar table it usually was. As the door closed behind the footmen, she came across the room and poured herself a cup of tea, adding only sugar. Placing it on a table next to one of her favorite chairs, she returned and picked up a plate to place her favorite sandwiches, biscuits, and scones. She added a healthy dollop of strawberry jam to her scone before returning to her chair and settling in. She picked a biscuit from her plate and bit into it. They had been fortunate to have on staff those who baked the best pastries. The only time she declined something new was if it was an item she detested to begin with. Today was quite enjoyable being on her own, not having to hold a conversation or smile all the time. She could just sit and be herself.

At that moment, as she was taking a sip of tea, the door to the drawing room flung open. She jerked her head towards the noise. In front of her stood a very wet, red-faced and flustered Perry, Casper's son and heir.

"Excuse me, milady, he pushed right past me," the butler said.

"Not to worry," she said, staring Perry down. "He has two minutes to make his peace and leave."

The staff nodded as Perry's face was more flustered. "Who do you think you are? Putting the house up for sale. It's not even yours to do what you please with. My father gave you the house for your use while you are alive. No mention of ownership being transferred."

"Tea?" she offered.

"Tea? Woman, I'll not stand before you while you offer me a cup of tea."

"Your choice. Now what can I do for you, Perry?"

"I want the title and all money from this sale."

She shook her head and picked up her teacup. "There has been no sale. I'm sure you recall your father gave me that house. You know that better than anybody."

"When I heard of a sale pending, I came rushing over."

"I don't know where you're getting your information, but whoever it is, is incorrect."

"Bloody hell, woman. You're lucky to leave with anything but the clothes on your back when Papa died."

She arched her brow. "Your father was a cruel man, Perry. I hope you do not turn into him."

"Hmmph! Since you can't seem to be rational about this matter, I'll take it to my attorneys and let them handle the matter."

"Feel free. Make sure, however, that all future communication is handled between our attorneys. I have nothing further to say to you," she said. It was taking all her strength to keep her voice calm. "My man will show you the front door."

"This isn't the end of this!" Knowing he had no choice but to leave with the butler and footman, Perry retreated. The sour look on his face showed Roxanne just how much anger consumed him. She was sure it was due to his father and how he demanded his children to be the best. The man had been a tyrant. He and his heir deserved not one further thought from her.

She returned to her tea, watching the rain plummet down outside. Roxanne wondered how Graham's day was going since she hadn't heard from him and was curious to know if he'd met with the bishop or not. Then she remembered he had business meetings and thought Arthur was included on some of them.

Men! They were strange creatures, and she knew they thought the same of the female sex. Sometimes it was as though they thought women should be mind-readers and know what their plans and schedules were. She counted herself among the lucky ones as she had lived through both types. Casper barely acknowledged her existence and Graham, for the most part, was thoughtful and tried to make sure she was kept apprised of his comings and goings.

Roxanne hadn't noticed she had been picking at a piece of scone on her plate until she heard Arthur's familiar voice. "Are you going to eat that or smash it into a thousand bits?"

She arched a brow and laughed at his comment. "My mind was elsewhere."

"Obviously."

"I had an unexpected visitor a while ago. That's not right. He stormed in, past the butler and footmen. Perry dropped by in a fit of anger because he thought the house had sold and had no intention of allowing me any of the profits."

Arthur picked up one of the cucumber sandwiches and ate it in two bites. "The man has no manners. It must run in the family."

Shaking her head, she agreed and offered her brother tea, handing him an empty plate so he could fill it with what he wanted. "I agree. He's as nasty as his father was."

"Well, you got rid of him. At least for now."

"Yes."

Waiting until he finished his second sandwich, he pursued Roxanne. "How was your day? Did you get everything done you set out to do?"

"Yes, until the rain came in, then I headed back. Have you seen Graham today? I thought you had a meeting together."

"He showed me a ship he's interested in purchasing. Quite amazing the changes these ships have undergone transforming from sail to steam."

"So it's not a play toy like some who purchase for personal use."

"Graham's not that egotistical. At least I don't think he is." Arthur chuckled. "Never say never, though I will say he researches his purchases in quite the detail, and buying a steam ship for his leisure would take a lot of researching."

"Do you know if he was able to see the bishop and obtain the license?"

"I thought you weren't in a hurry to remarry?" he teased.

Picking up her teacup, she placed it back on the tray. "I made an exception. Now could you please answer my question?"

He loved to tease her, always had, and he wasn't going to quit anytime soon. Something he and Graham shared, especially when he was younger. "Why don't you ask him yourself? I invited him to dinner tonight."

Roxanne used the moment to put on her most exasperated face and sighed. "Why didn't you say so?"

"You didn't ask," came the reply.

"Excellent. Have you informed Cook of the addition?"

"Yes, I have. Do you really think I want to hear the wrath of the woman if I forgot something like that? I know she can usually be accommodating but would rather avoid her annoyance with me."

"I know you would. Doing so might cut off your favor with her. No more favorite sweets made especially for you. At least until she got over her anger with you."

She knew she had him boxed in because he refused to agree or disagree with her statement, so instead he changed the subject.

"Did you have a good day?"

"Yes, but with the weather changing like it did, I never finished everything I needed to do. I do have a dress and my dressmaker is going to hurry with the alterations so she can bring it to me for a final fitting," she said, knowing Arthur really had no interest in details women might have in answer to a question. He had better learn, because at some time he would marry, and listening would be a virtue his bride would appreciate. At least at first.

"I'm glad the woman can work miracles on such short notice."

"That's why she's one of the best."

Arthur set his plate down, picked up his teacup, and swallowed the remaining contents. "I hate to leave such delightful conversation, but I need to take care of some matters in my study."

"I always enjoy a good verbal sparring with you, dear brother. I will see you right before dinner." He rose to his full height, looking down at her. Nodding with a smirk, he disappeared from the room, leaving Roxanne alone once more.

Nothing would delight her more than to be a fly on the wall so she could hear and observe everything that went on in that sacred male room. Their father had used it as his sanctuary like most men, and she imagined Arthur and probably Graham would as well.

WHEN ROXANNE STEPPED into the drawing room a few hours later, instead of Arthur and Graham being present to greet her, she was confronted with an empty room. Shaking her head, she found a favorite cream damask chair near the fire and sank into it. They were probably in Arthur's study discussing something they didn't want her to hear. Since they were in business together on a couple of projects, that was probably why they were locked away. Typically, discussion such as this was put aside until later in the evening, but the two of them obviously could not put it away until after dinner.

Upon hearing the door open, she looked in the direction of the thick doors. Expecting to see Graham and Arthur, she was disappointed to find the butler coming closer and carrying a letter.

"Where are Hawksbury and Arthur?" she asked.

"His Grace asked me to inform you that something important came up and they had to tend to it. Hawksbury asked me to give you this."

Roxanne accepted the letter. "Thank you. I'll take dinner in the dining room as planned. Let me know when dinner is ready."

"It is ready whenever you are, milady."

"Then let's go."

She held on to the letter, rose to her feet, and followed the man to the dining room. Though she had wanted to see Graham, the most she could hope for now was this. Dinner alone in the cavernous room. A room that had seen its fair share of family, friends, and dignitaries over the decades.

Roxanne sat down at the end of the table where her brother usually sat. As she waited for the first course to be served, she took a glance at the letter the butler had given her moments ago. She opened it and scanned its contents. Graham apologized for the last-minute cancellation for dinner, and he promised to make it up to her. He went on to tell her he had an appointment to obtain the special license from the bishop in the morning.

She pulled herself away from the letter and laid it to one side as a footman set a bowl of asparagus soup before her. Picking up her spoon, she tasted the warm, creamy liquid. It was one of her favorites, and Cook always did an excellent job.

In between courses, Roxanne tried to read the rest of Graham's letter. Besides meeting with the bishop, he mentioned he would call on her tomorrow afternoon so they might visit his house so she could visit with Mary, and she could have a walk through the house. Of course, he ended the letter with flowery words and his undying love. She ought to be angry with them both but found she couldn't be. At least he'd taken the time to inform her of what was going on and why he and Arthur hadn't shown up. Most men wouldn't go to the trouble to sit and write their wives to let them know what was going on. No, Graham was unique. She hoped that wouldn't fade after they wed.

Finished with dinner, Roxanne sat back in her chair for a moment. She'd tried everything presented to her as she didn't wish to insult the cook since dinner had gone from three to one.

Retiring to the drawing room, she declined tea, instead choosing a glass of brandy. She certainly deserved it, and after pouring a snifter with the deep gold liquid, Roxanne walked over to her favorite place to watch the weather and gardens. The French doors let in much needed light even during the dark cloudy days or storms like today. Though the rain had finally let up, Roxanne noted lightning on the horizon.

Glass in hand, she took a sip of brandy before turning and walking out of the room. It had been a long day, and she would finish it off with time for herself.

CHAPTER FIFTEEN

RUE TO HIS word, Graham showed up at noon. He wore a dark-gray suit with a crisp white shirt and lighter gray cravat. She sighed at the sight of him as she realized why he'd easily played the part of a rake when he was younger. He was always meticulously dressed, and over time she noticed how he used it to drive women crazy.

"I apologize about yesterday. There is a deal Arthur and I are trying to shore up, and the seller was trying to change a couple of items in the original agreement."

"It's forgotten. You were kind about making sure I knew what was going on," she said.

"I met with the bishop this morning and secured a special license," he said, flashing a cheeky grin.

"That's wonderful. Now we can decide when and where."

"If it's going to be a small affair, might I suggest we hold it either here or my place?"

She nodded. "Since there will only be you, me, and Arthur, we could have it in the drawing room."

"Okay. Drawing room here. Wedding breakfast here. Now what day?"

"My dress should be delivered by Monday. Would Wednesday morning work for you?" she asked.

"I'll check, but I think yes it will," he said, leaning over and kissing her. "Shall we go to my house?"

"Yes, I can't wait."

"I'm glad to see you're excited because I am as well. I never thought this would ever happen."

"I don't know why you wouldn't. You've got so much to offer a woman."

"And that woman is you. Only you."

She placed a kiss on his cheek. "Come, let's move on to your house before we find ourselves getting delayed because we can't keep our hands off each other."

"I'm not responsible on what transpires."

He placed his hand on the small of her back and guided her out of the room and toward the front door. She accepted a shawl and watched as he picked up his black hat. They walked to his waiting carriage. The ride was so short to his family home, they could have walked.

"What would you like to do first?" he asked as he led her to the red drawing room.

"Have you discussed with the nanny about my upcoming role in Mary's upbringing? If she's awake, perhaps we could start there. If not, you may show me to our bed chambers."

"I have spoken with the nanny in detail. Perhaps we can stop by the nursery first and see if she's awake. Afterwards, we go to the bedchambers."

"Excellent," she replied.

Following Graham across the reception hall to the split staircase with its wrought iron railing she had always admired, she began to ascend the steps one at a time as he followed. She looked about as they continued their walk. There were minimal furnishings in this area. Not that there should be with the stairs. Artwork was scarce. Everything had a purpose.

The nanny cradled Mary in her arms, rocking her as she hummed something soothing. She glanced in their direction and smiled. "She's just eaten, but if you'd like to hold her, I'll get her cradle ready."

Roxanne neared the nanny and gently took the babe out of the woman's arms. Sitting down in the rocking chair, she peered down at the little bundle, who looked at her through her long dark lashes. Violet eyes met hers before the soothing motion shut them.

"She is a gorgeous child, Graham."

"Yes, I'd have to agree."

She shifted her eyes to him. "She also seems to have a calm disposition."

"Just like her father," he quipped with a grin.

Shaking her head, she stroked the babe's cheek with a finger. "You're anything but calm."

"You really know how to hurt a man," he replied, with a mock look of horror on his face.

"I'll be glad once everything around her is settled."

"It won't be long. My attorney assured me everything was close to being resolved."

"I'm glad to hear that. Everything needs to be settled now rather than later when Mary might get swept up in the proceedings."

"I couldn't agree more. She's just a babe, a small child and doesn't need to be used as a pawn in anything."

Roxanne noticed the nanny hovering in the background, almost out of sight. She nodded at the woman. "Let's allow Mary to stay on her schedule. It's important at this young age. I'll come visit again once I've settled in."

Giving the older woman the child made her sad for a moment. It was an odd emotion, and she didn't understand why she should be sad when in fact she should be grateful the babe would have only the best life had to offer.

As she and Graham reached the end of the corridor, he stopped, leaned over, and brushed her lips with his. "You're going to be an amazing mother."

"I don't know how you can say that when I only spent ten minutes with her."

"All of that's about to change, but in those few minutes, I could see how much of yourself you had to give."

"You don't have to play the rake with me, Graham, with your flowery words. Just be yourself."

He stopped in front of a closed oak door, placing his hand on the knob. "I can assure you I'm not. This is the real me." The door opened and she passed him and into the chamber.

"This will be your bedchamber. You may do whatever you like to make it your own."

She walked around the room, her fingers occasionally touching a piece of furniture or object. The room was done in lavender with shades of purple worked in as accent color. She couldn't have chosen a better color. There was a closed door, which she immediately knew led to his domain.

Sensing her hesitation, he neared. "That leads to my chambers, but it is my desire that we share the bed, and you simply use the countess's chambers for dressing."

"I've never had that option before," she whispered.

"Now you do." He diverted her attention away from the door to the other side of the chamber. "There's a dressing room along with a bathing chamber. I hope it meets with your approval. The house has the latest of everything, so when you want to bathe, you have hot water almost instantly."

She walked through each room with a smile on her face. "This is more than adequate, Graham, and I can't think of a thing I'd change right now."

"When you decide you want to, let me know and I'll hire the workmen."

Roxanne lovingly placed her palm on his cheek. "Would you care to show me your bedchamber?"

"Yes," he groaned. Taking her hand, he led her to the painted white door.

On the other side of the door was a large room done in shades of blue and gold. At one end of the room was a large, mahogany bed situated on a pedestal. It was quite regal, and

Roxanne thought it fit Graham's personality perfectly.

"Did you have this room re-done?"

"Yes. My father had had it done in dark, oppressive colors. It was almost depressing to come in here."

"I can tell you had a hand in the job. It is very much you with the colors."

"Thank you." He reached for her hand once again.

There was a writing desk that sat at the far end of the room, near the hearth where a settee and chairs were placed. Masculine but not overly so.

"Is this one of those 'if these walls could talk' rooms?" she asked, turning away from him so he wouldn't see the grin on her face.

"I've never brought a woman here. You will be the first and only."

She neared him and placed her hand over his heart. "You're serious, aren't you?"

"I've tried to tell you that part of my life is over. Has been for a while. I'm not that man."

"I believe you. Now kiss me and prove it."

"My pleasure, milady."

He closed the space between them. He cupped her face with both hands and lowered his lips to hers. It started out as a lazy, slow kiss but as he probed her mouth deeper, she responded with fiery passion. She moaned as he traced the seam of her mouth. Knowing they needed to show some sense of decency, he gently pulled back, breaking the kiss.

"Again," she moaned.

"As much as I would love to spend time ravishing you, I don't think this is the wisest of times. Anyone could come knocking on the door or worse."

Placing her hands on his chest, Roxanne looked up at him. "I know you're right, and Wednesday will be here before you know it."

"Not soon enough for me," he said. "Are you hungry? Because I believe I asked for lunch to be served on the terrace. No reason to waste a beautiful day."

"I'm famished. I think we've covered everything for now. I'm going to wait before I make any changes."

"Whatever you wish, my love."

Graham took her hand and led her out of the bedchamber and down to the terrace. A table was set for them, and the minute a footman saw them he had the food brought out and placed on the table. A platter of rare beef cut into slices was served. Another held baked chicken while cold asparagus awaited them along with a fruit and cheese platter.

"This looks so delicious. I'm certainly happy I didn't have a heavy breakfast because I have to try everything here."

He beamed at her words. "The beef is exceptionally good, and you must try the cheddar. It's made on my estate up north. I'm told it's some of the best."

"I believe I had this at your estate. It's some of the finest I've tasted."

They ate in relative silence, which made Roxanne happy that they could do that. Some couples felt they had to talk all the time when they were together. There was a slight breeze that made her pull her shawl closer.

"If you're cold, we can move inside," Graham said.

"No, I'm fine. Really."

The butler stepped through the doors and walked up next to Graham. "I'm terribly sorry to interrupt, but there's a gentleman here to see you. He has no appointment with you but says it's urgent he speak with you."

"Who is he?"

"Mr. Gregory Crenshaw."

"Tell him I'll see him, but he only has ten minutes."

The older man nodded, turned, and disappeared as quietly as he'd arrived.

"I'm sorry, my dear, but I'm sure this is about the ship I'm looking to purchase."

"You go ahead. I'm going to finish my meal and enjoy this marvelous terrace and gardens."

"Thank you. I won't be long."

She nodded. "I'd like to see the photography equipment you purchased for me. It's still in Arthur's attic where you had it delivered."

"It's still waiting for you."

He unfolded his lean body from his chair and leaned over to kiss Roxanne. "He has ten minutes."

"Yes, well…"

"I don't like people wanting to speak about business by coming to my home without an appointment or invitation." He turned and hurriedly walked to the door and disappeared.

Roxanne thoughtfully bit into a piece of cheddar. Why did the name of this man Graham had gone off to see sound familiar? She knew she had heard it before but couldn't put a face with the name. Perhaps he was also a friend of Arthur's and that's why the name was familiar to her. It would make sense since her brother and Graham ran in the same circles. Whatever the reason, it frustrated her. Normally she had perfect recall, but not with this. Perhaps she hadn't been paying attention to one of their conversations. It wouldn't be the first time she hadn't had total recall about something she'd overheard her brother speak about. Though fascinating, men could be quite boring in the way they spoke. It frustrated her, making her more determined to find out who this man was.

GRAHAM WALKED AS quickly as he could towards his office. He couldn't believe the audacity of Crenshaw. To show up unannounced simply wasn't done except in the case of an emergency, and there was nothing in his and Arthur's dealings with Crenshaw to warrant such a bold move.

As he entered his study, Graham was met by a footman the butler had placed to keep watch of the stranger. Graham nodded at the man to let him know he could leave his post.

To his disbelief, he found Crenshaw seated in front of his desk with a glass of whiskey in his hand. A move Graham found to be bold.

"Crenshaw, you've got some nerve. In the future, make an appointment. You've got five minutes to explain yourself."

The man shifted uncomfortably in his well-worn leather chair. "A second ship of mine has arrived in port this morning. She wasn't due back for another week."

"This is the one we discussed?"

"Yes. She would pair very nicely with the other."

Graham ran a hand through his thick locks as he contemplated the man's words. "And you thought this something that couldn't wait?"

"There is another gentleman who expressed an interest some time ago. As he's out of the country and I have not heard from him as to how to proceed or if he's interested, I thought I'd approach you and the duke."

"Have you spoken with the duke?"

"No. I was nearby and decided I'd take a chance to let you know about this other ship."

Graham tapped his finger on the desk. "The duke lives close by. You could have gone and given him the news. Not that it matters."

"I'll keep that in mind. I was unsure how to proceed so I just took a chance. If you hadn't received me, I would have gone to the duke's residence."

"Get a proposal to me on the sale of both ships. In the meantime, I will inform the duke," Graham said.

"Very well."

"I've given you ten minutes so if you'll excuse me, I need to get back to my guests. My man will see you out."

Looking Crenshaw straight in the eyes, Graham left the

room. Rather than immediately return to Roxanne, he stood in front of one of the front-facing windows just out of view to make sure Crenshaw really left and which direction he would go. The man turned as he went out the gate and stood, staring at the house as though knowing he was being watched.

Graham studied the man. He hadn't been completely comfortable with the man, considering the history Crenshaw had with Arthur and Roxanne's family. Now he was beginning to doubt everything about the man. Even the sale of these ships. He needed to think this over carefully before he brought up his doubts to Arthur.

When he stepped foot back onto the terrace, he found Roxanne close by admiring one of the flower beds near the steps leading to the gardens. It took her a moment to acknowledge him. She smiled warmly and met him at the bottom step. She lit up his life just to be near her, making his heart full.

"You seem disgruntled. Didn't your meeting go well?"

"It wasn't enough to warrant an unscheduled visit. What he had to tell me could have waited."

"He sounds ambitious, a risk taker." Roxanne linked her arm with his and began to talk. "A turn in the gardens might help alleviate some of your stress."

Graham closed his eyes for a moment to take in her essence. Vanilla and oranges was burnt into his being. He felt himself calm as she led him along the crushed shell path. "How do you do it? I feel better already."

"It's something I taught myself. I found whenever Casper was in residence, which wasn't often, that the tranquility of the garden alleviated whatever stress I felt."

"I found a good ride on horseback or a walk to the lake on the Kent estate helped me immensely."

Neither said another word as they continued to walk. It was as though nothing needed to be said between them. They were that relaxed each with the other.

"I forgot to mention I had the photographic equipment I

bought for you moved here. Why don't we head back to see it?"

"I hope this isn't too hard to learn."

"You are an intelligent woman. Never doubt yourself."

"I try not to."

Their walk took them back to the house. He led her up the steps where he took her hand and led her back into the house. The staircase came into focus, and he led her up to the top where they ended. A separate set of stairs led up to the third floor. This was where the nursery was located. To the right, they went down a hallway painted white. Doors leading to other rooms were all closed. Graham stopped at one door and pulled a key out of his pocket. He unlocked the door and walked in. Roxanne hesitated a moment but quickly joined him. There were crates and crates, all sitting unopened. She walked closer and spotted toward the back of the crates a single open box. As she peered closer, she noted a camera sitting on the straw of the crate.

"Look, there's a camera," she said, pointing in the direction of the item.

"Yes, there is. I must have opened the crate when it arrived."

"Perhaps we can have it all unpacked so we can look at all of it."

He grinned. "I can do you one better. The proprietors of the shop where I purchased this offered to come and set everything up and give some lessons on how to use the camera and how to develop the plates."

"That would be wonderful, but will they work with a woman?"

He arched a brow as he heard the frustration in her voice. "Yes, they will. I informed them this was all for my intended and it didn't appear to bother them at all."

"If they're as good at their trade as you say they are, they aren't going to be able to bear anyone possibly doing harm to their lifelong passion."

"Good point."

"Why don't you arrange it with them. See if they'd come to

Kent after our wedding. We'll have it all moved there since that's where we'll be."

He nodded. "I think that's an excellent idea. There will be no end to what you can take pictures of."

She gazed up fondly at him. "I'm sure it's getting late so I probably should return home."

"Don't worry about etiquette. You're a widow and a dowager. The same rules don't apply."

"I know, but I just want to make sure I'm not monopolizing your time."

"You could never do that."

She giggled, holding her hand over her mouth.

"What's so funny?"

"The idea that you're so worried about tainting my reputation. We'll be married in a few days and none of this will matter. I remember there was a time in the not so recent past where you wouldn't have thought twice about any of this. You had a devil may care attitude."

He barked out a laugh. "You know me far better than you let on or I give you credit for."

"I take it that's a compliment?"

Graham nodded. "Yes."

She could tell with the way the shadows were lowering that it was late afternoon, an afternoon she would never forget. "We still need to plan out Wednesday. There are some things we've not touched on."

"Would you like to discuss this over tea?"

"That would be nice. There isn't much to talk about, but it would help me especially."

Graham swung his head around. There was a strange knock on the door. The butler. Graham ordered tea for the two of them. He guided her to a gold settee and chair arrangement as they waited on tea.

"I hope this meets with your expectations," he said lowly.

She flashed him a grin and looked down at her folded hands.

"You know it does."

For the next hour they discussed their wedding day. Roxanne needed for her belongings to be moved from Jameson House, no later than the day before their nuptials. She would keep what she needed to prepare herself the following morning. Following the wedding breakfast, the couple would make the short drive to their home.

Graham revealed he had the afternoon through the following day planned out for them and he wasn't about to reveal to Roxanne what the plans were. He knew that would bother her, and she did her utmost best not to let any emotion show.

"I guess that's everything and that I ought to return home."

He stood to his full height and helped her from her chair. "I'll have the carriage brought around."

"You don't have to accompany me. There are probably things that need your attention here."

"Trying to get rid of me so soon?" he quipped.

"Of course not."

It was a short ride to Jameson House. Once they entered the house, the butler greeted them. "His Grace is in the drawing room with a guest."

"Who is it?" Roxanne asked. She did not know anyone who would call this late in the afternoon.

"A Mr. Crenshaw."

Roxanne's gaze jumped to Graham. "Isn't that who came to see you earlier?"

"It is."

She nodded to the butler and turned and walked to the staircase that would lead them to the drawing room. With Graham close by her, they entered the room. Towards the far end of the room she found her brother in deep conversation with Mr. Crenshaw.

Arthur raised his head at the sound of them walking across the hard wood floor. "Sister. Hawksbury. You've met our guest, Mr. Crenshaw?"

"Yes," Graham responded, taking Crenshaw's hand in his to shake. "He called on me earlier. Is he trying to convince you to buy this second ship?"

Arthur took a sip of whiskey and nodded. "He made no mention of calling on you. And yes, he's driving a hard bargain for the sale of this second ship."

Roxanne, who'd made sure she sat down near Crenshaw, leaned forward in her chair. "Mr. Crenshaw, I feel as though I know you from sometime in the past. Your name is just too familiar."

Arthur spoke up. "Father and Mother were going to India with his father."

"That's where I've heard it. How could I forget?"

"I have always found it amazing that our parents' remains were never found. What of your father and the other guests?"

Crenshaw shifted his weight in his chair. "Your parents were the only guests that journeyed on that train. My father did make it and right now he's living in India."

Something wasn't right, and Roxanne could feel it in her bones. He was lying. There was something off in just the small amount of information he'd given her. He was uncomfortable and fidgeted; more importantly, he wouldn't look her in the face. Instead, he averted his gaze.

"I imagine it's a fascinating place. Our parents certainly thought so. This was to have been their second journey there." She watched him through hooded eyes, to see what his response would be.

Nothing was different. He was still hesitant in his answers. She would discuss this with Arthur and Graham in greater detail once Crenshaw left. The man was hiding something, and they needed to be prepared and ready when they began looking into his background.

"India's like no other country. It's a world all its own."

"It sounds like it might be."

Deciding she had perhaps said too much in front of Mr. Crenshaw, Roxanne stood and smoothed her skirts with her hands. "If you gentlemen will excuse me, I need to check on a few things."

Hands were shaken, good afternoons said, and she turned and walked out of the room. There really wasn't anything she had to do, but interrogating her brother's guest seemingly was not well received by either Arthur or Graham. For the time being, she would make herself scarce by going to her bedchamber. She had a couple of letters she needed to respond to. That would take some time. Maybe after that, Mr. Crenshaw would be gone and she could rejoin her brother and Graham. She wanted them to discuss this with her. It wasn't something that could be ignored. Crenshaw knew more than he was letting on, and they needed to get to the root of it. They also didn't need to be purchasing any ships from him until they knew everything there was to know.

She began to pace her room as she contemplated what her next move should be. A discussion with her brother and Graham seemed like the best course of action. Maybe they knew things they hadn't shared with her. It was certainly worth trying. Maybe they were or would look into the man.

There had never been a satisfactory investigation into her parents' deaths. Whether it was because the incident happened so far from England, it was nearly impossible to get answers or after all this time it would be impossible to get any satisfactory answers, even if this Mr. Crenshaw knew something. She didn't know, but now there was a fire inside her that wanted answers. Arthur and Graham might have notes or correspondence about the matter. If she got ahold of that, she might be able to piece parts of the puzzle together and draw her own conclusion.

What happened to their parents should have never happened. The train did not go through any hostile areas and stopped randomly along the way. At least that's what they'd been told.

Maybe this was all an illusion. A fake scenario for something grander than what any of them knew. Graham and Arthur would probably be against her spending so much time researching the case when she had a wedding to plan. Little did they know she had much of the wedding day taken care of. At least, through the wedding breakfast. None of this was going to deter her from looking into Crenshaw.

CHAPTER SIXTEEN

ROXANNE COULDN'T HAVE asked for a more perfect morning. Pinks and shades of purple lit up the sky. A good soaking rain the night before had helped clear the air, making being outdoors quite pleasant. So much so that Roxanne made the decision to move the small wedding outdoors to the edge of the gardens in front of a fountain. After the ceremony, guests would be treated to a scrumptious wedding breakfast.

Afterwards, she and Hawksbury would embark on a short carriage drive to his house. She had no idea what he had planned once they arrived, but a bed was probably involved. For the remainder of the day and tomorrow there would be no interruptions. Just the two of them, locked away in the earl's suite where they would share and enjoy getting to know each other in the most intimate way.

A wedding trip would wait until next year. There was much on Graham's plate and planning the trip this far in advance would give them time to decide where they wished to go. It would also give Graham a chance to carve out a block of time from his busy schedule. It was ideal and she was excited thinking about it. There was so much she wanted to see. During her three years in the south of France, she hadn't traveled far from her home.

"The priest has arrived. Would you like me to show him the spot you have chosen?" Arthur asked. He looked quite dashing in his dark-gray suit paired with a white shirt and black cravat. He would make some woman a wonderful, caring husband. Roxanne couldn't understand why he hadn't found a bride of his own. She planned to start looking for him. It would be easier for her to do so. But that would have to wait until she was settled in at her new home.

"I'll come with you. Has Graham arrived yet?" she asked as they headed toward the house together.

"I believe he arrived right behind the priest."

She smiled. "Good, we're all here and all ready."

Arthur took her by the elbow. "I'm so glad you and Graham found each other. You both deserve a happy ever after."

"Thank you. Never thought I'd be marrying a former rake, but that makes it interesting."

"Let's go get you married."

They walked up the steps to the terrace and found Graham and the priest talking between themselves. Both men looked up, but for entirely different reasons.

"Shall we go inside?" Graham asked, trying not to stare at her.

"With it being such a beautiful day, I thought we could marry in front of the fountain. If that's okay with everyone."

"Splendid idea," Graham said.

"I concur," Father Evans said in agreement. "It's too perfect not to marry the two of you anywhere else."

Everyone was present, including Arthur's butler and house-keeper. They'd been in Arthur and Roxanne's lives since the two were babes, and both had felt the two should be included as their witnesses. The group gathered in front of the fountain. The sky was a brilliant shade of blue with only the occasional puffy white cloud floating by. It was indeed the perfect day.

Roxanne's voice was strong and clear as she repeated her vows, her eyes never leaving Graham's. The world seemed to stand still as she was unaware of anyone else other than Graham and the priest. The next moment the clergyman was pronouncing them husband and wife. Graham leaned over and kissed her firmly on the lips, the hint of a smirk as he ended their first kiss as a married couple. Turning to face their guests, they were greeted by Arthur who beamed with pride.

The appearance of a footman meant it was time for the wedding breakfast. With Roxanne's hand on her new husband's arm, they journeyed back into the house and to the dining room. A footman had a chair pulled out for her, and Graham helped her get situated. As soon as everyone was seated, a prayer was said and the first course of beef consommé served. The main course that followed was a favorite of Graham's—rare roast beef with Yorkshire pudding. Vegetables were served with it. Next came a selection of cheeses rather than the usual salad course. Dessert consisted of the wedding cake made of fruit cake.

If anyone had asked her what was served, Roxanne would be unable to tell anyone. She was still in a fog and stayed that way until she and Graham left for his—no, their new home. New to her at least.

Saying goodbye and thanking Arthur turned out not to be as easy as she imagined. They had formed a close bond over the years, but especially since Casper died. He stepped in and took charge, making sure she had anything she desired and was comfortable. The difference of the young man she left when she was forced to marry Casper to the man she came back to were like night and day. He would do anything within his power for her, and she would do the same if the situation ever presented itself. She was proud to call him brother. Even though he would always live nearby, she would always miss him.

"Are you ready?" Graham finally asked.

She nodded. "Yes."

Roxanne climbed into Graham's waiting carriage. He followed, sitting down next to her. While he was getting settled, Roxanne waved and peered up at the structure that had been her home for a large portion of her life.

And now, today, her life had forever changed. She was a newly married woman, a countess. A woman who, in a short span of time, had gone from having disdain for her spouse to finding herself hopelessly in love with the man she had just married. She had been given a second chance at love, marriage, and life itself, and she had made a pledge to herself after she accepted Graham's proposal that she would be the best wife and mother she possibly could be.

"Is there anywhere or anything you'd like to do over the next few days?" he asked, taking her hand.

She felt herself flush. Now why was she acting like a virgin bride? She and Graham had been intimately involved, so what was this about?

Graham caught her face, which had reddened, and barked out a laugh. "Besides the obvious."

"Um, no. Nothing comes to mind now, and it would depend on how much time you have."

The pad of his thumb drew circles on her cheek. "I have all the time in the world for you."

"Flattery will get you everything."

He arched a brow and smiled. "That's what I was hoping."

"You certainly are full of yourself today."

"That's because I just married the woman of my dreams. I never thought this day would come."

The carriage slowed and turned into the short drive of Roxanne's new home. As the vehicle came to a stop and the door opened, she noted the staff was lined up for her to meet. She was the countess and woman of the house, and she knew it would take a while to settle in. Names of the staff would come to her in time. She imagined some of them might be as nervous as she was.

Graham stepped out of the carriage and waited for her. He took her outstretched hand and helped her from the carriage where he led her a short distance to where everyone was waiting. He started by introducing Roxanne and then, with the aid of the butler, began to walk and greet staff members. It went better than he imagined, and he noticed his bride listening closely as the butler gave her a description of what each staff member did.

Looking around the reception hall, Roxanne tried to take in details she might need later. No expense had been spared when the house was built, and she knew only the best was chosen. She looked around for Graham who was in discussion with the butler and housekeeper. Whatever they were discussing didn't seem dire. She figured he was just going over details of the next couple of days.

He walked across the hall to where she stood. "I was just going over dinner and details. Would you care to go upstairs?"

"Yes, it's been a long day and it's barely past noon."

He placed his hand on her elbow and led her up the grand staircase to the family rooms. They continued to the next level where the family bed chambers were. Leading her down the hall, he stopped in front of what was her suite. "Would you like to freshen up?"

"I would like to change into something more comfortable." She could tell he understood her meaning and tried not to smile.

"I'll be in my rooms. Just enter through the adjoining door when you're ready." With that, he opened the door, then kissed her as she began to pass by him.

She slipped out of her shoes and walked about the room. It was quiet, but she had given her lady's maid two days off. Unheard of, but she didn't want to chance her and Graham's intimacy being disturbed or seen by anyone. This was their time, and since they were postponing their wedding trip, they needed as much time alone as they could possibly manage.

She made her way to the dressing room and undressed. She picked up a gown and nightrail her maid had put aside while she was unpacking Roxanne's clothes while the wedding was going on. She put it on and looked into the mirror. The gown was off-white and was prettier than she remembered. She nodded, giving her approval to the woman in the mirror.

Sitting down at her vanity, she unpinned her hair, and, deciding to wear it loose, she picked up the brush and began to brush it. Applying some perfume and adding some rouge to her lips,

Roxanne decided she was happy with what stared back at her, though she silently cursed her sweaty palms. She dried them off with a towel and rose from her chair.

Deciding there was nothing further she could do, she crossed the room to the adjoining door. Holding the handle, she attempted to open the door, but it wouldn't budge. It was locked. She knocked on the thick door, hoping to gain Graham's attention, but got no response. Surely, he must be wondering where she was or what was taking her so long.

There was only one other thing she could try and that was to go out in the hall and walk to his door. She figured it would be unlocked. Opening her door, she stuck her head out in the corridor to make sure there was no one wandering around. She bolted out of her room to his door. She tried the door, but it was locked and again he didn't answer her knocks.

She concluded he must be taking a bath, so she went back to her room and began looking around for a key. There had to be one near the door. There was nothing above the door and further detection led her to the writing desk. Roxanne had noticed a small bowl perched to one side of the desk. She looked into the blue bowl and at the bottom, a key waited. She took it back to the door and inserted it in the lock. The door swung open, and she walked through. Graham was nowhere to be found until she walked to the bed and found him lying on his stomach, and naked as he was the day he was born, snoring. She smiled, unsure what to do next. Quietly she walked through the two rooms before deciding that she too was tired. There was certainly more than enough room on the bed for them both. Perhaps a quick nap was what she needed as well.

Not wanting to wake him by moving the covers about, she removed her slippers and arranged herself on the bed near him. The next thing she remembered was the feel of his hot breath on her neck as he kissed and nuzzled her. If he was trying to awaken her, his efforts were working. He lifted himself to his knees and quickly, with hands holding her tightly, moved her to the middle of the mattress.

He mounted her, bending her knees and then grasping her shins. Never had she felt as exposed as he looked her over. Cock in hand he sank into her. She was his, and he was letting her know she was not only his wife, but also his lover. He pounded into her as hard as he could, taking her in deep, hard strokes.

Roxanne began to feel something inside, her body needing and wanting more as she succumbed to the intensity of the orgasm he gave her. He continued to thrust hard and deep before he shuddered into her the next few times. His cock jerked inside her as her inner muscles clutched him.

"That was incredible," he said hoarsely as he rolled off of her and tucked her against his body.

His hands wandered. He could certainly turn it on and off at will. A gentleman one moment, a demanding lover the next. He took a nipple between his teeth and slowly bit down. The combination of teeth and his beard prickling her skin sent her to another realm.

He stared down at her, his dark hair falling forward. He could be dangerous and dominant if he wanted to be. He sucked at one of her nipples again until it was hard. His mouth pulled away from her breasts and moved down her body. When he reached his intended destination, he spread her legs wide as he dipped his mouth to her cunny. That same feeling began to overcome her. Rather than helping her finish whatever this was he'd started, he stopped and sat, his hard cock in his hand as he pulled it.

"Open your mouth. I want to teach you what pleases me."

Eyes wide open, she stared but accepted him as he buried his cock deep in her mouth. He began to push then withdraw his cock in slow, precise movements. It was natural, a part of their essence. She found her tongue darting over his hardness.

When he withdrew, he laid her on her back and entered her. This time she met him stroke for stroke as he drilled into her. She finally trembled beneath him as her eyes widened. Her back arched to take him deeper as he called out her name before his cock spilled his seed deep inside her. She called out his name as she climaxed.

"Graham?" she finally said as she ran her hand across his chest.

"Yes?"

"Will it always be like this?"

He kissed the top of her head. "God, I hope so."

"You know this is new to me. Casper never wanted anything to do with me once he learned I was with child, and he wasn't a particularly caring lover."

"I'll try to remember that and be a little more conscientious for the immediate future."

Remembering her gift for her husband, Roxanne smiled and wrapped a sheet around her. "I almost forgot… no, you made me forget. I have something for you. I just need to retrieve it from the countess's rooms."

"I'm intrigued," he said, propping himself up on his elbow.

It was all Roxanne could do not to stare at his chest as she walked to the door separating the two rooms. His upper body was muscular, and he had a distinct patch of dark hair on his chest. She diverted her attention to something else, anything else, because she found herself wanting to return to the bed. She breathed a little easier as she entered the living area in the countess's suite. She had wrapped the book a couple of days previously and placed it in a drawer for safekeeping.

Picking the volume up, she held it to her chest before retracing her tracks back to their shared bedchamber. When she walked through the door, she found Graham nowhere to be found. Placing the book on the bedside table, she removed the sheet she'd been using to cover herself and crawled onto the mattress.

She called out for Graham, not wanting to look for him. He may have needed some time for himself. "Graham? I'm back."

Silence filled the room, but a moment later Graham appeared holding two glasses and a bottle of champagne. "I thought we should celebrate." He moved to a table by the window, set down the two glasses before uncorking the bottle. He then filled the glasses and passed her one. Interlocking their arms, they toasted to their new future and new life together.

Graham opened a drawer and withdrew a box. He turned and carried it to his bride, placing it in her hands, saying nothing.

Roxanne, in turn, placed the wrapped book in her husband's hands. Sitting on the bed still, she carefully opened the box. She gasped as inside lay the most exquisite sapphire and diamond necklace. In a separate box she found not only a matching bracelet but earrings and a brooch. She was at a loss for words.

"I don't know what to say, Graham. These are magnificent. I will treasure them always."

"I'm glad you like them. They belonged to my mother, and before that they had been my grandmother's. My father's mother. As my bride and countess, it's only right that you wear them."

"Thank you. I will cherish them always. I don't believe I've ever seen such a deep shade of blue."

"I know. My mother would have adored you, so it's only fitting you enjoy them as much as she did."

They shared a kiss before he ripped the paper off the book like a child would do. He stopped once he realized what he was holding. "Shakespeare. It's in pristine condition." He opened the book and saw it was a first edition. "A first edition? Do you know how difficult it is to find a first edition, not to mention one in such amazing condition? I will cherish it always."

Taking the necklace from its box, Roxanne held it to her throat for an idea of what it would look like. It was exquisite, something she would never have expected. The cut and clarity of the diamonds and sapphires were amazing. She looked up from the mirror and saw Graham watching her. He was now behind her and picked up the bracelet, putting it on her wrist. That was followed by him securing the necklace so she could get a real idea of how breathtakingly beautiful both pieces really were. "I will treasure them always."

"Only the best for my bride," he said.

"What shall we do tomorrow?"

"Anything or anywhere your heart desires, though I must say I'm a bit hurt you don't want to spend all our time in bed making love."

"You'll get over it," she quipped.

"Now I'm really hurt," he pouted, thrusting out his lower lip for maximum effect.

"We could go on a picnic in the gardens."

"The gardens? You don't want to go to one of the parks or drive a ways out of town? Or did you have the gardens in mind for maximum privacy?" He waggled his eyebrows and grinned.

She uncharacteristically snorted at his remarks. "This is supposed to be time just for us. There'll be plenty of opportunities in the future. Let's enjoy each other's company because I don't want to share you with anyone."

"I agree. I was afraid you might get bored if we stayed here."

"I could never get bored if you're with me. You believe in living life to the fullest. That's one of the things I love about you."

"That's all?" he mocked.

"Well, I do love your spontaneity. It's rare in a man."

It was true. Graham did have some unique characteristics. He loved to do things on the spur of the moment, finding it unnecessary to always plan things out. And while a good majority of men thought women didn't have a head for anything outside of the household and should stay there, Graham treated her as though she were an equal. At least life with Graham wasn't going to be boring.

"I suppose the spontaneity is left over from my days as a rake," he said with a devilish gleam in his eyes.

"So you admit to it!"

He chuckled. "Admit to what?"

"That you were a rake."

"All men are rakes, in one form or fashion. Most, though, grow out of it."

"So you say," she said.

"Yes, in fact, we should do something that'll throw people off balance."

"Such as?"

"Let me give it some thought."

Roxanne began removing the jewelry and carefully putting it back in the boxes when Graham started smiling.

"I know what we can do! We can go to the park and take Mary for a walk in her pram."

"That'll sure get people gossiping," she replied.

"Well? Shall we do it?"

"Yes!"

He had a smug grin on his face. He loved her willingness to try things ordinary women would never try because it was something society might disapprove of.

A soft knock on the door redirected their attention. Graham stood and neared the door when Roxanne called out to him.

"You are going to cover yourself, aren't you? You're not going to answer the door naked?"

"Why not? No one should be there. I instructed our meals be left at the door, that I would take care of the rest."

She shook her head and took a deep breath, afraid she might burst out laughing. "Someone might be in the shadows, thinking you'll answer the door with no clothes."

"If it's a show they want, it's a show they'll get," he said. He had a devilish grin pasted on his face. Being bold obviously was left over from his earlier days after university.

Roxanne stood and, with a sheet around her, walked into the bed chamber so if there was someone at the door, they wouldn't get an eyeful. She strained to see if there was someone present, but all she heard was Graham mumbling to himself and the door shutting.

"You can come out. Dinner has arrived."

She came out of her hiding spot and reentered the room. He was standing over a tray he'd just placed on a small round mahogany table.

"That smells heavenly," she said. She walked to the table where Graham handed her a plate.

"Cook's rosemary chicken. It's one of my favorites."

"Apples, pears, cheese, bread, wine. Everything we need."

Graham picked up the bottle of wine and two glasses. "I'll pour us some wine while you lay everything out."

"We could eat at that small table," she said, referring to another small table; this one was in front of windows and overlooked the small and functional gardens.

"Whatever you want is fine by me."

He joined her and placed two glasses on the table and began to pour the dark red liquid in each. Roxanne placed a plate in front of both chairs and sat. The two of them were famished, having not eaten since the wedding breakfast. Roxanne had been so nervous she barely ate.

"I think the wedding was very nice, don't you? I'm so glad we had it outside," Roxanne said.

"Yes, I must agree."

She picked up a piece of apple Graham had sliced with his knife and bit into it. "I've been meaning to ask how your investigation of the man who owns those ships is coming along."

"Slowly. The man seems to be a chameleon. He can blend into any situation. Trying to find someone he's actually done business with is proving a daunting task."

"Well, if I know anything about you and Arthur, you're both persistent."

CHAPTER SEVENTEEN

HYDE PARK ON a typical sunny summer afternoon was full of what members of the ton had either stayed behind in London or had returned, albeit temporarily. Couples walked together by themselves or with another couple. It was bustling with all who wanted to be seen.

Graham and Roxanne had taken the pram and Mary from her nanny who would walk a discreet distance behind them. Graham set the pace and guided everyone down one of the busier walking paths. This seemed to be where everyone was congregating. The pair leisurely began their walk. They acknowledged people in passing but never stopped to talk. It was too soon to speak to anyone. Roxanne wanted to get a feeling of how people were reacting to seeing the pair pushing a pram, and she wished for one of the ton to come and inspect.

It wasn't but a few minutes before Roxanne came upon a small uprising in the form of two titled women who had no scruples. Not wanting to not be the first, they scurried up to where she and Graham were stopped as Graham pointed out a hot air balloon being prepared for its short voyage over the park.

"Does the child belong to a friend?" the older of the two women inquired, peeking into the pram's interior and immediately beginning to make silly noises to Mary.

"No, she's ours," she said. She didn't dare look at Graham as it would ruin their whole plan.

"Yours? I had no idea or heard you were with child."

"I kept it to myself until I couldn't."

"Do you plan on staying here?"

"Yes, either here or in Kent."

"Well, if you need to talk somewhere, I'll make myself available. It can't be easy raising a babe by yourself."

"I'm not alone. Hawksbury and I are married. I have a nanny, who does a marvelous job."

The woman flushed at her error. "I apologize. I had no idea."

"No need to apologize. You had no way of knowing."

"I don't mean to be insensitive."

"Like you said, you had no idea." She turned to Graham. "I think it might be a good idea to head back to the carriage. The skies seem to be darkening."

They said their goodbyes and headed back in the direction of the carriages. She didn't want Mary getting soaked. It certainly wouldn't help anyone, for that matter.

"Be prepared for the calling cards and invitations to start coming in," Graham said. "You're going to be quite popular."

"Which was not my intention, but this could prove to be interesting."

She felt drops slowly falling from the darkening sky. Stopping for a moment, Roxanne placed a dry blanket over the pram opening. Maybe this would work until they could get to the carriages.

As soon as they placed Mary in the second carriage with her nanny and the pram secured, the pair rushed into their waiting carriage just as the sky opened up and rain started pouring.

Roxanne sat back against the squabs and giggled.

"What is so funny?" Graham asked.

"That we accomplished what we intended. Our surprise marriage and Mary will be the talk of the ton thanks to those two ladies."

"We did that, though I'm a bit disappointed we weren't able

to take a longer walk."

"You'll get your chance again," she said.

"We're going to do this again?"

Roxanne nodded with a grin. "Yes."

"I'm beginning to believe my wife likes to stir the gossip mill."

"You know me too well, husband."

He glanced outside the carriage and turned back to her. "Since we're back at the house, I thought we could have a pot of tea brought up to our bed chamber and we can get out of these wet clothes while we wait."

"That sounds splendid. You can go over any correspondence that has arrived."

Graham had other plans. "Actually, I was thinking after the tea arrives and I've at least seen who's written that we could be a little naughty."

"Naughty? Like yesterday?"

He gave her a devilish grin without saying a word.

To her surprise, she caught a glimpse of the house as the carriage pulled down the short driveway and stopped in front of the steps. "We're home."

"I'll order the tea and such and join you upstairs," he said.

"Excellent," she replied. "Do have some of the ginger biscuits sent up with the tea. I smelled them baking in the oven this morning and have wanted one ever since."

He walked her across the reception hall to the stairs. "I'll be behind you momentarily."

Nodding, Roxanne held on to the railing as she walked up the stairs. Standing in front of the door, she swung it open. Kicking off her short boots, she went to the countess's suite. She was sure by the neatness of the room, her maid had more than likely come in once she and her husband left the suite. There were also vases of fresh flowers throughout the two suites which hadn't been there before. It was a thoughtful gesture, trying to make the rooms a little more hers.

She returned to Graham's suite as soon as she was out of her damp clothes and into something dry. He appeared as though he had just arrived. He had divested his suit jacket and thrown it over the back of a chair. There was a small stack of correspondence in his hands.

"Tea should be here momentarily," he said.

Roxanne neared. "Anything interesting?" she asked as she neared a little closer to him.

"There's a missive from your brother, but I haven't read it yet."

"I thought you weren't working for at least three days. Whatever Arthur thinks is so important can wait."

"It might be important."

"If it is that important, he can physically come here."

"True, but maybe he doesn't want to interrupt our time," Graham said.

"Arthur is considerate like that."

Graham placed the letter down on the writing desk, walked away, and began removing his vest and shirt, tossing them to the floor. He picked up another shirt folded on a chair and put it on. He walked back to the writing desk where Roxanne still stood.

He picked up the letter and opened it carefully. He read the contents before re-reading the missive. "Well, this is interesting…"

"What's that?"

"Arthur thinks we scared our ship seller off because both the ships we were talking to him about have suddenly left London. He goes on to say that offices are closed up and any of the dockworkers were as surprised as Arthur when he asked about the ships and their owner."

"Is there anyone who might know?"

"Possibly, if he didn't bribe them. We'll get to the bottom of it," Graham said.

"It's a good thing your transactions never went any further."

Graham walked over to a sideboard and poured two whiskeys. One for him and another for his bride. "We're not going to give up. There's an excellent chance he knows what happened to your parents."

She accepted the glass and took a sip. "I would continue. He's going to slip up again. Someone will come forward with information about where he is."

"If he hasn't left for the Continent. It'll just take longer to locate him."

A light knock on the door reminded them tea had been ordered. Graham went to the door and accepted a small trolley which even held sweets and tiny sandwiches for them to nibble on. He placed it near the desk and stood back to allow Roxanne access to fix things as they both wanted.

"Come and take what you want to eat. I'll fix your tea." She looked down at the tray while he picked up a plate and began to fill it.

He took his plate and found a place to sit where he could spread out. Food in front of him, tea to the right. Roxanne placed his cup down and walked back to retrieve her own. He had just taken a huge bite out of an egg sandwich as she sat down next to him. "You're certainly hungry."

"I am," he replied. "I've got an idea. Would you like to hear an idea I came up with? And I promise you it has nothing to do with business."

"Yes, do tell."

"There's a new production of Shakespeare's 'Macbeth' playing at the theater. We could go afterwards and have dinner. I thought it might be nice to get out for a few hours."

"I would love to go. And as much as I've loved spending all this intimate time with you, I know we need to get back to reality."

"We do. I thought we could go to Kent when I've got things taken care of here."

She reached for a slice of seed cake. "Just let me know and I'll get everything prepared."

GRAHAM FOUND IT impossible to sleep, even with having made love twice to his bride. Oh, he had fallen asleep for about half an hour, but sleep eluded him for the rest of the night. Looking over at his bride, he sighed and rolled onto his back. How could she sleep so deeply and calmly?

He flung his arm over his head, thoughts still dancing through his head. Ever since he and Roxanne had spoken about Arthur's missive of the missing two ships and the seller scarce as well, he had not been able to shake off a gut feeling about the man. He was sure he'd seen the man somewhere else but could not place where.

Was there any truth to the news that the man somehow knew what happened to Roxanne and Arthur's parents? Perhaps Arthur's decision to go through his father's correspondence might shed light on this. It didn't sit right that he couldn't figure out where he'd seen the man before. He tried to recall all the places he'd been over the past month. Nothing and no one stood out. Perhaps he saw him in passing and nothing more.

Shutting his eyes was of no consequence. He couldn't begin to sleep. Quietly, he got himself out of bed. Waking his bride would not be good. She needed her sleep as he'd kept her awake until the early mornings since their wedding. Naked as the day he was born, he found his way to the sitting area and poured himself a brandy. Perhaps one would help slow down his thought process.

He sat down at his desk and picked up Arthur's missive, re-reading it for the umpteenth time. He wanted to try and make logical sense of what was on the page. The ships having left was the most troubling. On the other hand, they may have simply been emptied of their cargos and sent elsewhere for maintenance work. There were a good many shipyards in England and Ireland, and it was quite common to make sure a ship was seaworthy after a voyage. He made a note of it to discuss with Arthur.

The office being locked up and appearing empty was disheartening. It might have been a temporary office and had been relocated. Something else to check out. He was making everything sound logical, and Arthur had seen warning signs. He would make sure the two of them talked. They weren't detectives and wondered if they shouldn't find one better than they already had.

As he took another sip of brandy, the mystery of where he'd seen Crenshaw came to him. This had to be it. It was logical; he just hadn't seen the connection. The man was none other than Roxanne's mysterious bookstore stalker. He wore a beard and moustache at the time and had since shaved to disguise himself. He had certainly been interested, what with all the questions Roxanne said he'd asked. He'd been in plain sight all along, and if he or his family had anything to do with Arthur and Roxanne's parents' disappearance, he would find out. Now that he had a name to go with the elusive man, he felt better.

"Don't tell me you've been sitting here all night," Roxanne said lowly. A sheet wrapped around her was the only thing she wore, and the sight stirred him.

"Okay, I won't. Truth is, you're right. I woke up and couldn't go back to sleep, so rather than toss and turn, I made the decision to come out here and see if I couldn't figure some things."

She was behind him, her hands on his bare shoulders. "Did you figure anything out?"

"As a matter of fact, I did. You remember the stranger at the bookstore?"

She nodded. "Yes. You know who he is?"

"I do. He's Mr. Crenshaw. It took me this long to figure it out because he was sporting a beard."

"You're sure?"

"Absolutely. I will need to speak to your brother about this."

She ran a hand through his hair; her other remained on his shoulder. "So that's your plans today?"

"A few hours. After I speak with Arthur, I'll see about the theater for tonight. And you?"

"I'm going to let the staff know we'll be going to Kent in two days, spend some time with Mary, and catch up on correspondence I've been neglecting."

"Do you think Arthur would mind if we used your family's box?"

"I don't think he'd mind. He rarely uses it as he's not particularly fond of plays."

"Or opera," Graham said.

She clapped him on the shoulders. "He'd rather converse with debutantes than have to sit and listen to an opera."

"He's a duke; he's expected to attend affairs like that. He had best get used to it."

"I agree but he's also an eligible, unmarried duke, so unless he's courting someone, no one would give a second thought to him not attending."

A jolt of thunder caused them to both pause and then burst out in laughter. "You see what happens when you discuss your brother and marriage?" Graham said.

He stood and rose to his full height. Facing her, he pulled her next to him. The sheet covering her fell to the floor. Lowering his lips to hers, he nudged her mouth to open with his tongue. The deeper the kiss, the more aroused he became. Roxanne was having the same sort of feelings because she clung to him as though her life depended on it. The storm raged on directly above them, the skies opening up. Thank goodness they were safe and sound inside.

Gasping for breath as he broke the kiss, he gazed down at her. "It's only around five. What if we continue this from that huge bed?"

"Who needs a bed? I'm sure you can show me what you like outside the comfort of a bed."

"You have no idea what you've unleashed, madam."

"Promises, promises."

CHAPTER EIGHTEEN

THE FIRST THING Roxanne noticed when she walked into breakfast was the neat stack of correspondence to the right of her place at the table, but the small porcelain bowl contained a good number of calling cards. It seemed the ton was eager to not only meet her, but to find out all the juicy tidbits about the infant.

Without looking at a single scrap of paper, she walked behind Graham, placing her hand on his shoulder for a moment. "What's all this?"

"Seems you're quite popular all of a sudden."

"Ah yes, word is out about our marriage and our daughter." She moved on to the sideboard where she picked up a piece of bread and handed it to a waiting footman.

"What are you going to do?" Graham asked.

"Go through everything, though I doubt I'll have time for this sort of thing. We leave for the country tomorrow, and I doubt I'll have time for callers. But I will acknowledge everyone." The footman placed a plate in front of her with the golden colored piece of bread. She slathered it with marmalade. "And you? What have you planned for your day?"

"A meeting with your brother to decide the exact course of action to take with Crenshaw."

She set the toast back on the plate before taking a bite. "Wouldn't it be wise to involve the police with all this?"

"That's one thing we'll need to make a decision about before we head to the country. It will also mean giving all our hard work to them and I'm not ready to do that. Some of the force are quite lazy and don't take to members of the aristocracy doing their own detective work. But what is one to do when the police don't take us seriously?"

"I see your point. If you decide to go that route, check and see if they've had other complaints about Crenshaw."

He pushed his chair back and began to unfold his tall frame. "I'll mention that to your brother. See what his thoughts on the idea are."

"I'll leave the details to the pair of you. The only thing I ask is that the two of you keep me up to date."

"I will. Now, if you'll excuse me, I need to get started." He leaned down as he began to leave and kissed her softly on the cheek. "I'm going to miss you."

"As will I."

She listened to his footfalls as he walked toward the door. Picking up a cup of tea, she took a sip and leaned back in her chair, savoring the distinct notes of this new blend. It was a popular blend because of the hint of cinnamon infused with the black Chinese tea.

Gathering up the calling cards from the blue and white bowl, she began to go through them, looking for any sort of note that may have been added to the back. Then she did the exact same thing with the correspondence she found with the calling cards. These would prove a bit more time consuming, but she would take the time to reply to each one. After all, she had a new title, and she was still the dowager duchess. She wanted to leave a good impression with her peers.

She sat down at the writing desk in the countess's room and sorted everything out. She had always been meticulous about how she did things and it drove some people crazy. Everything had its place and order. Opening the drawer, Roxanne took out a small book in which she kept notes and things that needed to be done in. Placing it to the left side of the desk, she next pulled out a small stack of heavier card stock and envelopes plus a sheet of parchment to write her reply on. She picked up the first card and, with fountain pen in hand, began to write.

The calling cards were the easiest to reply to, but when she started on the actual letters it slowed her down. She needed to read each before deciding how to respond. For the most part she took a simple approach, thanking the writer and then letting them know she wouldn't be in town and available, but that she looked forward to getting together once she returned.

Finally finished with her daunting task, Roxanne peered down at the large stack of envelopes. She would find the butler shortly and let him make sure her correspondence was sent out today. She then opened the leather notebook and found a blank page to begin writing things needing to be purchased before they left, what she needed to take with her.

The list of what she needed to purchase was fairly short. The village always carried what she needed and, if not, one of the merchants would order for her from London. Plates for the camera would be a must, and the easiest way to do that would be to write the emporium where the equipment was purchased and have them send her a decent supply. She wanted to make sure she had plenty of them on hand so she could get some shots of the estate, the streams and old trees. The beauty she saw on the whole estate would be her focus. She would also begin photographing Mary on a regular basis. Babies grew so fast, it was sad that most were only seen by their nannies. At least now, parents would have an alternative to formal portraits.

Taking her pen, she quickly wrote a missive to them and what she needed and asked that it be sent to Kent rather than London. Taking all the correspondence she'd written in one hand, she then walked downstairs to the drawing room where she used the bellpull to summon the butler. Once she handed the man all the letters, she would go back upstairs to the nursery where she'd speak to the nanny about putting some time aside so she could, for now, have some time with Mary. Right now, the babe slept more than she was awake, or at least that's what she assumed, and once she began to mature, Roxanne would extend the amount of time she spent with her. And as she grew up, there would be lots of mother-daughter activities, hopefully with sisters and brothers. She and Graham did want children, and hoped that they would be blessed soon.

She found the older woman in the middle of packing when she arrived at the nursery. Roxanne crossed the room, not wanting the woman to see she was smiling. Smiling at how much had to be brought along for Mary. It easily rivaled what she'd be taking as far as quantity.

They chatted for a while about Mary, children in general, and how to raise well-adjusted girls and boys in the ever-changing world. The woman also gave Roxanne a brief rundown of her background and how she came to be a nanny. She also had high praises for Roxanne for taking her husband's bastard in and raising her as her own. It was not something many women would do.

The sound of Mary waking up and vocalizing caused both women to smile. Roxanne insisted she would go in and take care of her even if it meant changing a nappy for the first time. She had watched Nanny do it, so Roxanne figured she should have no problem, but a fussing, hungry babe, one who was flailing her arms and kicking her legs about, proved to be almost more than she could handle. She talked softly to the child, reassuring her everything would be fine in a matter of minutes.

It took Roxanne a couple of tries, but she had the wet nappy replaced by a dry one. By the end of it, Mary had calmed down and followed what Roxanne was doing by listening to her voice. Roxanne picked her up and found the older woman standing in the doorway with a smile and a bottle of milk.

"She likes you," she told Roxanne. "She doesn't always calm that quickly."

"I just talked to her. I think I got her taken care of. At least she's dry."

"I'm sure you did fine. Would you like to feed her?"

"You don't mind?" Roxanne asked as she followed Nanny to a rocking chair. She sat down and arranged the infant in her arms and took the bottle of milk from her.

"Of course not. Why would I? She's your daughter, and she needs to get to know you as well if not more than me."

"I just wanted to make sure. I have a couple of friends, and their nannies don't care for the child's schedule to be disturbed."

"I would be sacking them or sitting them down and going over what their job entails."

Looking down at the babe sucking the milk bottle, Roxanne found herself in awe of how such a small thing could twist herself around everyone's finger or heart. How could her own mother give her up without a second thought? At least the woman had taken her to Graham, the child's father, and not left her at an orphanage or who knew where else. Still, she worried the mother might come back and try to claim her child. Graham had his lawyer taking care of that sort of thing.

Mary was quick to finish her bottle and fell asleep to Roxanne's rocking. Nanny took her and placed her back in her bed. She thanked the woman for the fine job she was doing with Mary. Walking out the door to the nursery, she felt at peace and was surprised such a small person could do that.

She walked down the stairs and to her dressing room to see if the maid was preparing and packing things for the journey. The chamber was completely devoid of anyone. Perhaps she was downstairs with some of her dresses that needed ironing. But the further she looked, she noted the trunks sat right where they would have been placed but none had been opened. Walking into the sitting area, Roxanne could hear Graham's valet hard at work next door. Going over to the desk, she gathered the journal she used to write anything in. Reminders, lists, anything she needed to remember went in the book. She placed it in the pocket of her skirt and went in search of her maid.

People raised their heads and tried not to stare at the mistress of the house as she quickly walked past them and in the direction of the housekeeper's office. Unaware of why the countess would come to the kitchen could be anyone's guess. The housekeeper led Roxanne into her office and closed the door quietly.

"What may I help you with, milady?"

"I know you might find this silly, but have you seen my maid?"

"Have you looked to see if she's packing?"

"Yes, that's where I just came from. It doesn't look like she's even been in there."

"That's not like her. Let me do some digging. Perhaps she's helping one of the other girls. Wouldn't be the first time."

"Thank you."

"Not to worry, milady. Are you settling in properly? Let me know if I can do anything for you."

Roxanne nodded. "I will, thank you. I best leave you to your day."

"I'll come see you once I've located that girl."

"Very well. When I return from Kent, you and I will meet and go over the household accounts."

"I'll have them ready."

She left the housekeeper's office with an odd feeling and couldn't determine what it was. She would discreetly make inquiries once she arrived in the country and would see how long the maid had served Graham's family. Some of the domestic help had been with their families for generations. Perhaps that was the case here.

As she went through the kitchens, the cook approached her. "What would you like for lunch, milady?"

"Oh dear, is it that time already?"

"Yes, ma'am."

"How about something simple like cheese, bread, and some sort of meat. Oh, and a pot of tea."

"One pot of tea. And where would you like to eat?"

"The breakfast room unless the weather will permit eating on the terrace."

Eating outside was always a preference, especially in the summer. It made up for all the time lost by the elements.

SHE HADN'T HEARD Graham come in. After not being able to locate her lady's maid, Roxanne began laying out what she wanted to take to pack. No one had seen the girl when she snuck off the premises with all her earthly belongings. Consensus was that the maid had a secret lover and had run off with him. Foolish girl.

"Roxanne, what in bloody hell are you doing? You have a lady's maid to do that."

Turning to face him, she waggled her eyebrows. "You mean had a lady's maid. Past tense. Seems mine must have a lover or something because she took all her belongings and left. Unannounced, not a word. It's a good thing we aren't leaving until Thursday."

"I'm sure one of the other maids could help you."

"I can take care of this on my own."

He neared and placed his hand on her arm. "Come, take a break."

"Very well. I'm curious as to how your day went. Did you find Mr. Crenshaw?"

"Come, let's sit down and I'll tell you all about my day."

She followed him into the sitting room where he poured her a glass of wine. He served himself a whiskey before settling into a well-worn leather chair. Roxanne made a mental note to herself that the chair needed to go to one of the estates or even his study. Like most men, her husband was oblivious to the furnishings around him and whether they were aesthetically pleasing to the eye.

"We found Crenshaw. The office we thought had been vacated is a small office he keeps to hold business transactions in when needed on the docks. His main offices are in Mayfair."

"And the ships?"

"Interesting turn of events. He sold them out from under me and Arthur."

She took a sip of wine and shook her head. "I see. Obviously, he's not a good businessman. Untrustworthy comes to mind as well."

"It's going to make our work a little harder."

"Perhaps you could ask him if he could recommend a superb ship builder. If he names one, ask him to accompany you for a meeting."

He set his glass down and scrubbed his face with his hand. "That's an excellent suggestion. Your brother and I are supposed to meet with someone who can keep tabs on Mr. Crenshaw."

"That is money well spent. Did you find out to whom he sold the ships?"

"Another mystery we have to solve."

"And you will. So far, the pair of you have easily found out things I would have thought were unattainable."

"True. Sometimes I feel like we're being conned."

Standing, Roxanne sat back down next to her husband. "How's that?"

"It's like we're always two steps behind Crenshaw."

"It almost sounds like he has someone on the inside."

He arched a brow. "You mean like a member of the staff might be his eyes and ears here?"

"Yes. Possibly someone in Arthur's staff as well."

"Bloody hell. I hadn't even thought about that connection," he exclaimed. "It's perfect. Too perfect."

"How can you flush them out?"

Graham picked up her hand and kissed the back. "Speak with the butler and housekeeper first. They may know or suspect someone, especially if they're asking on a more personal note.

Also, ask if anyone new has been hired. They would be more likely."

"Maybe this will work."

"All we can do is hope," he replied, shifting his weight so he was even closer than before. With his hand, he ran the back along her cheek before leaning over and kissing her.

Before he could take things further, Roxanne pulled back. "Now's a perfect time to speak with them."

He looked at her blankly before he realized what she was talking about. "You're right. Why don't you find them and ask them to meet us in my study?"

"Me? Why me?"

"You are the lady of the house. This is a perfect way to assert yourself in your new position."

"Very well." She sighed. "I'm not sure how much they need to know."

"I'll figure that out as we go along."

"This is the best chance we have had," she said.

Deciding to meet in Graham's study in fifteen minutes, Roxanne left her husband and headed to the kitchens. It should be busy at this time of day, and hopefully no one would pay much attention to both the butler and housekeeper slipping away.

The pair were in the butler's office. This made things easier. She could just make the request once.

"The earl needs to see you both in his study. It should only take a few minutes," she said. The request seemed to startle them at first. Probably because she was new in her position as countess.

"Do you know what it's in reference to?" the butler asked.

She nodded. "I do, but you should really let the earl explain it. If I tell you, it'll take too long."

"Very well," he said, glancing at the housekeeper. "Shall we?"

Graham was standing in front of the fire when Roxanne entered with their two guests. He motioned for them to sit while Roxanne went for a dark-blue upholstered chair.

He explained what he thought might be going on. That he

was fairly certain information from within the house was being passed on to someone outside the household. It shocked both, so Graham pressed on and inquired if there was anyone new on staff, or someone who'd been on longer and might be dissatisfied with their position and might not think twice about selling information.

The housekeeper was quick to reply. "The countess's lady's maid has disappeared. Gone without a trace."

"Anything suspicious about her?"

"No, not really. Very quiet, did a good job, but wasn't one to volunteer to help out when needed."

"Anything else?" Graham asked.

"No, milord, but if I remember anything else, I'll get word to you."

After they left, Roxanne turned to her husband. "They know nothing."

"No, they don't, but I can assure you they'll be more observant. If anyone will get to the bottom of this, that pair will."

"That's good to know."

Graham moved to a sideboard and poured two brandies. He turned back around and handed her a snifter. They remained silent as each took a sip of the French brandy.

"Are you ready for the quiet of the country?" he asked.

Swirling the liquid, Roxanne gazed fondly at her husband. "Yes, I am. I'm looking forward to the peace and tranquility. I'm looking forward to being able to work in a garden. And you?"

"I'm looking forward to riding the estate, maybe get some hunting done."

"Hopefully it'll help being out of the city to help you think more clearly about this Crenshaw matter."

"Yes, I hope so. Being out of town will also give us some time alone. If you know what I mean."

"I know perfectly good and well what you mean. Are you saying we can't be alone here?"

"Not really. We can ride or take a gig and find all my old

haunts where I used to go to be alone."

"Sounds like you've got everything planned."

"I'd like to think so. Oh, and did I tell you I purchased a new croquet set?"

"What's wrong with the one you have?"

"It's quite old and there are parts that have been lost throughout the years."

"That'll be a great way to entertain."

He chuckled. "I was thinking more about you and I playing. Alone."

"In that case, I really look forward to it."

"Watch what you wish for, love."

His warning did not deter her. Friendly competition was always beneficial, and Roxanne had one more game to add. Trap shooting. Something she excelled at.

"I would love to do some trap shooting if you still have your equipment," she drawled.

"Of course I do. You are familiar with the sport?"

"Oh my, yes. I'm quite good at it. Or so I've been told."

"I look forward to it."

She arched a brow. "As do I. Competition is always good for one's health."

He finished off his brandy as he studied the clock. "I imagine dinner is ready or about so. Why don't we continue this later?"

"Fine, I'm taking my photography equipment. I'd like to take some pictures of the estate and, of course, you and Mary."

"Excellent."

She graced him with a smile. "It's something we can learn together."

"I had not thought of that, but you're right. I find the entire medium quite fascinating."

Setting her glass down on a table, she stood and walked over to Graham. She kissed him on the cheek, placing a hand on his shoulder. "Shall we go to dinner?

CHAPTER NINETEEN

ROXANNE SLEPT MOST of the journey to Kent. Not that it was a long-distance drive, but the motion of the carriage lulled her to sleep. They had gone to the theater the night before, followed by dinner. Sleep had been hard to come by once they arrived home. Five minutes in the carriage was all she needed to fall deep asleep.

Word had been sent that the countess was without a lady's maid and would require one to be assigned for at least the summer season. This was her first visit as the lady of the house since they had married. Roxanne knew that meant the staff would be there to greet their new mistress. It was tradition. Hopefully, the housekeeper had everything in order and a girl picked out to be her lady's maid.

An unobscured view of the manor was impossible until the carriage turned in front. The house seemed to know no end. Hawksbury Manor was huge when compared to some of its neighbors. The house was of Georgian design with bricks with a simple wide staircase finishing the entrance.

"Are you ready for this?" Graham asked as the door to the carriage opened and a step was let down. He had a grin on his face, trying to irritate her, knowing she was nervous.

"Of course. Nothing to it."

Graham jumped down from the carriage and offered her his

hand. She placed her gloved hand in his and gracefully stepped down.

"Milord, welcome home," a familiar voice rang out. The butler had been here forever. Roxanne had always thought the man was a hundred years old when she spent summers in Kent.

"Thank you, and may I introduce my bride, Lady Hawksbury."

Curtsies were made by the female section of the staff. Mrs. Langford, the housekeeper, in turn introduced a black-haired young woman. "This is Miss Boyd. She will be serving you unless you'd rather choose."

"No, there is no need. I'm sure she'll do fine." She turned to the young woman. "I would like to change as soon as the trunks arrive. You will find a periwinkle day dress. That's what I wish to wear."

"Yes, milady." Boyd curtsied and left the group.

"I think she'll do quite nicely," the housekeeper said.

"Yes, I believe you're right. If it is convenient for you, I'd like to meet to go over household accounts tomorrow."

"Yes, milady. That will work. We'll choose a time later."

"If you'll excuse me, I need to see to the earl's needs and change."

"Very well. Please let me know if you'd like tea," Mrs. Langsford told her.

She looked around but didn't see Graham anywhere. Probably off checking things out at the stables. She entered the house and looked around the grand hall. The gray and white marble floor made the already large room even more inviting. She looked up to see if the fresco was as beautiful as ever.

As she neared the staircase that led to the family rooms, Graham caught her off guard. "I didn't mean to leave you alone, but I saw the wagons and carriage with Mary come to the back. I wanted to make sure the journey had been satisfactory."

"That was thoughtful of you, and don't worry, you don't have to be with me all the time. It's not like I haven't been in the house before."

"I know."

"I was just going to change. If you'd like to show me the way, I'd appreciate it," she said.

"After you change, we could go for a walk. Perhaps the gardener will be working nearby. I can introduce you and we can talk with him about a space for you as well as the greenhouse. In any case, I'll show you the greenhouse."

She followed Graham, and they soon stopped in front of oak doors. She had been making mental notes so she'd remember her way. Graham pushed open the door. The room was large, and the windows overlooked not only the gardens but a large meadow leading to a wooded area. It was a stunning view. She turned back around to her husband who was standing with his arms crossed, watching her with an amused look on his face.

"This is beautiful. The view is outstanding."

"It is, isn't it?" Graham offered a hand and walked her over to the door that adjoined the two suites.

The earl's quarters mirrored the countess's rooms. Apart from the furniture, the two rooms were laid out the same. Of course, there was the matter of the color choices in the countess's rooms. It seemed the previous occupant, Graham's mother, had a fondness for shades of pink.

"This is very much you," she said, walking around the earl's room. The colors, which were shades of green and gold, were quite masculine, but Roxanne could see spending a lot of time here. The room itself was welcoming, which was more than she felt in the countess's rooms.

"I thought so as well. As a child I was rarely ever allowed in here or my mother's chamber."

"Same with me. Arthur and I had a standing weekly appointment to spend about an hour with our parents, and it was held in the music room. My mother, though, would have us brought to her room. She would have treats for us and allow us to pretty much be children."

He took her hand and kissed the back. "Come, I'll lead you

back so you can change. How about I meet you in the drawing room in an hour?"

"That will work." She looked around the bright and bold room and cracked a smile.

"I know the colors are a little too pink and bright. If you want to make any changes at all, please feel free. That includes the wall coverings and paint. This is your space, and I want you to enjoy it."

"Thank you."

"See you in an hour," he said, planting a kiss on her lips and disappearing into his own set of rooms.

When she met up with him an hour later, Graham looked refreshed. He'd also changed clothes. The trip had been dusty despite having had rain recently. This was a time of year when the weather was never predictable. Some years there was no rain and others it did nothing but rain the entire month.

"I understand Mr. Foster is working on cleaning up the fruit tree orchard. We can walk there and on the way, I'll take you by the greenhouses."

"He has a crew to help him?"

Graham nodded. "Yes. The estate is self-sustaining. Part of what tenants receive in addition to a small pay are things made or grown on the estate like cheese, fruit, vegetables, honey. Each year I give each tenant a wheel of cheddar. It's efficient and they can concentrate on their tasks when they know where their next meal is coming from."

"That is remarkable."

"If tenants are happy, it shows in how much they can work."

She nodded and put her hand on his arm. "There is a lot more than that that could be done."

"I agree. My mother used to see children on the estate and village had shoes and coats for the winter. At Christmas, every family receives a goose or whatever is plentiful."

"Amazing. Does this continue?"

"Yes, but I'm not sure to what extent. You'd have to ask

Cook or the housekeeper."

"I would like to be part of this. As countess I should be involved in these."

He stopped near one of the greenhouses. "This is the one I thought you'd like for your use for your plantings or seedlings. It's a bit older than the other but this has a working pineapple stove."

"Really? Now I'm intrigued."

"Come, why don't I show you?"

Leading her over to the glass door, he let her pass in front of him. The interior was humid and hotter than outside. For some species, it was far better for them to grow.

"Once this is cleaned up, it will be perfect," she said.

They departed the greenhouse and began to walk outside toward a grove of trees of various shapes and sizes. "Once we get you settled in, you and I will spend a day introducing you to the tenants."

"I would enjoy that. Can it be done in just a day? The estate is huge."

"Yes. I can use the time seeing if they have anything needing done, like a new roof on their cottage. Things that must be done now before winter arrives."

She pointed out an apple tree that was beginning to be weighed down by the fruit. "What do they use the apples for? Besides eating?"

"Depending on variety, some are used for cider, others are made into pies. There's much more like canning for use in the winter. The possibilities are endless."

Roxanne tucked her hand into her husband's arm. "Is that your gardener, Mr. Young?"

Graham studied the man who was studying the sky with two others. "Why yes, it is."

"I fear we're going to get rained upon," Graham said as they neared the gardener.

She made the mistake of looking up and saw the sky was

blackening. "Oh my, we best head back to the house or we'll be soaked."

He stopped by a large apple tree. "Stay here for a moment. I need to have a quick word with Mr. Young. Then we'll race to see who can get to the manor before the rains begin."

"You can be such a child. Hurry because I refuse to run all the way to the house."

She stood against the tree trunk, watching him quickly walk to where the small group was. She couldn't hear what they were discussing but knew part of their conversation had to do with the impending rain. All heads suddenly tipped upwards at the sound of a crack of thunder. The group dispersed and Graham headed towards her in almost a sprint. She met up with him and the pair hurried towards the house.

Thunder boomed and lightning lit up the darkening sky. Rain had yet to start falling and she said a silent prayer that it would wait until they were to the house.

As they finished crossing the meadow and garden, drops began to come down from above. Graham grabbed her hand and led her up the steps to the terrace and into the drawing room. One large burst of thunder with lightning lighting up the sky and the storm opened up with all its wrath.

Laughing, Roxanne sat down and removed her boots. "The weather has been very unusual this year. I hope the rain subsides and we can have some nice summer days to enjoy outside."

"As do I. Too much rain can be bad for the crops."

She stood up with her boots in hand. "Let me take these upstairs so my maid can see they get dried and cleaned. I'll find something dry to put on."

"Would you care for some company?" Graham asked with a smirk.

"I'm sure I can manage."

He pursed his lips. "You know how to spoil things."

"I'm not doing such a thing. Besides, I'm sure your valet and my new maid are both busy getting our things organized."

"Very well. I should see if there's anything needing my attention. I'll be in my study."

"Would you like me to have some tea brought to you?"

He shook his head. "No. Maybe later."

"Very well," she said, brushing a kiss on his cheek. "I'll see you shortly."

"Don't take too long."

"I want to go check in on Mary and see how well she's taken to the move."

"She's a mere babe. I doubt she knows she's not in her bed in London."

"Would you care to wage a bet on that?"

"I would be a fool to wager on something like that. Something I'm not well-versed in."

"Smart man," she said with a smile.

THE RAIN SEEMED to be here to stay. Graham was sure he would go mad if he looked at one more ledger or wrote one more letter. He'd brought along a new novel, a murder mystery he'd had to force himself to limit how much he read. Something fun was needed by both him and Roxanne. They'd played cards, billiards, which she was quite good at, and still the time inched along.

Then the idea hit him. The ballroom would be a perfect place to play croquet; it was certainly large enough. The course could be set into two parts to make it official. He could add some challenges to make things interesting. Roxanne was always up to a challenge, and she also played to win.

Wickets were the only thing holding him back. The ones he'd purchased were, of course, for outside, to be fixed into the ground. He could modify a couple which would mean they would be mobile and moved after each use. He thought hard as he walked to the ballroom. What could be substituted?

Walking into the ballroom, which also doubled as a dining room for large parties, he found everything neat and in its place. Chairs and tables normally used for events were pushed up against the perimeter walls until next time. He cringed at the thought of hosting an event because once she settled in, Roxanne would insist they have a party or ball. Seeing this room would only emphasize her plans. If playing croquet indoors helped the time pass, then he would survive one evening of dancing and dull talk; it would be worth the effort. He couldn't wait to see her face when he challenged her to a lively game of croquet. She was so competitive about everything that a modified game such as this would drive her crazy. He would enjoy watching her try to beat him.

Armed with some brilliant ideas for his newly invented game, Graham walked out of the ballroom and back to his study. He needed to write everything down along with some rudimentary drawings of each wicket.

Walking to his study, Graham noticed how unusually quiet the house was. Not something he noted before this rain began. He imagined the housekeeper had some of the staff busy with various projects. Things like polishing silver alone would keep a great number of staff occupied. There was a lot of silver to be cared for.

When he opened the door to his study, he was glad there was a fire started in the hearth to ward off the dampness. There was more correspondence on his desk. He picked it up and noticed one in Arthur's familiar handwriting. He opened it and began to read.

The detective he and Arthur hired regarding Crenshaw had sent word he was on to something and would be personally delivering an updated report. Arthur would host him and they'd both be present to receive whatever news the man had. Graham kept reading the letter. Both ships which had disappeared were safe and sound in a shipyard in Liverpool. There was no confirmation the ships had been sold, and the only information he could gather was that both ships were in for regular maintenance. Progress was being made, even if it was slower than Graham liked. The information would be correct and well detailed.

He rose from his chair to find some paper he could use to make renderings of wickets for his friendly competition with his bride. They would have to be simple as making these wickets would be used indoors and had to be right. He poured himself a whiskey as he sat back down with his paper. Taking a swallow of whiskey, he found his pen and began to sketch. He had a couple of ideas how these wickets should look for indoor use, but without knowing what materials would be used made it futile. Searching for the materials first might be a better option. And what more perfect place to look than the attics. They held life from eras gone by. He put his pen down and picked up his drink as he then sat back and held his glass in his hand. He should find what he needed there. Otherwise, he would have to go to the shed where most of the wood and related items were stored. And that meant more work on his end.

Making a couple of thoughts about the upcoming meeting with Arthur, he closed the book and finished his whiskey and raised himself from the chair.

The top floor of the manor home was used for several things. There were two separate entrances. One where the nursery was located. The other was in another area of the house. Besides a huge attic space, it was also where staff lived. He chose to start with the massive sized attic. Last time he'd been inside the attics was to look for a vase his mother had insisted had been stolen from her by staff. She had everyone looking for the crystal vase. That was when he discovered that the entire floor connected as one. There was a mere wall that separated the two attic spaces. There was an easy explanation for it, but blueprints and mention of what it had been intended to be used for were lost to the ages. He opened the door with a key he had been given when he became earl.

Walking inside, the first thing he noticed was how stuffy the room was and how eerily quiet it was. He wasn't sure exactly what he was looking for, so he began to slowly walk and look at what wasn't covered. He found a chest sitting off to one side. By the looks of it, there was some extensive damage. He pulled a drawer out. Simple enough. He could use a few drawers, cut out holes in the bottoms, and use them. No one would ever know unless someone decided to use the chest, and it would have to be sent for repairs.

A smirk crossed his face at the thought of someone finding holes in the drawer bottoms. All he needed now was to get them done.

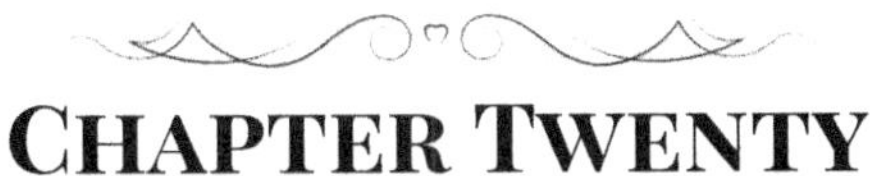

CHAPTER TWENTY

THE RAIN CONTINUED for the next two days. Graham spent most of his time setting up the indoor croquet field so he and Roxanne could play, though he knew she was certain she'd win every time against him. To try and keep that from happening, he began to play so he could learn the idiosyncrasies of this makeshift course.

His wife had, to his knowledge, respected his request that she not enter the ballroom until he was finished. Graham wasn't sure she observed his request or not. If she had been in the ballroom, she was hiding it quite well. Even some of his comments about the progress he made went unnoticed.

Walking to the breakfast room to join his bride, Graham glanced outside. The rain was still coming down, though he thought it had slowed for the moment. He entered the room and found Roxanne eating some toast, which seemed to be her favorite breakfast food.

"Good morning," she said. "You certainly got up early."

He nodded to a footman for a plate. "I couldn't sleep and ended up in my study trying to go through everything."

"Hopefully this rain will stop soon," she said as she took another bite.

"One can only hope, though I think today's activities will lighten the mood."

"Everything is ready?"

"Yes," he said. "Oh, on another matter, Arthur sent me a note that Crenshaw will be arriving tomorrow. He asked if we could host dinner because something came up in his cook's family and she had to take some time off."

"That should be no problem. I'm sure the staff will delight in something to do like a dinner."

"Thank you. I'll leave the details to you."

"Would you do me a favor?"

He nodded as he took a forkful of egg. "Of course."

"Would you take me to the attics? I'd like to see if there's anything that could be used."

"Ah, you mean for when you renovate?"

She arched a brow. "Not necessarily. I just wanted to have a look. Sometimes people cast things aside like what's in the attic and don't know enough about the piece to know it's an antique. Or a copy."

"Interesting. I would have thought there might be a list of what's up there."

"If there is, it's gotten lost or hasn't been found in a ledger or file."

"Anything else you'd like to do?" he asked, waggling his eyebrows.

Taking a sip of her cooling tea, Roxanne pursed her lips. "What do you have in mind?"

"I thought we might find an abandoned room or somewhere else that's private and spend some time together."

"I'm intrigued. If you'd like to, we could do that this afternoon. Unless you have something more pressing to do."

"Absolutely not. You are my only priority."

"That's nice to hear, dear," she said in her best old woman imitation. She put her teacup on the table, trying her best not to laugh.

"You certainly are saucy this morning. What's going on?" he replied.

"I thought we were going to participate in a lively game of indoor croquet. Or have you forgotten?"

"Forgotten? Hardly. How could I forget when I am going to prevail as the champion?"

She snorted, followed by a very unladylike laugh. "You? When was the last time you played? With the children of friends? No, I'm afraid I'll be the one walking away with that honor."

His head was cocked with a look of disbelief as he listened to his bride make her claim. "I'll have you know I've played at lots of house parties and the only way a woman might win is if I let her. The men held back because they knew what I was about."

"What were you about? Being the notorious rake or the charming gentleman I know you to be?"

He chuckled, folding and putting the newspaper he wished to read aside. "Why, the charming gentleman, of course."

Roxanne arched her brow and smiled. "Perhaps you can be the naughty rake for me? Just this once?"

"Your wish is my command, milady."

"Good. Now, shall we go look in the attics or do you have other things to attend to?"

The door to the breakfast room opened, causing them to both turn and look as Arthur strode through the door. "Good morning. Horrid weather we're having."

"Yes, it is," Roxanne sniffed. "What brings you out in it? Must be something important."

"It is. I need to borrow your husband. There is a matter we need to discuss."

"Sounds serious," she said.

"Something about Crenshaw's upcoming visit?" Graham inquired.

"He's still coming tomorrow. I thought we should prepare for his arrival," Arthur said, turning to his sister. "You are still prepared to host dinner tomorrow?"

"Of course," she replied. "While you two are in your meeting, I'm going to go over the dinner with the cook and housekeeper."

Graham put his hand on her shoulder as the men left the room for his study. As he did, Roxanne reached for the teapot to pour herself a fresh cup. She couldn't help but give him a saucy smile.

While they were discussing this upcoming meeting with Crenshaw, Roxanne decided to go ahead and speak to the cook about tomorrow evening's dinner. Then she would sneak into the ballroom and see what this croquet layout looked like. She needed to know what to expect if she wanted to show Graham up by winning their "tournament". He wouldn't know what hit him, even though he'd played multiple times. Of the two, she was sure she was the better player. He never took it seriously, as he thought it a way to try and flirt with the ladies and not a type of competition.

After checking in with the cook and housekeeper, who both assured her everything would be ready for the dinner, Roxanne left the kitchens and headed to the ballroom. It seemed a waste to her to have a room that was specifically used for entertaining. The rest of the time it was unused space. Wasted space.

As she walked into the room, she couldn't help but remember the cream damask wallcovering. In the daylight, even gloomy like today, she could tell the room needed to be redone. The wallcovering had been there for years, and if one looked close enough they would find it had faded and was peeling at the edges. Since they had no parties planned, at least for the foreseeable future, it was low on her list of projects.

Finding a wicket, Roxanne smiled. She had to give him credit for originality. Using drawers with holes cut into the bottoms in place of the metal wickets was genius. Looking around for mallets, she was disappointed not to find them lying about. Graham must have tested his course since it was not regulation. If he put them away, she had no idea where he hid them. Before she could look further, a deep, familiar voice boomed from behind her.

"What are you doing in here?" Graham asked.

She quickly turned around to face him, only he wasn't alone. Arthur was standing just behind him. She felt like a child who had finally been caught doing something she had been told not to.

"I... I got turned around leaving the kitchen."

Surely, he wouldn't reprimand her in front of Arthur. "I'm sure you did, considering all the closed doors."

"Exactly,"

"This is quite ingenious," Arthur said. He kneeled beside one of the wickets. "Where did you get the idea to use drawers?"

"I was in the attic, hunting for a way to either anchor down the wickets normally used or something entirely new."

Roxanne turned and quickly looked at Graham. "Would you like to play, Arthur? Unless you have somewhere else you need to be."

"Yes, you must. Anything that important can wait a few hours," Graham added.

"You wouldn't mind?"

"Of course not, brother. Your presence will deter my husband from any unsavory cheating." Roxanne knew Graham would be on his best behavior with a third person playing.

"I beg your pardon," Graham said. "You're accusing me of cheating?"

"Not really. You simply get overenthusiastic, which is perfectly acceptable."

"Let's play! Anything needing my attention can wait," Arthur said.

"Yes, let's. I'm dying to try these wickets."

Graham nodded. "Yes, let's. I'll bring the mallets so we can choose which one we want."

"You can explain any rule changes that might need to be made as far as the course size and wicket change," Roxanne said.

"Good idea. I'm sure most of them can still be used," he replied.

Arthur and Roxanne watched as Graham strode over to the far wall. He stopped by a table draped in a Holland cover.

Pushing the cover up, he bent over and pulled three mallets and balls out from under the table. He then placed the balls on the table and took two of the mallets to the pair.

"Decide which you want. Balls are on the table," he said.

"Why do you get the red mallet?" Roxanne asked her husband.

"My game, my choice."

She looked at her brother, ignoring her aggravating husband. "We're left with green and orange. Do you have a preference?"

Arthur picked up each mallet and tested its weight and feel in his hands. "I know you like green, so I'll take the orange."

"That's fine. I'm happy we got all this sorted out so easily." She turned to Graham who had the three balls and the red mallet with him. "Do you wish to explain the changes, if any, before we begin?"

"Yes, please do," Arthur said.

"There aren't many. Obviously because we're indoors, we cannot hit the ball as hard as we might otherwise. After playing the course, I have decided that it will take going through the course twice."

"How will we know where the start and finish are?" Arthur inquired.

"The one which has been decorated with apples will be our first and last wicket. A complete game is not possible, but I believe two turns will be enough."

"Who will start? You, Graham?" Roxanne asked.

"You flatter me, my dear. I thought you could start. Ladies first and all."

"Very well."

Picking up her mallet, Roxanne made her way to the starting point. Not that she would admit it freely to either her husband or brother but the entire concept of being able to play indoors was remarkable. She would file it away for future parties. It certainly was better than charades.

She stood in front of the wicket and studied her surroundings.

Tapping her ball firmly, it rolled right through the improvised wicket. Both men cheered her on. She stood close as both went for their first shots. With everyone cleared, Roxanne made her second shot which put her close to the next wicket.

The game went along without incident through the first round. Moving forward, Roxanne noticed a slight change in the air. While it had been a relatively boring game thus far, she was not expecting for Graham to hit his ball through the next wicket and right into her ball. The two cracked as they met, sending Roxanne's ball completely off course. She glanced at him out of the corner of her eye and saw the devilish smirk on his face. Her brother also seemed to be enjoying seeing her knocked off course, putting her behind both men.

The gloves had come off and there was no going back. It was time to plot her revenge.

Slowly, ignoring the men, she walked over to where her ball sat. The ball was out of bounds which meant it would take extra shots to bring it back inside. She would be in last place for the time being which didn't sit well with her as she had no intentions of finishing last. The best thing to do was walk around the next wicket and see what she might encounter.

"Roxanne, are you ready? It's your turn," Arthur said.

"Yes." She walked back to her ball and stood behind it with her mallet. This wasn't going to be easy as each shot was a penalty until she was back on track. Both of their balls were well within range of hers. Since Arthur was closer, she aimed for it. It rolled and she watched her ball go through the next wicket.

Instead of showing his disappointment, Graham smirked. She wasn't sure why he was reacting that way, but she didn't like it. He was quick to point out where she stood. She may be last still, but she gained ground.

Coming in last by the end of the first game encouraged Roxanne to ask for a rematch. Knowing what everyone's weaknesses were made her confident she would win the next.

"That was fun. Why don't we do another?"

"I would have thought you to be more of a brat since you lost and want to never see this ridiculous game again," Arthur said.

"Actually, I'm beginning to like it. Besides, what do any of us have to do today with all this rain?"

Graham was the first to answer her. "I'm in for a second round. Arthur?"

"Sure, why not. Should be more fun this round."

They were halfway through the second game when Roxanne saw her chance to get ahead of them. It would mean a more aggressive shot to pass them both, possibly throwing one or both out of bounds. That was all the satisfaction she needed.

What happened during this shot would be long debated. Graham and Arthur both thought Roxanne to be too self-absorbed in her shot. She stood there, behind the ball for a couple of minutes, looking ahead, then back down at the ground.

Roxanne barely remembered what would come next as she swung the mallet as hard as she could, hitting Graham's ball and sending it through the air. The next thing everyone heard was the sound of glass shattering. She had just sent both balls through the French doors and into the rain.

She smiled in satisfaction at what she'd done while both men stared at her as though she were a monster or something. Neither knew she had the force in her to drive a ball so far and so hard.

"I guess it's safe to say Roxanne is the winner." Arthur mused.

"Can't argue with that," Graham agreed.

Seeing what havoc she had caused hit home for Roxanne. She dropped her mallet and hurried over to the broken glass. Not wanting her to be walking around in all the shattered glass, Graham stopped at her side.

"Be careful. You don't want to cut yourself on the glass," he said.

"Oh Graham, I'm so sorry. I had no idea I was going to hit so hard."

He leaned over and kissed her cheek. "A window can be replaced."

Before he could say anything more, the door burst open as the butler, followed by two footmen, charged into the ballroom. From the look on their faces, it was obvious they had heard the glass door shattering. The trio stopped in their tracks to observe the damage.

"I think we're going to need the door glass replaced. For now, cover it to keep the elements out for the moment."

The butler simply stared at the damaged door. "I'll see to it immediately, milord."

"There is a lot of shattered glass, so advise everyone to be careful of where they walk."

"Yes, milord."

Graham pivoted on his heel and turned his attention to Roxanne and Arthur. "I guess we'll have to try again another day."

"Preferably outside," Roxanne said.

"Absolutely outside," Graham agreed.

Roxanne headed over to the door. "Come, let's get out of the chill."

"I'll take my leave," Arthur said, turning to Graham, "unless there's something else we need to talk about."

"No, not that I can think of. I'll see you in the morning," Graham replied.

They stood in the grand hall and bid Arthur good day. As the door closed behind him, Graham put his arm around her waist and pulled her close. "Would you care to go visit the attics now?"

"Yes, but after I warm up. Let's go to the drawing room and stand in front of the fire."

"Are you sure I can't warm you up quicker?" he whispered in her ear.

"Oh, I'm sure you can."

Taking her by the hand, he led her to the staircase where they walked until they found the door leading inside the attic. He unlocked it and pushed the door open. She walked through and looked around at all the furniture and long-forgotten trunks and boxes.

"It's musty up here. Are you sure there isn't a leak from the roof or perhaps one of the windows?" She scrunched up her nose, reminding him of a rabbit.

"Attics are supposed to smell like this."

"But…"

"If you're worried about roof leaks, I can assure you there are none as a new roof was put in place last summer."

She nodded as she made her way to an old trunk. "Good to know."

Looking across the room, Roxanne noticed what appeared to be a door leading to who knows where. "Where does that lead?" she asked, pointing across the attic.

"I have no idea. Let's go check it out. It may simply be the door that leads to the other side of the attic."

"You don't know?"

"Not for certain. You have to remember staff rooms are up here as well."

"Well, let's go see for ourselves."

They picked their way through all the old furniture and trunks to the closed door. As they stood before the door, Graham found it to be locked. No key was to be found anywhere close to the door and he mumbled under his breath. Turning around, he found his bride checking old vases and bowls for the key. Still no key.

"I will ask about a key and if there isn't one, I'll have a new lock installed."

"Good. I really want to find out what's behind the door now," Roxanne said.

"Is there something in particular you were wanting to find?"

She shook her head. "It can wait. It's damp up here and I'm getting cold."

"Can't have that," he replied, adding, "there's another place I want to show you. In fact, it could end up being a place for us to go if we want complete privacy."

"Promises, promises," she giggled.

"You think I jest?

"No, not at all."

He led her back to his bedchamber and shut the door behind him. Leading her across the room, he motioned to his lips, indicating to her not to speak. Graham stopped in front of a dark panel to the right of the bed. He pressed on the panel in one specific location and the panel slid to the side like a pocket door. Leaning down, he picked up a lantern sitting on the floor and lit it. He slid the door back to its closed position and began to lead Roxanne farther into the dark.

It was a priest's hole, albeit one in a peculiar place. Graham didn't speak, which she took to mean she shouldn't either. At least for now. They finally came across a room to the left of the corridor. She felt confused looking at what was in front of her.

A large comfortable bed took up one corner in the back. There were three tables, one of which was specifically made for this room by the looks of it, a couple of chairs, lanterns, and baskets.

"Priest's hole?" she whispered.

"No, because there is one on the main level."

"Then why is it here?"

"I believe it was a place the earl could go when he wanted privacy. Either that or a place to hide in troubled times."

"What about the rest of his family?"

"The earl probably would have sent his family somewhere safe. If not, there would have been plenty of room."

She gazed around at her surroundings. "It would have been quite cramped."

"There are three other rooms along the way. All like this. Nothing has been done to them in years so they're dusty. There is another room I believe was used for food and supplies."

"What if they needed to exit the house without being seen?"

"This corridor leads down to a tunnel that continues to an old building that's out of sight because it's hidden by a grove of trees."

"Wouldn't someone find it?"

"That's always possible, but the opening is well hidden."

"This house has quite a history," she said.

"It does and fortunately, my ancestors wrote it down when it happened. There are lots of diaries in the library in addition to letters."

"I will have to find them and read them. I've always been fascinated with what might have happened in these older estates, not just my family's."

He pulled her against his hard body, not saying a word.

CHAPTER TWENTY-ONE

GRAHAM JOINED ARTHUR in his study the following morning. The rain had stopped at least for the time being, but the skies overhead were still gray and menacing. Today was their meeting with Crenshaw about whether or not they had a deal for the ships, and for them to try and understand the man. His father had been the guide to India for Arthur and Roxanne's parents. They had never returned, and Arthur wanted answers.

"Crenshaw's an hour late. I wonder if he's even going to show."

Graham ran his hand through his hair and sat back in the brown leather chair. "He'll be here. I'm sure the roads are in a dreadful state after all this rain."

"True. I simply hate being kept waiting."

"Don't we all."

The detective they'd hired had expressed to them how hard Crenshaw made it for anyone to keep him in their line of sight. It was obvious the man had more debts than he could handle. His spice trade had shrunk in the past year. He wasn't paying attention to what had been a thriving business. Crenshaw seemed to want to make fast cash. One was to guide tourists as his father had. It was lucrative, but not to his expectations.

A knock on the door as it was being opened caused both Arthur and Graham to jerk their heads back around to the door.

"Mr. Crenshaw, Your Grace," the older man said, and Crenshaw went around him and into the study.

"That'll be all," Arthur bid the butler with a nod.

With the butler gone, Arthur guided their guest to where they had been seated moments ago. "How are the roads from here to London?" Graham asked as the man sat down.

"Muddy and rutted. There are sections of the road where you need to make sure not to get into one of the ruts left by an earlier carriage or you'll get stuck."

"Hopefully the rain is gone, and everything will get a chance to dry out," Arthur added.

"It'll take at least a week if not longer, but at least everything will be greener for it," Graham said.

Crenshaw grunted. Obviously, the man did not make small talk or like it because he jerked the conversation back around to him and why he was there. "I must admit the two of you are quite persistent."

"Really?" Graham shot back. "Because the only thing I see us being persistent at is trying to find out why the sudden change of mind and why the ships were moved north."

"In regard to the ships, they were in need of maintenance work before going back out to sea."

"There are plenty of good shipyards here to do that," Arthur said.

"True, but I wanted a more thorough inspection before sending the ship back out. I had a scheduled time, so it isn't as though it was a last-minute decision," Crenshaw said.

"So you intend on keeping the ships?" Graham asked.

Crenshaw peered down at the floor as though knowing this question was coming but still not sure how to answer without causing a potential argument among them.

"Yes, I intend to keep both. I apologize if you feel I misled you. I thought and thought about it and realized I wanted to keep my father's dream of not only trading in goods from India but also taking people who wish to see the beauty of the region."

The room fell silent. Graham and Arthur glanced at each other. They had expected this since the investigator had advised them of his findings. Neither of them believed Crenshaw's story. Arthur felt Crenshaw didn't want to sell to them because it might lead them to things he didn't want to be rehashed. His parents' unusual deaths and how nothing added up. The answers they received about the incident were ever-changing depending on who they spoke with.

"No one can fault you there," Graham said, stretching his long legs in front of him.

"Though you could have just told us the moment you changed your mind," Arthur added.

The man shifted uncomfortably in his seat. "You're right. I didn't handle that right."

"I find it interesting that you accepted our invitation. You could have just as easily told us your decision and how you came to it in a letter. Especially with the roads as they are," Graham bit out. He couldn't just let this man go this easily. He had to find out what happened to Roxanne and Arthur's parents. If he let the man go, they might never find the answers they were looking for.

"It was something I felt needed to be done in person," Crenshaw said.

"We appreciate that," Arthur replied.

Crenshaw rose to his full height. "Again, I appreciate you seeing me. I need to get back to London. Hopefully one day we might be able to do business together."

"You're going back? So soon? I thought you accepted my invitation to dinner," Arthur said.

"My apologies, but I cannot. I need to go now because I don't care to travel in the dark with these roads in such a state."

Arthur and Graham both stood up and faced Crenshaw.

"We appreciate you coming all the way out here. Good luck with your ventures," Arthur said, shaking Crenshaw's hand.

"Yes," Graham added. "It shouldn't take you too long to get the import business back up and running. I'll have to get some information about your trips to India. My bride and I are to take our wedding trip next spring and India would be a far better choice than Italy."

Crenshaw gave an odd look but quickly headed to the door. "You needn't see me out. My carriage is still out front."

"I wouldn't be a very gracious host if I didn't give you a proper send off," Arthur said.

Arthur led Crenshaw and Graham to the front hallway. The butler opened the door, handing Crenshaw his hat. He stepped into his carriage and a moment later, the horses began walking down the drive.

"That was certainly odd," Arthur said as the two men stood and watched as the carriage slowly made its way down the long drive.

"He knows something. I think we made him uncomfortable because we're close to whatever he's hiding."

Arthur nodded in agreement. "Shall we keep on looking into him, or did today satisfy you?"

"Keep on with what we've been doing. He may think that's the end of it, but he will trip up."

"You're right. He may start breathing more easily because he believes he's ended any arrangement we might have had, but he'll fall flat."

"I should be getting back. We'll still have dinner as planned. Roxanne would be most unhappy since I'm sure the meal is being prepared as we speak."

"We can't have my sister unhappy. I look forward to it," Arthur said.

Graham took his leave, heading home on the same rutted roads as he earlier used. Crenshaw would not get away with whatever he was involved in. Especially after today. He might try to minimize his involvement in his father's business, but Graham, on his own, had discovered the reason behind that.

He'd noticed Crenshaw's uneasiness while in their presence. The man had one thousand and one reasons to be uneasy, but

Graham believed he'd found a major one. On Crenshaw's right hand was a ring. Not any ring, but one that Arthur's father always wore, boasting it had been worn by every duke. Graham had recognized it because of the ruby at the center and he'd seen it on the late duke's hand since his childhood. He would tell Arthur his finding this evening.

Was Crenshaw aware of where the ring came from? Had his own father gifted it to him with some wild story about its origins? So far, this was the most solid lead they had.

His thoughts turned to his bride as his carriage slowed down and it turned right down the drive to his home. She wasn't going to be happy about their guest backing out, but she'd play the gracious hostess through the evening. If there was one thing he'd discovered about his bride, it was her ability to put on a mask and pretend everything was fine. He knew her better than that. But with Arthur as their only guest, she might let out all her anger and frustration on the two of them. She wanted closure on her parents' deaths, as did Graham and Arthur. She'd told him that much. God, he loved her, every single thing about her.

Finding her on the terrace soaking up the sun which had come out brought a smile to his lips. She was one of those women who didn't necessarily conform to the ideas men had about what women should or should not do. He couldn't think of another woman who would come out and simply enjoy the sunshine.

He approached her from the side, kissing her on those pouty lips, and nuzzled down her neck. "I hate to disturb you. You look so peaceful."

"I am. The sun feels wonderful after those days of torrential rain."

He took a seat to her left and covered her hand with his. "I have to agree."

"How did your meeting go?"

"It was rather unusual. He probably wasn't there for fifteen minutes before he took his leave."

"What do you mean, 'took his leave,'" she asked.

"He explained to us why the ships had been moved and why he was now uninterested in selling them."

"But I thought he was going to stay and have supper," she said with a hint of frustration.

"He had some excuse about wanting to get back while it was daylight because of the roads being so bad right now. Don't worry, Arthur's coming."

"Of course he is," she snapped.

"We aren't going to give up so easily."

She shifted in her chair. "If the man doesn't want to do business, what else can you do?"

"It seems he's going to begin offering guided trips to India and the region. That I thought was quite interesting."

"I wonder if he's going to be involved in the actual trips?"

Graham shrugged his shoulders. "I may have mentioned that you and I might be interested for our wedding trip. That caught him off guard."

"You didn't. I have no desire to travel there, at least not for my wedding trip."

"It was a ploy to see how he'd react."

She said nothing except to nod her head thoughtfully.

"You want to hear the best thing?"

"Yes, of course."

"The man wears your father's ring."

"What? You didn't confront him about it?"

He arched a brow. "I didn't realize it until after he'd left."

"You need to confront him on how he came in possession of the ring."

"I intend to, but I need to think it through before I go accusing him of theft."

"You're right, of course, though I can't imagine there's a second ring out there that looks like my father's. Yes, we need to think it through."

He patted her hand. "Enough about that. We can talk it

through with Arthur when he arrives. I'm sure he'll have thoughts on what we need to do next."

"I think you're on to something, especially hearing this. He's hiding something."

He waggled his eyebrows. "Have you plans for this afternoon?"

"No. I have already gone to the nursery and seen Mary."

"And how is she?"

"Perfect. She's smiling now, though Nanny says it's nothing more than gas."

"What does Nanny know? I'm sure it was a true smile."

"Of course it was. We have the most perfect daughter."

It made Graham's heart fill with love and pride to hear his wife refer to his illegitimate daughter as her own. Not all women would have it in them to even allow the child of a paramour to take up residence in her house, let alone have anything to do with the child. The child would be non-existent. But Roxanne was gracious. Despite the horrid years she spent in a marriage of convenience, she never lost track of who she truly was.

THE EVENING APPROACHED and dinner would be upon them in a short time. As Roxanne raised her glass of wine to her lips, she noted the chiming clock on the mantel read eight. Arthur was late, which was uncommon for him. He was one of the most punctual men she knew. He'd always been that way. She placed the glass on the table beside her before smoothing the skirt of her plum silk gown. It was a gown she'd picked up in Paris on her last trip. Her trip home. She loved how the lavender color used as trim set the gown off.

She hated that the owner of two ships they wanted to purchase had not gone as planned. Graham had mentioned they weren't going to let him go that easily. He and Arthur would keep the investigator and continue their quest to find out more about this man. Especially now that they discovered the ring Crenshaw wore had belonged to her father. It confirmed her suspicions something bad had happened to her parents while en route to India. How else would he have it? Her father never removed it, and he wouldn't have started then. She would support whatever Arthur and Graham decided.

A familiar pair of voices could be heard on the other side of the door. She wondered how long her brother had been here, or if he was just arrived.

"Look who I found in the grand entry," Graham said.

"You know you're late, don't you?" came her quick response.

He nodded as Graham motioned him over to the sideboard. He poured each of them a healthy swallow of whiskey. He knew Roxanne wanted to pounce and ask her brother and him a long list of questions. Arthur nodded when his glass was half full. He thoughtfully swirled the amber contents then took a swallow.

"Yes, but it couldn't be helped."

"Why's that?"

He took another sip before walking toward her. He sat down on a cream-colored damask chair. "There was a horse in the meadow. Not one of mine and I'm unsure who it belongs to. I tried approaching it, but the beast fled."

"Could it be one of Graham's?"

"No. At least, I didn't recognize it as one of his."

"From Arthur's description, it's not one of mine," Graham said.

"A feral horse?" Roxanne asked.

Arthur shook his head. "Doubtful. We would have encountered it before now."

Knowing they were dancing around the subject, Roxanne decided to see her brother's reaction to the ring which would have been his. "Graham says that Crenshaw is wearing a ring belonging to our father. Did you see it?"

Arthur scrubbed his face with one hand. "I really didn't notice."

"Do you think it possible? It could answer a lot of questions."

"Anything's possible," Arthur replied. He polished off his whiskey and sat back.

"I agree with Graham about continuing your investigation. I think you need to find the answers, and using an investigator, you should have far better chances."

"Agreed." Graham nodded his head. "One of us should get word to our investigator so he can continue."

"I can do it. I have a meeting in London. I won't be there but for a few days, but I could definitely speak with him and give him all we found out during our meeting with Crenshaw."

"That would be an enormous weight off our shoulders," Graham said.

Before anyone could get another word in, dinner was announced. The men followed Roxanne into the dining room. She sat to Graham's right as they were seated. She tried to keep the conversation light as they went through the first couple of courses. It was the entrée that got them talking. Roxanne had decided to try the cook's acclaimed pork roast. Graham had boasted about it when she asked if he'd tried it before. It was served with potatoes, carrots, and peas. By the silence around the table, she knew she had made the right choice.

A cheese and pear plate was next. It included Stilton, mild red cheddar made on the estate, as well as the sharp cheddar also made on the estate. She was amazed at how good the cheddars were.

As she and Graham were to visit tenants, she would give each family some cheese. It would be a nice gesture and a way for her to get to know the families who helped to keep the estate in perfect working condition. Seasons would be changing soon, and everyone would be working to make sure they were ready for the cold of winter.

"Graham, have you ever thought about selling your cheese? That is, if you make enough." Roxanne asked.

He shook his head. "I've thought about it, but sadly, no. Occasionally a wheel to one of the pubs. To seriously sell it, we'd have to make more and since it's aged, it would be a year or two minimum before it would be ready to go to market."

"What else is there? I would like to take each family some cheese."

"Honey," Graham replied.

"Arthur? You should do something like this."

He shook his head as he popped a piece of cheese in his mouth. "It's never been done. Repairs were the only thing Father ever did."

"Now's a good time to change that."

He grinned. "Perhaps once I've married."

Roxanne shook her head, wagging her finger at her brother. "Oh no, you're not going to go there and use not being married as an excuse not to do things."

"I'm not going to discuss this with you."

"Roxanne," Graham said lowly. He knew this to be a sensitive subject matter with Arthur, though he knew his wife only meant well when it came to her brother. However, she was like a dog with a bone. Once she took an interest in something, that was that. All bets were off. In this case, it was getting her brother married.

"What? Can't I be concerned that my brother has no heir and isn't making any strides to fix the situation? He's not making an effort to find a wife on his own. That's why I will help."

Arthur picked up the brandy snifter Graham had placed in front of him and swirled the dark liquid. "I need no help. I'm not going to accept a loveless union."

"No one said you should," she said, her lips pursed.

"Good, I'm glad to see we agree on something."

He polished off his brandy and pushed himself away from the table. "This was a lovely dinner, sister."

"You aren't leaving, are you? The night's still young."

He nodded and stood. "I have to catch up on things I didn't take care of earlier."

Roxanne nodded. "I understand."

Arthur came around the table and kissed his sister on the cheek. "Good evening," he said before turning to follow Graham out of the dining room. As the door closed behind them, Roxanne finished off the brandy sitting before her. It was still early, and she wasn't ready to turn in. Instead, she would go to the drawing room and relax. She could play the pianoforte for Graham, but she wasn't sure if he'd sit through her playing. She was still not as good as she had been before Casper. He never wanted her to play when he was around and discouraged her playing by cruel means. Closing her eyes, Roxanne tried to forget Casper's brutality.

She sat in front of the fire, staring at the flames. She'd poured herself another brandy and sat with it in her hands. Taking a reflection of the evening, she was not comfortable that Arthur thought her assisting in his quest for a wife was interference. He'd used an excuse that he was up to the task himself. She knew that was merely an excuse. She knew he had a history of choosing the wrong women through no fault of his own. It went without saying that most women he chose were after two things: his money and his title. Fortunately, it didn't take long to figure this out. The women could be quite bold. All they needed was for Arthur to feign to show interest by dancing more than once with a particular lady, sitting with another for too long. The rules went on and on. She would continue what she had started doing. Find her brother a wife.

"Are you ready to retire?" Graham asked. He put his hands on both her shoulders. He bent to kiss her on the cheek.

"It is still early, but yes, I'm ready to go up. I can read some."

"Reading is not what I had in mind, Lady Roxanne."

"No?"

"No. Come, let me show you the way."

She rose and strode to where her husband still stood behind her chair. She extended a hand which he took and pulled her close to his chest before ravishingly kissing her. A few minutes later, he led her up the stairs to their bedchamber.

CHAPTER TWENTY-TWO

GRAHAM LOCKED THE door behind him to ensure they wouldn't be disturbed at any time. He strode over to Roxanne who was already sitting on the bed, her slippers and stockings in front of her on the floor. She stood again as she tried to rid herself of her gown.

"Here, let me help you," he growled into her ear. By the time he had her stripped down to her chemise, his cock ached in the confines of his trousers. She stood before him, removing his cravat and pulling at his shirt in order to take it off. "I'll get it. You get out of that and get up on the bed."

After divesting his clothes, he noticed Roxanne lying on the mattress, propped up on one elbow watching him lustfully. Her hand breezed over her breasts and continued on. She parted her legs and touched herself, her eyes on his jutting tool. Sensually, she licked her lips, sending Graham almost over the edge. He needed her here and now, fearing he wouldn't last much longer. The mattress moved as he put his full weight on the bed. He covered her with his muscular body as he spread her legs even wider. He kissed her deeply, their tongues in a wild lover's duel. His hand dropped to between her legs, to her heat. Rubbing her lightly, he inserted a finger as far as he could. She gasped at the sensation. Moments later he removed his digit, replacing it with two. This time she moved with him as he brought her to new heights. Crying out, she arched her back to take him deeper. Removing his fingers he guided his cock between her legs and thrust. Roxanne cried out once again at the sensation of him stretching her as she wound her fingers through his hair, his mouth crashing down.

They said little more than a groan for the next few moments. Then he thrust hard one last time and filled her with his seed. He kissed her wildly before pulling out of her wet cunny. Slowly, he lowered himself on her, his elbows keeping him from putting his full weight on her.

"We need more of this," she whispered in his ear.

His breath returning, he laughed. "Yes, we do. We need to try it in the attics. We need to try it by the lake…"

"There's no privacy at the lake."

"Yes, there is. I just haven't shown you yet," he replied with a wink.

Roxanne wriggled under him with such force he had to move, lying next to her propped on his arm. She sat up and glared down at him. "How would you know this? Did you take your paramour out there? Did you make love to her while you were there?"

"Whoa, whoa, whoa, Roxanne. Why would you think such a thing? I have taken no one there. My mistress never set foot on any of my private properties."

She pursed her lips. "How do you know you can't see anything if you haven't taken someone there?"

"It was a place your brother and I came to as boys. We knew we could hide there and that no one could see it from the house."

"Really?" she asked meekly.

"Yes," he replied with a sly grin. "We could swim naked in the lake if we wanted without worrying you would come."

"Still, I could have."

"You were not allowed near either of the lakes. Not the one here or the one on your family's estate."

"True. Father was very strict about that."

"So you'll let me take you to the lake some time in the near future for some spirited shenanigans?"

"Yes. Now can we get some sleep?" She stretched and lay against the pillows.

He looked at her with mock horror. "You mean you don't want to have a second go? You hurt my feelings, madam."

"Not now. I'd rather sleep first, and I don't buy that nonsense about your feelings being hurt."

He wrapped his arm around her and pulled her closer until she had her head on his chest. "Then sleep it is. Good night, my love."

Hearing no reply from her, he looked down and found her asleep. She was beautiful even asleep, and he couldn't believe how lucky he was to have, after all these years, reconnected with her in the deepest way. For Graham, sleep eluded him as it normally did. He would finally succumb to slumber early in the morning. Perhaps his wife could help change this.

The reason for his sleepless nights was due to, or at least he thought was due in part to whatever happened during the day. Tonight, it was not only his wife, but the strange meeting he and Arthur had with the man they knew deeply had knowledge of the disappearance of his wife's father and mother that captured his brain. He couldn't get it out of his mind that the man thought he could play innocent in the matter. Some of his remarks, plus Arthur's father's ring on his hand, made Graham certain the man knew far more than he was letting on. He was old enough that he could have even played a part in their deaths.

Why, he could have done it himself. Why, was the huge question. Why were they murdered? No one had ever come up with a satisfactory answer or conclusion. Bandits had been the reason, and being that neither the duke nor duchess had survived the incident made that became the official version. No one believed it. Any attempt on the family's part to reopen the case was met with a huge lack of cooperation from law enforcement. They made it abundantly clear that the case was closed and would not be reopened no matter who requested it. That refusal to help in the case spoke volumes. He and Arthur would get to the bottom of it all.

Feeling his eyes grow heavy, Graham wondered if he could truly fall asleep. Perhaps if he concentrated on one thing, shutting his mind down, he could sleep. The next thing he remembered was his bride snuggling as close as she could to him. Cold. She had to be cold as they had nothing covering them. Slowly he found a piece of the cover and pulled it up over both of them. He hadn't realized how cool the room had become and wondered if it were time for someone to come restart the fires. It was going to be hard for him to keep from making love to his wife. His cock was so hard, it wasn't going to allow him to sleep until he either took himself in hand or relieved himself with her.

AFTER A QUICK coupling, Roxanne fell back to sleep well satisfied. Graham waited a while until he was sure he wouldn't wake her by getting out of bed. Still, he rose quietly and, grabbing his robe, he walked over to the windows to see what sort of day it was going to be. Dawn was just beginning to show its pinks and purples. A perfect day for a ride. A ride with his wife; a ride to the lake where he was intent on proving to her they had more privacy than needed.

First, though, he would dress and have breakfast before he spent most of the morning in his study. Today would entail more than his usual days. His estate manager was expected with his monthly report. Sometimes it was lengthy, sometimes not. He expected it would be lengthy because there were activities about to take place. Livestock, harvest. Everything being prepared for when they did happen. Roofs of tenant houses needed to be repaired if necessary. He didn't want anyone having a leaky roof in the cold. This was where he'd find out if any repairs were needed to the rock walls or stables. Fortunately, his estate manager knew the land as well as Graham did. He'd taken over when his father was no longer able and proved himself over and over again. He was someone Graham could leave for months at a time and know the estate would be just as he left it. The man kept up to date on all the farming changes, new inventions to help make things easier. Graham tried to remember everything he had on a list sitting on his desk. He knew he was interested in how much money was being brought in by the various products made on the estate.

Roxanne had an idea regarding the tenants that he wanted to discuss with his manager. It was done by others, but not with the personal touch she wanted to give it. She wanted to be the one who gave everything out to them. She had given him a list of what she needed. Foodstuffs that would last better during the colder months than in summer. He had no hesitation letting her represent him. She was, after all, the countess, and as such, she wanted to be one who was seen by tenants. That she wasn't some entitled aristocrat who sat in her manor and never mingled with anyone outside her social standing spoke volumes.

ONCE THE ESTATE manager arrived, the pair sat at a round, mahogany table and went over every entry made in the past month. After which, he told Graham what needed to be done before it got too cold. They settled on what was priority, after which he brought up how Roxanne wanted to take foodstuffs to the tenants. She wanted to give out shoes and coats, but that would be done another time and would probably be set up somewhere close to the manor. He told the manager he could deal directly with the countess regarding what she needed.

As the two finished up their meeting, Graham happened to mention taking Roxanne to the lake. He was told there was a group of workmen cutting the brush back and cutting the grass. Graham was glad he'd thought to mention it because he certainly didn't want to ride over there and be surprised they weren't alone. That would be for another time.

He bid him farewell and returned to his desk now filled with papers, which he now gathered and placed together in a pile to his left. He could always take the camera and plates with them. Then they would both get some practice with this.

Deciding it was time to find his bride, he took one more look at the top of his desk. As far as he could tell, there was nothing so important it couldn't wait.

Roxanne was descending the stairs when he went in search of her. She was a breath of fresh air, dressed in a light-blue day dress. "Did you have a good meeting with your estate manager?"

"Yes, it was excellent. We got a lot accomplished, and he is looking forward to meeting with you about the delivery to the tenants."

"Wonderful."

"What have you been doing this morning?"

She smiled broadly. "I've just spent the past hour with Mary and her nanny."

"I can see you enjoyed your visit immensely," he said.

"Yes, she's such a joy to be around. To be that innocent. It's too bad that all changes as the years pass."

"A lot of that has to do with the environment a child is raised in," he said.

"True, but even if it's the best, sometimes a child is just going to be unpleasant. There is little that can be done to change it. It's the way they were born."

"Fortunately, we won't have that arise in any of our children."

"What do you have in store for us this afternoon? Unless you have other matters to attend to," she said.

He rubbed her cheek with the pad of his thumb. "I was hoping we could ride to the lake, but I understand there is a work crew down there cutting back weeds and shrubs."

"That's too bad. I was so looking forward to seeing it."

"Another time," he said.

"Yes."

Just as she was going to add an idea she had, the butler came out of nowhere with a letter for Graham. He took the paper and studied it after dismissing the older man. It was from Arthur and if he was sending him a missive this soon, the investigator must have found something new and sent Arthur a report.

"That's Arthur's handwriting," she said, standing next to him.

"Yes, it is. He may have received a report from our man."

"Go find out. I'm going to take a walk around the gardens in the meantime." She lifted her skirts and strode in the direction of the drawing room.

He hated keeping things from her, but she had the habit of getting emotional about how matters should be taken care of. He opened the letter and stood to read it. Information they'd been trying to get answers for were anyone's guess. Crenshaw's movements seemed to be taking a turn they feared they would. The man, with another couple, had taken a ship out at high tide this morning, headed for India.

Their fears were real. He was following in his father's footsteps and taking people with him, acting as a private tour guide. Just as his father had done with Arthur and Roxanne's parents.

He walked towards his study. He needed to think this through. Was there anything they could do now? Could their investigator get an idea which route Crenshaw would go? Would it be wise to try and write this couple and warn them that their host may not be as honest as he appeared?

Graham decided to send Arthur a reply with his ideas and suggestions. This wasn't a matter that could wait because if the trio got too far, the harder it would be to find them until they arrived in India.

They were close to finding out the entire truth, and the last thing they needed was to get into too big a rush and spook

Crenshaw off. He'd done it before, and they didn't need to have a repeat of that episode. Arthur would agree with him; especially now that he knew the man wore his father's ring. He knew all Arthur and Roxanne wanted was the truth of what really happened to their parents, and he would do his utmost to see the truth was known.

CHAPTER TWENTY-THREE

ROXANNE'S WALK IN the garden turned into a note taking trek. She made penciled notes about various flower beds, flowers, and shrubs. Some were made for a future discussion with the gardener, others were just for her own records. Things like moving plants and shrub trimming.

She finally found herself in front of an elaborate fountain Graham's grandfather had installed for his countess. She understood it to have come from Italy as it was quite intricately made. Her sketch pad was on the terrace. Why hadn't she brought it? Wanting to sketch the fountain for a possible painting, Roxanne rushed back and got her charcoal pencil and sketch book.

Sitting on a bench, the sun behind her, she began to sketch. She rose and occasionally strode over to the fountain to look at the intricate beauty it possessed. Certainly, she had seen beautiful and elaborate fountains in her lifetime, but she'd never found herself wondering what Graham's grandfather was thinking when he chose this one. Now she was speculating and determined it was because of her husband. This was part of who he was. His heritage.

While sketching, she wondered why the late earl would have put the fountain in this location. It wasn't at the center of the gardens, but rather off to one side, hidden by shrubs and roses.

With the location and benches placed around the fountain, Roxanne concluded that it was placed in this spot for privacy. Privacy for the late countess and her husband to share together. Unfortunately, there was no one still living from that time, which saddened her because she couldn't ask questions or hear stories about the fountain. Perhaps some of the older staff members might recall hearing stories about it. Even Graham might possibly have some memories of the fountain. He rarely spoke of his family so she doubted he would remember.

She felt the splash of a large raindrop on her shoulder. Looking up at the sky, she saw the sun being pushed out of the way for a summertime shower. Shutting the sketch pad so it wouldn't get ruined, she stood up and walked back to the house as fast as she could before the rain came down in sheets.

As soon as she entered the drawing room, she ordered hot tea to warm her up from the dampness. As she waited for her tea, Roxanne went and retrieved a shawl from her room to ward off the dampness. Returning to the drawing room, she sat near the fire and began making notes and observations of her experience at the fountain.

Then she began laughing. Graham had planned to take her to the lake, but his plans were thwarted by the fact a work crew was busy working there. Had they been able to go, they would have been soaked on their way back to the house and who knew what state of undress they might have been in when the rains came.

Her thoughts were interrupted by the footman and butler bringing her tea into the drawing room. Not needing anything more, she dismissed the pair. She went over to the cart and found a teapot with two cups along with a plate of seedcake and scones. Pouring herself a cup of tea, she placed a scone and raspberry jam on a plate. She walked over to the ivory-colored couch where her drawing pad sat on the table in front of it. Placing her plate down on the table, she moved her sketch pad to the couch before she put her cup of tea down on the table.

Settling herself on the couch, Roxanne opened the sketchbook she had been working from and turned to the sketch she had started of the fountain. She studied it closely. There were still a lot of details she needed to sketch before she could start painting, but for the most part she had captured the fountain well.

She was concentrating so hard on the sketch that she hadn't heard Graham enter. "Did you do that on your walk?" he asked.

"Yes. I plan to paint it once the sketch is done."

"It's quite good. Why not paint it outside, in front of the fountain?"

"I may, but I always like having a detailed sketch in case it rains for days or weeks on end. I'm even considering photographing it at different times of the day," she said.

He walked over to the tea cart. "That would be quite interesting; the light at different angles." He poured a cup and walked back with his tea and the seedcakes and scone.

With everything placed on the table, he picked up a piece of seedcake and bit into it. No fork. Just eating it like a naughty boy might. He didn't stop until he finished and once he did, Graham licked his fingers, making sure he got everything. Seedcake was one of his favorites and his cook made sure there was always some on hand.

"Did you get everything settled with my brother?"

"Yes, just needed to respond to a couple of questions and ideas he had."

"I see."

"We're both sure that Crenshaw had something to do with your parents' disappearance. Whether he did it on his own or plotted with his father is unknown. We're going to continue our investigation, but carefully so we don't scare him away."

Roxanne spread some jam on the scone and took a bite. She waited to finish before she spoke. "I completely agree with that logic. I may not have had a close relationship with my father, but the man was still my sire. He didn't deserve this."

"No, he didn't and neither did your mother. We'll get to the bottom of it, I promise you that. It may not happen tomorrow; it may be next year, but we will get to the bottom of this."

"Enough of business. It is still raining. How would you like to spend the rest of the afternoon?"

"I don't know. I hadn't thought about it."

She waggled her eyebrows. "We could always go to the secret passage and see where we might utilize it."

"I thought we had."

"We will need to take whatever we need. Blankets, pillows. Things to make us comfortable," She smiled wickedly in his direction.

He gulped down his tea. "What are we waiting for?" Graham stood, wrapping the remaining seedcake into a napkin. He took her hand and guided her from the drawing room. His most willing countess.

Life would never be dull for either of them. Despite having started out on the wrong foot, he had fallen in love with Roxanne. Being persistent had paid off. It took a while, but he showed her he was not the man she remembered. No longer was he a rake who lived to have fun with women and life. Now he was a man deeply in love with his wife, his countess. With that came responsibilities he never believed he would have. A family of his own to love and protect. An unexpected chance at fatherhood and a woman who accepted the child to raise and took him for who he was. Hopefully, soon she would be with child. His child.

Life would be perfect with a houseful of children. There was a time in the not-so-distant past he would have shaken his head in disbelief. Mary changed all that. Roxanne changed all that. He now found himself fulfilled as a man.

He glanced behind him at his wife who still had her hand firmly in his. Turning back around, he grinned. Life was perfect.

About the Author

J R Salisbury writes Victorian era English and Scottish historical romance with perfectly imperfect heroes and strong, sassy heroines.

Writing has always written. It was the continuous encouragement of a high school creative writing teacher to further her craft. Bit with the self-publishing bug in 2011 she started out her on-line eBooks as contemporary romance before switching to her preferred and loved genre, historical romance. Her books can be found at the majority of on-line bookstores.

Raised outside Seattle with three years in the South American country of Chile, traveling is in her blood. Dividing her time between Atlanta, GA in the United States and the UK gives her a unique perspective on history.

Author Links

Website: www.jamiesalisbury.com
Facebook (historical): JRSalisburyHistoricalRomance
Facebook Profile: JamieRSalisburyAuthor
X (aka Twitter): @JamieRSalisbury
Book Bub: jr-salisbury
Instagram: authorjamiesalisbury
Email: jamiesalisburyauthor@gmail.com